CRIMSON TEMPEST

SURVIVAL WARS BOOK 1

ANTHONY JAMES

AN UNNAMED PLANET, KARNIUS-12 SYSTEM

YEAR 31 OF THE HUMAN-GHAST WAR.

The repair bot had been busy for a long time. It was slow and methodical, blessed with an infinite patience. For over fifty years it had been working on a single task, which was to bring the vessel's mainframe back online. The damage was extensive, but the robot continued unabated even though it was almost out of power. It hadn't been programmed with anything as pointless as human emotions to make it care about how long it took, or even whether or not it would be successful. All it could do was go through the trillions of tiny steps required to bring the ship's main computer systems to an operational state. Given the time and the materials, the robot could have constructed a completely fresh core, though its power cell would have decayed long before it could accomplish such a monumental task. There was a second core hiding behind the first. This core was almost undamaged, though it was unable to access any of the spacecraft's systems except by routing through the first. It waited with patience.

Success came without witness. On the ship's main bridge, a screen winked briefly into life, before fading again. A different screen illuminated, a hundred billion lines of code scrolling up and vanishing in the blinking of an eye. Deep within the ship, the mainframe became semi-aware again. The screen on the bridge flickered and then went out – the ship's core wasn't wasteful and it didn't need to expend even this infinitesimally small amount of energy. The bridge screens were for human pilots and this ship hadn't carried a crew.

For the next three seconds, it checked the status of the onboard systems. There was extensive damage to almost every system and subsystem. The single remaining repair bot had the primary task of repairing the core, with the propulsion, weapons and life support systems a lower priority. As such, there was little the mainframe could do for the moment. The transmission systems were offline – damaged, but the ship considered that it could re-route power away from the primary, secondary and tertiary communications systems, in order to activate the emergency antenna. The concern was, the emergency system lacked the capability to broadcast with full encryption.

The *ESS Crimson* ran through the possibilities and decided the risk was worthwhile. It sent the signal and waited for a response.

CHAPTER ONE

THE GAME of cat and mouse had lasted almost two days. So far, the damaged Ghast light cruiser – a Kraven class - had managed to keep the gas giant Gyer-12 between itself and the pursuing ship *ES Detriment*. It was a dangerous game for all parties. The two ships weren't built for extended periods in low orbit and the snub nose of the *Detriment*'s hull glowed a dull orange from the heat of the planet and the blossoming clouds of silicate which spilled thousands of kilometres above the tempestuous surface.

Captain John Nathan Duggan was standing on the cramped bridge, embedded deep within the five-hundred-and-twenty metre length of the Vincent class warship. *Gunners* was the nickname given to them by their crew. They were an ancient design, yet modular and easy to patch in new technology, which was enough to keep hundreds of these workhorses still in service. There was something glorious about serving on ships like this and their crews had the shortest expected lifespan of anyone in the Space Corps. It either made them proud enough to fight like demons, or they tried to get a placement elsewhere. Many grew to love working on the Gunners and if they'd been offered a transfer to a Hadron class, they'd turn the chance down. There was something about fighting on the edge that appealed to certain people and they'd never want to serve elsewhere.

There were no windows on the bridge – a single long screen against the bulkhead projected a 360-degree view of everything around the vessel, whilst displays and readouts flashed with continuously-updated status reports. There was only just about room for four people, with the cracked leather seats giving no illusion of comfort. An ancient design flaw, never fixed on subsequent revisions of the Vincent class, meant that the air conditioning wasn't strong enough to keep the bridge at anything like an acceptable temperature. It was hot and the air carried tangy odours of oil, grease and electricity.

Duggan wiped the sweat from his forehead with the back of his hand. He was angry – furious almost, that the Ghast ship had evaded them for so long.

"What the hell do they think they're playing at?" he asked, not for the first time. He wasn't expecting an answer and got none. "Anything on the fars?" he asked.

"No ping. Not even an echo of a ping," replied Second Lieutenant Frank Chainer. He had his face glued to a bank of glowing green screens in front of him. To Chainer's left and right, the ship's sensors spilled out page after page of readouts. Sometimes a trained comms man could spot an anomaly to indicate the presence of something too subtle to register on the screens. Chainer took another shaky gulp from his hi-stim drink can.

"They still outgun us, Captain," said Commander Lucy McGlashan. "And we have no idea how long their distress beacon was sending before we destroyed it."

Duggan growled. He knew he was being stupid. Stupid and stubborn. They'd caught the Ghast ship unawares and Duggan had decided to take a shot at it. The *Detriment* had two batteries of the latest Lambda missiles, one of which had evaded the enemy ship's Vule Cannons and torn a vast hole in her engines. With the Ghast ship drifting, Duggan thought he'd scored a win. Then, without warning, it had happened. Everything on the *Detriment* had gone dead – stone, cold, dead. Every light and every screen winked out of existence, as if a mysterious hand had pressed a central power button. They'd been lucky that the Ghast ship's momentum had carried it out of weapons range. After exactly one minute, everything had come back online, as if nothing had ever been wrong. The crew had checked the error logs, but as far as the ship's compact mainframe was concerned, nothing whatsoever had happened.

By the time the sub-light engines had fired up again, the Ghast ship had dropped into the gas giant's orbit and used the iron and silicate atmosphere to hide itself from the *Detriment*'s sight. Duggan couldn't even leave his ship high and stationary for the Ghasts to come to him – the enemy light cruiser could evade detection simply by staying low beneath the swirling gases of the atmosphere. It was now a matter of luck as to if or when Duggan could force another engagement.

"How long till they can get their deep fission drives online?" Duggan asked.

"I'd only be guessing, Captain," said Lieutenant Bill Breeze. "Their technology works like ours, but not like ours. We made a big hole in their hull. Our sensors suggest we took out twenty three percent of their engine mass. It all depends on how good their ship's core is at rerouting. Hours, days or weeks. Take your pick."

Duggan already knew this – he just couldn't stop himself from asking again. He felt clenched up tight as if he had to do something, but with no control over what. There wasn't even any room for him to pace in order to work off steam, and he didn't dare leave the bridge for long enough to spend a couple of hours in the ship's gym.

"They can't stay lucky forever," Duggan said quietly. On the screen ahead of him, the computer-enhanced image of Gyer-12 drifted slowly to the left, against a background of distant stars which showed as magnified specks against the pure blackness. Staring out into those black depths gave Duggan a feeling he'd never been able to put words to. The emptiness had frightened him once – now he craved it. In the background, the air conditioning thrummed and the integrity warning system continued to bleep softly at the intense stresses being placed on the alloys that comprised the hull.

"Got a fission signature, Captain," said Breeze, the loudness of his voice cutting across the low noise of the bridge.

"Where is it? How far?" asked Duggan at once, crossing over to stand at Breeze's shoulder.

"One hundred and eleven thousand klicks anti-clockwise with a thirty-degree offset from our orbit. They're almost a third of a circuit ahead of us."

"Can we get to them before they jump out of orbit?"

"Not a chance. Not unless you want us to burn up," said McGlashan. "Thirteen minutes till we can get close enough for the Lambdas."

"Unlucky thirteen," said Chainer.

Duggan swore. "How long till they can go to lightspeed?"

There wasn't a planet dense enough to keep that hidden from the *Detriment*'s sensors. If the Ghast ship had managed to get enough of its fission engines online, it could outrun the smaller Vincent class.

"The output from their engines means they'll be gone in five minutes," Breeze announced. "Nope, they've stepped it up. Make that three minutes."

Duggan increased power to the *Detriment*'s sub-light engines. The warning bleep increased in volume at once and a faint vibration began underfoot. *Hold it together, old girl.*

"Eleven minutes till engagement," said McGlashan. Her face was a pattern of reflected light strobes as she focused on the screens in front of her.

"One minute till they're gone," said Chainer.

"We're not going to make it," McGlashan told them, as if they hadn't already guessed.

"The fission signature's faded, Captain," announced Breeze. His face showed a mixture of elation and fear. "Whatever they tried, it didn't work."

"And now we know exactly where they are."

"They must know we've picked them up," said McGlashan.

Duggan ran his fingers across a couple of the screens on a console in front of him and then touched another to override the ship's safety warning. The *Detriment*'s speed increased another five percent and the vibration became a shuddering. The warning bleep turned into a continuous tone to let the crew know that the hull temperature had gone ten percent above its design maximum.

"The boys and girls below will be getting worried," McGlashan told him.

"I want those bastards," said Duggan. With a grunt, he relented and backed off the power. There was no point in taking the risk for such a small gain. The Ghast ship would be lost in the atmosphere by the time they got to where the fission signature had come from. He looked across and saw McGlashan take a deep breath and shake her head to free the droplets of sweat from her eyebrows.

"Nine minutes," she said.

In front of Duggan, another screen lit up a bright blue. Letters formed on the screen: Priority Message Delivered. It wasn't the time for distractions, but the *Detriment*'s comms system dutifully rolled the lines of text onto the screen. *Return to the Juniper. No delays. Teron.* Duggan swore again when he read the words.

"What's up?" asked McGlashan.

"It's Admiral Teron. He wants us back at the *Juniper*. Without delay."

"He could have picked a better time," said Breeze.

"He won't notice a few minutes, will he?" said Duggan, dismissing the message.

"Wouldn't want the Ghasts escaping after all this effort we've put in," said Chainer.

Minutes passed and no one dared to break the silence. Duggan drummed his fingers on the grey metal console before him. He felt a line of sweat soaking through the back of his uniform.

"Three minutes."

"Anything on the fars?"

"Nothing. No, wait. Maybe." Duggan looked over. Chainer was frowning.

"What do you mean, *maybe*?"

"I thought I saw something just for a moment. Maybe."

"We can't work on maybes, Lieutenant," said Duggan. "Get the Lambdas ready," he said to McGlashan with urgency clear in his voice. "And launch countermeasures. Immediately."

McGlashan was good – one of the best. She didn't question the order. "Shock drones away. Bulwarks ready."

"Got incoming," said Chainer. "Fifteen, twenty. Fast moving. Missiles, Captain. Four waves."

"Beginning evasive manoeuvres!" Duggan barked. A deep grumbling thrummed into the structure of the metal walls as the ship's computer fired them into a randomised pattern of turns and rotations. A wave of giddiness swept through Duggan as the *Detriment*'s life support systems struggled to cope with the incredible changes in gravitational forces that would have otherwise crushed the fragile bodies of the human crew.

Where're those bastards hiding?" asked Duggan. "Can you get a fix on them?"

"They must have doubled back, Captain," said Breeze.

"I reckon," said Duggan. "They're either very lucky or very good." *Or perhaps this Ghast ship just has better sensors than the Detriment.* They'd been making advances over the last few years. It had plenty of people in the Space Corps worried. "ETA on the missiles?"

"First wave in thirty seconds, Captain," said Chainer. "Got another fission signature. This one incoming. It's a big one. Dropping out of Light-J on the far side of Gyer-12."

"One of ours?" asked Duggan, knowing that it couldn't be. The Corps had nothing out here in no-man's land. At least, nothing bigger than a Gunner.

"Cadaveron," said Chainer.

"Damn," muttered Duggan. It was a Ghast heavy cruiser – the *Detriment* stood no chance against it. "At least their navigator screwed up and took them the wrong side of the planet."

All around the bridge, status warnings burned orange on the readout screens in a seemingly endless procession of information thrown up frantically by the *Detriment*'s mainframe. A multitude of warning bells clamoured for attention, their volume low yet impossible to ignore. Neither Duggan nor his crew showed outward sign of fear. They'd been in the Corps for years – decades even. Each of them had seen almost everything that could be imagined. In the end, fear got them nothing. They either lived or died and often it was luck that saw them through.

"First wave of missiles within fifteen thousand klicks."

"Launch more shock drones."

"Shock drones away."

The view screen lit up, so brightly that it was almost a pure white. The bridge computers stepped in quickly and reduced the intensity so that it wouldn't burn the eyes of the crew.

"First wave of missiles down," said Chainer. "Next in ten, fifteen and twenty seconds. They've packed them in."

"Bring the fission engines online," said Duggan.

"Fission engines coming online," Breeze responded. "Eighty-three seconds till we can go."

"I've nearly got a fix on them, Captain," said Chainer.

The view screen lit up white again. This time there was a greyish tint, as if the ship's computer had adjusted it badly. There was a shuddering accompanied by an almost imperceptible tilt to the left.

"Right-hand Bulwark got the last one," said McGlashan. "They're getting closer."

"Deploy shock drones."

"Shock drones away. Lambda batteries ready to fire. Waiting for a fix."

"I've got a fix."

"I see it. Lambdas gone, Captain."

Again, there was the whiteness on the screen and the shuddering came. *Both Bulwarks this time,* thought Duggan. *Too close for comfort.* On the weapons display in front of him, twenty Lambda missiles raced away, tiny dots that could rip a hundred-metre hole in the heaviest of armour. The latest versions were still better than anything the Ghasts had, at least as far as he knew.

"We can fire another twenty in ten seconds," said McGlashan. Her eyes were alive and glowing with the excitement.

The last five of the Ghast light cruiser's missiles detonated five thousand klicks away, confused by the swarms of one-metre metallic shock drones. The drones had tiny single-use engines that could propel them hundreds of klicks in only a few seconds.

As they flew, they transmitted signals in all directions and on a billion different wavelengths in the hope that they would confuse or destroy the guidance systems of incoming missiles. If they failed, there were always the Bulwark cannons, but when they fired, everyone knew it was time to cross their fingers.

"Lambdas will impact in twenty-five seconds," said McGlashan.

"They've launched another five missiles, Captain. Impact in thirty-two seconds. I'm getting something else from them. A power surge."

For the second time, everything went dead on the *Detriment*.

CHAPTER TWO

THE BRIDGE DESCENDED into a darkness that was utterly impenetrable. Every screen winked out at once, the air conditioning stopped thrumming and the faint vibration of the *Detriment*'s huge engines stopped.

Duggan spoke into the void, his voice calm, yet with an unmistakeable edge to it. "Anyone getting a response from their consoles?"

"Nothing, Captain."

"Dead."

"No response."

"Keep trying."

None of the crew said anything further, waiting for Duggan to speak.

"Thirty-two seconds to impact at last report," Duggan said. His hand reached out for the solidity of the plasmetal control panel in front of him. With the absence of sight, his brain marvelled at the absolute smoothness of the material beneath his fingertips. In his head, Duggan counted down from twenty-five, slowly and calmly, permitting himself a deep breath every five digits. The seconds stretched on forever, time on the bridge going so slowly that it might as well have stopped. A long time ago, Duggan had watched a documentary about life aboard the old submarines hundreds of years passed. How the sailors must have waited in the confines of those tiny spaces, never knowing if death would take them until it almost inevitably did. *And they call this progress.*

After a lifetime and more had passed, Duggan's count reached zero and he breathed out noisily. "Drones must have got them. Let's hope they didn't launch any more."

"This makes you realise you're alive," said Chainer.

"Everything's still completely out," said McGlashan.

"It lasted for one minute last time. There can't be long left."

"You think it's the same thing again, Captain?" asked Breeze.

"The Ghasts have used a new weapon on us. I would love to find out if there've been any other reports on the front. For the time being, let's hope that when the lights come back on we don't have six waves of incoming missiles."

"I'm mashing the release command for the drones," said McGlashan. There was a smile in her voice. Duggan couldn't remember the last time she'd been phased. At least not badly.

The lights came on, as if that hidden power switch had been flicked again. Darkness vanished, to be replaced by displays and readouts filled with updates and status reports. Duggan had been so caught between expecting death and expecting light that the brightness caught him unawares and he had to squint and shield his eyes. The structure of the ship shuddered as energy flowed through one hundred and thirty million tonnes of engine mass.

"Resume evasive manoeuvres. Status reports," Duggan commanded.

"We're on a random course already, Captain. The engines are continuing as they were."

"Shock drones away, that's our last cargo."

"Scanners clear. No missiles and no Ghast light cruiser."

"Bringing fission engines back online. One-hundred-and-seventy seconds. It seems like whatever shut us down has slowed up the mainframe."

"Any sign of debris, Lieutenant?"

"Checking. Nothing at the moment."

"Could they have got away? Hidden themselves?"

"There wasn't enough time to escape. Scanning."

"Any transmit logs from the Lambdas?" asked Duggan.

"Nothing at all, Captain. If they scored a hit, the transmits didn't reach us or our sensors were offline and unable to receive."

"How long till the Cadaveron gets here?" There was no chance they'd have failed to detect the fission engine build up from the *Detriment*.

"At least eight minutes. Plenty of time," said Breeze.

"Plenty of time," echoed Duggan, wondering why he didn't feel convinced. He looked at the displays in front of him – at the carpet of white-spotted blackness in the background of the gas giant. It told him nothing at all. There were times when sight was reduced to an almost useless sense and there was still that primeval feeling of helplessness when it happened.

"I'm picking up a cloud of fragments, Captain," said Chainer. "Decaying orbit approximately ten thousand klicks from the last known position of the Ghast ship. We got them."

"You're sure?"

"Definite, sir. No! We've got homing mines! Three of them only ten klicks!"

"How'd you miss those?" snarled Duggan, preparing himself for the impact.

"Sorry sir, no time to pick them up when the power came back."

In the vacuum outside, three one-foot diameter mines clamped themselves to the *Detriment*'s starboard side. They armed themselves and exploded within half a second. The shaped explosions sent a ripple through the spacecraft's hull, inflicting a violent trauma to the *Detriment*'s thick armour plating. Insulated from the worst of the blasts, the occupants on the bridge felt little more than a trembling through the walls. A stark red emergency light filled the room.

"Status report!" shouted Duggan.

"Engines still at ninety-five percent, sir," said Breeze.

"Have they breached the hull?"

Breeze looked up, worried. "I'm reading damage to the lower infantry quarters."

"Sergeant Ortiz, please report at once!" Duggan said through the onboard comms. "We've taken a hit over the lower infantry quarters."

The comms crackled and spat, a cacophony of background shouting. "It's gone to shit down here, sir. Life support's shut us out of the below quarters and we've got men in there!"

"I need to know what's happening, Sergeant!" Duggan blew out his breath and sprinted through the narrow exit door from the bridge. He dropped down the access steps three at a time and charged through the tightly turning corridors of the spacecraft's interior until he came to the area of the ship where the soldiers spent their time. The upper infantry quarters were cramped. Men and women from the *Detriment*'s small contingent of soldiers were gathered, shouting and pressed tightly in the narrow space between the wall-mounted bunks. There was an access hatch that led down to the lower quarters. It was closed.

"Sergeant, what's the situation?" asked Duggan, picking out the slender shape of the infantry officer. She was crouched over the featureless alloy plate that led below. It had a display panel that was flashing a blood-red colour.

Ortiz stood and faced him, anger visible in her deep-set

13

brown eyes. "Rogers, Morgan and Rivera are down there, sir," she said. "The mainframe slammed the access hatch tight."

Duggan shouted and kicked out at the nearest wall. "Captain to bridge. Anything you can give me on the status down here?"

The voice of Lieutenant Breeze returned at once. "There's been no breach, sir, but the engines dissipated a lot of heat through that area."

"How much heat?" asked Ortiz.

"Fifteen hundred degrees. Looks like the temperature's down below a hundred now. The hatch should open up soon."

"Where's Corporal Blunt?" asked Duggan, looking around for the ship's medic.

"They're gone, sir," said Ortiz quietly.

"Ship's sensors aren't reporting any signs of life," said Breeze.

Duggan sat down on one of the bunks and put his head in his hands. Corporal Blunt arrived, carrying with him a pack and a metallic box of hi-tech medical equipment. The man was thickset and looked younger than his years. He'd arrived just in time to hear the report from the bridge.

"Clear the room," Blunt instructed. "The hatch lock has just disengaged. I don't need anyone to go down there with me."

"I need to see, Corporal," said Duggan.

Blunt nodded and waited until the soldiers had cleared the room before he opened the hatch to the lower quarters.

Half an hour later, Duggan returned to the bridge. The destruction of the Ghast light cruiser against the odds would have usually filled him with elation. Now all he felt was anger and sadness that he'd lost three of his men.

"Good work ladies and gentlemen," he said, the words sounding hollow. "Point us towards the *Juniper* with no stop-offs."

"The *Juniper* it is," said Breeze.

Two minutes later, there was a whine and everyone on board

the *Detriment* was gripped by the unshakeable feeling that they'd been displaced, yet without being able to put exact words to the feeling. The life support systems sucked up almost a thousandth of one percent of the engine's output as they fought to stabilise the vessel's interior against the incomprehensible dislocation that was about to happen to the fragile bodies aboard. Then, the *Detriment* vanished from the orbit of Gyer-12, skimming away through space at many multiples of lightspeed. Far behind, the shattered pieces of the Ghast light cruiser tumbled lazily towards the planet's surface. The few sections which were large enough to survive the heat would crash into the surface over the coming weeks.

The Ghast Cadaveron, which had come in response to the distress beacon from the smaller ship, registered that the Corps vessel had entered Light-H – a speed somewhat in excess of that normally achievable by a Vincent class, but well within the capabilities of the heavy cruiser if it chose to follow. Its AI ran through the countless destinations in its databanks of known human outposts, before narrowing them down to the five most likely. None of these possibilities had a greater than three percent likelihood of being correct. Accurate lightspeed pursuit was almost impossible even with the processing power available to the most advanced warships. The Cadaveron possessed a colossal amount of firepower that would be wasted in the pursuit of a Vincent class. The Ghast ship left the planet to travel its own course.

Nineteen days later, the *Detriment* exited Light-H and re-entered normal space. The ship's sub-light engines fought to stabilise its speed and course for a few seconds and the brutal exit from lightspeed was replaced by a comparatively serene entry into a very high orbit of planet Kryptes-9. Along the way they'd jettisoned the bodies of their dead out in space, letting the infinity of darkness claim them forever. The men had been reduced to little more than carbonized lumps of matter, dehumanized as an added insult to their deaths. Duggan felt his blood boil whenever he thought about it. He'd not lost a man or woman in five years.

"You'll not hear the end of this little trick when we dock," said Breeze, his voice cutting through the silence.

"So we dropped in a little too close for comfort," said Duggan. "Teron said *no delays*. We're just following orders."

It was accepted practise for a ship to emerge from lightspeed travel at least an hour away from an orbital position. It wasn't entirely unheard of for a helmsman to plot a course that was fractionally awry and there were rumours that an AI had once managed to screw things up and nearly cause a disastrous collision between an Anderlecht class and the surface of a moon.

"Like he'll take the flack for that one," said McGlashan.

"*Juniper* ahead, Captain. Her AI isn't pleased."

"I'm sure it knows why we're here."

"I'll bet it knows more than we do."

"Amen to that," said Duggan.

Through the main viewscreen he saw the approaching orbital command and control station, magnified by the *Detriment*'s mainframe so that the details were sharp. The *Juniper* was a vast, metallic cuboid that rotated smoothly about its own axis, with a surface that appeared featureless from a distance, but which was covered in a myriad of sensors when viewed from close range. It had taken many decades to build and its construction had stripped at least three remote planets of their precious resources of certain rare metals that went into making up the ship's awe-inspiring power and propulsion systems. Duggan had once heard an engineer boast that the *Juniper's* engines could generate enough thrust to reverse a large moon's orbit. He didn't know if that was true or not, but had no reason to doubt what he'd heard. They'd not been fired up in anger for thirty years anyway and the *Juniper* continued to rotate in a smooth elliptical orbit, several hundred thousand kilometres above the surface of ice giant Kryptes-9.

"We've got clearance to land," said Chainer. "It's still not happy."

Duggan gave a rumbling laugh. He'd never learned to feel guilty for pissing off an AI. An hour later, he was in an airlift taking him from Hangar Bay 1 on the 705th floor, all the way to the 17th floor of the Military Command Unit. The Military CU took up several dozen floors and much of the *Juniper's* interior. It was one of the few operational command and control stations that remained after decades of cutbacks. The once almighty armed forces had been scaled back and scaled back, with the funds ploughed into whatever current issue the bigwigs thought would get them votes. It was short-termism at its worst.

At the 17th floor, the air lift slowed smoothly and its doors opened, allowing Duggan to exit into the Military CU. The lobby area was stark and clean – almost clinical in design. The temperature was several degrees too cold. The space he'd entered was huge and overwhelmingly metallic – like a spacecraft hanger with a low roof. People hurried to and fro, dressed in their contrasting uniforms, all trying to give the impression that they knew what they were doing.

Duggan was familiar with the place. As a captain with over twenty years' experience, he'd visited the *Juniper* on dozens of occasions. There'd been a time when he'd almost felt as if he lived here. The rest of his time had been spent scouting the edges of Confederation space for signs of Ghast activity. He set off across the floor, the hard soles of his boots producing a crisp noise from the metal underfoot. Duggan was an imposing figure – over six feet tall, with broad shoulders, cropped blond hair and a piercing stare from his green eyes that sent people scuttling out of his way as he approached. The CU had a row of reception desks with real people sitting at them, instead of automated check-in screens. The man whom Duggan approached looked up.

"Captain Duggan?" the man asked, polite and impersonal. The scanners in the lift had sent this information on ahead.

"I've been asked to see Teron."

"Admiral Teron, sir. I assume you know how to find him." The receptionist was a pro – he made his words neither a statement or a question, allowing Duggan to ask for more information if he needed it.

"Thanks," said Duggan. He knew exactly where he was going.

He walked along what seemed like several hundred metres of stark, silver-grey corridors until he arrived at his destination. Sensors checked his identity, whilst a nano-computer somewhere in the *Juniper*'s brain tallied his appearance with the diary of the occupant. Finding a match, it dutifully slid the plasmetal door open, permitting him entry. Duggan didn't pause and stepped through into the office beyond.

"Good to see you, Captain Duggan," spoke a deep voice.

"That wasn't what you said last time I saw you, sir," replied Duggan.

CHAPTER THREE

THE OFFICE WAS large and the left-hand wall was covered with screen upon screen, each of which flashed with numbers, diagrams, schematics. There were other monitors on the right-hand wall which received a feed from the orbital's monitoring sensors and showed alarms and statuses of the vital systems that kept the *Juniper* running. The orbital hadn't broken down yet, but there were thousands of technicians who lived aboard and worked long hours to keep it ticking. There was a large desk – made of real wood, which had seen better days. Behind the desk was a man – he looked at least sixty, though it was difficult to be sure how old anyone was, with the availability of life-extending drugs. Admiral Malachi Teron could have been over a hundred years old for all Duggan knew.

Teron was broad and grizzled, with short, white hair and a lined face. He had scars on his neck – light pink and angry from where he'd been caught by a Ghast plasma burst twenty years ago. His red uniform dripped with medals, testament to the campaigns he'd fought in.

"Take a seat," said Teron, his voice was harsh and with an

unnaturally rough quality that came from the injury he'd suffered. It was an order and Duggan took one of the two firm chairs.

"What do you want from me, sir?" he asked.

"You always liked to get to the point, didn't you, Captain Duggan?" asked Teron. The man exhaled noisily and sat back in his seat, running his thick fingers over his scalp. He looked tired. "Something's come up. Things are happening – important things, that need the right man to deal with them."

"*Things*? Is that the military term for it?" asked Duggan with the hint of a smile. "Come on, sir. Stop beating around the bush and tell me what's going on."

Teron paused for a moment in order to push a brown folder from one position on his desk to another. Then, he looked up. "Have you ever heard of the *ESS Crimson*?"

Duggan frowned and racked his memory. He'd probably flown in half the Space Corps' ships at one time or another, but this one didn't ring a bell. "*ESS* means it's old, right?" he asked.

"Very old, as it happens. Corps ships became universally prefixed with Earth-Star over forty years ago. There was only ever one ship built as Earth-Star Superior, which was the *Crimson*."

"What happened to it?" asked Duggan,

"It was top military kit - grade A advanced. Stuff that we'd not put on a ship before or even thought to put on a ship. A lot of it was theoretical at the time – a new branch of tech that had enough funding poured into it to have paid off the cost of building the *Juniper* twice over."

Duggan let out a low whistle. "I've not heard any of this before. That means it was either unimportant or top secret. I'm sure I'm not sitting here because it was unimportant. Why was there only one built?"

"Cutbacks. This was before the Ghast war started. I guess the paymasters decided that we didn't need to be pouring fifteen percent of the total military budget into something new and unproven."

"Why'd they even start it in the first place?" asked Duggan.

"When times are good, we build. When times are lean, we look to where we can save money." Teron shrugged as if it were of little consequence. "Besides, there were lots of benefits to the project in terms of fission drive improvements, missile tech and hull design. Those Lambda missiles you're carrying on the *Detriment*? You can thank the Hynus project for that. More than half of our current armaments and weaponry are rooted in the Hynus project. It's the main reason why the Ghasts haven't reached Earth yet."

"Hynus project?"

"That's what they called it. The Hynus project was eventually meant to produce more than twenty ships."

Duggan shook his head at what sounded like a short-sighted approach to humanity's defences. "They shut it down? And you still haven't said what happened to the *Crimson*."

"It vanished on its maiden voyage. One minute it was there, the next it stopped broadcasting. We sent ships to search for it, but there was no sign. The *Crimson* was faster than anything else in the Corps at the time and it was a long trip for the search crews to get far enough out to look. They were unsuccessful and it was deemed that some of the more experimental hardware on board had failed, resulting in the ship's destruction. Fortunately, it was unmanned at the time so there were no awkward questions to answer that might cause unwanted people to start sniffing around for the existence of the Hynus project. That was fifty-three years ago."

Something didn't add up and Duggan couldn't quite put his finger on what it was. "Why is this important now?" he asked.

"We've had contact from the *Crimson*. One of the vets on

Monitoring Station Alpha picked up a transmission from it, telling us to prepare for war."

"A legit signal?"

"One-hundred percent, copper-bottomed legit."

"What did it mean *prepare for war?*" asked Duggan.

"We don't know. The transmission was terminated before the men on the Alpha could get more details. The *Crimson* cut itself off, stating the channel wasn't secure. We've had no further response."

"What do you want me to do?"

"You've been instructed to find the *Crimson*. We've traced its signal to a system of planets in Karnius-12."

"Why me, sir?"

"It won't just be you. You'll be taking the *Detriment*, her crew and her soldiers. The thing is, we've not had a presence out there for many years – ever since the Ghasts drove us back. There are few resource planets anywhere close, but the Ghasts might still have patrols." Teron stared intently across. "We need that information. What have the *Crimson*'s sensors picked up? It could be nothing, or it could have important intel on what the Ghasts are planning. We just don't know."

"Sounds like a wild goose chase."

Teron ignored the comment. "There's more - I probably shouldn't tell you this, but we're going to lose the Axion sector. Within the year. The Confederation has increased our funding, but we've been playing catch-up for several years. We can't turn out new ships nearly fast enough to replace the ones we're losing. The Ghasts have the numbers and now their newest ships have the edge on ours. Total war, John. They've been waging it, while we've been sitting on our hands."

"I've seen what it's like out there, sir. They're really pushing us. I didn't know it was *that* bad. We've just come away from an engagement with a Ghast light cruiser with some sort of weapon that knocked our systems out totally for a full minute. On something as small as a light cruiser of all things."

"We know about their new tech, Captain Duggan. It's why we're going to lose Axion. Their disruptors are only one example out of several. They've got beam weapons that can melt our engines from over a hundred thousand klicks. New missiles that are up there with our latest. It's like they've jumped decades ahead of us. Our intel guys have no idea how they've advanced so quickly. We're working on countermeasures, but it's not looking good. We might live through this if we're given time. If the *Crimson* has information, then we need to do our utmost to find out what it is."

"Charistos and Angax are in Axion, aren't they? How many billions of people live there?"

"A little over three billion across the two planets. It's only a matter of time till the Ghasts discover them."

"What do you think they'll do?"

"I don't know - we've never been faced with the question before. Perhaps they will try and impose their own leadership." Teron looked into the distance. "Do you remember what they did to that mining planet out in Late Ganymede?"

Duggan did remember. It was something that had reverberated across the Confederation and finally made people sit up and take notice. "They dropped something into the atmosphere. A bomb of some sort that we'd never seen before."

"Yes they did. It scorched twenty percent of the planet's surface and killed almost everyone who was living there. Over a million people – gone, just like that."

Duggan shifted uncomfortably in his seat at the memory. "How many of their ships are carrying this new weaponry you mentioned? They caught the *Detriment* pretty easily with it."

"One in four maybe, but that's only for the moment. We're only going to see more of it. You've already seen that it doesn't

23

make them invincible. However, it can turn the tide and that's going to be enough."

"Maybe if I hadn't been sent out to the frontiers I'd know all this."

Teron had the good grace to look pained. "People are still pissed at you. Important people."

"Damnit, the *Tybalt* was eleven years ago!" Duggan shouted, banging his fist on the table. He'd once captained an Anderlecht cruiser. As an up-and-coming young officer, he'd always been tipped for greatness. An explosion in the *Tybalt*'s weapons systems had put an end to that and consigned Duggan to a dead-end role on one of the Space Corps' smallest warships. He'd been cleared by a court martial, which was the only thing that had stopped him being kicked out of the Corps in disgrace. It hadn't been enough to save his career.

"Nothing will change. You know that."

Duggan leaned back in his seat and sighed. "So, you need me to pilot a ship to Karnius-12, find out what happened to the *Crimson*, and discover what it meant by telling us to prepare for war?"

"There's more to it than that - we need you to bring her back. Intact if possible, so that our technicians can interrogate the ship's databanks. It's imperative that you attempt to recover the vessel. Do you understand?"

Duggan stared back at Teron. "This is wrong, sir. It's going to be in pieces spread across a thousand kilometres of rock, or floating in space somewhere. And I'll bet I could download the entire contents of a mainframe as old as the *Crimson*'s onto a cube the size of my thumb. Why do we need it back?"

"I haven't been given that information, Captain. I have my orders, too."

Duggan stood, the glare from the room's monitoring screens

casting a multitude of shadows across his face. "How long?" he asked.

"Now. Your ship and your crew will leave immediately."

"We've got a big hole in the hull."

"The *Juniper*'s repair bots are fixing a patch over it as we speak. It won't look pretty."

"And we lost three the men."

"Their families will be notified. I've had another three assigned to your ship. Good men."

Duggan left the room. Nothing was looking pretty about this mission.

CHAPTER FOUR

DUGGAN RETURNED to the *Detriment* in Hangar Bay 1, which was a vast, open space enclosed by huge sheets of reinforced alloy. The *Juniper* had never been intended as a military launch platform, but each of her three bays could comfortably accommodate an Anderlecht class cruiser if needed. It wasn't uncommon to see one docked and the *Juniper* was guarded by three such ships in near space at all times. The *Detriment* was looking somewhat worse for wear, scarred and pocked, with the snub nose blackened from too many sub-light catapults through the atmospheres of the planets she'd fought on.

Hangar Bay 1 was surprisingly empty of personnel – here and there, Duggan saw technicians, carrying hand-held scanners which could analyse the integrity of a ship's hull in precise detail. The onboard mainframe could do most of this stuff these days, but the *Juniper*'s AIs were always good for a second opinion – they had vastly more processing grunt than what was available to the *Detriment*'s almost obsolete silicon-based systems. The *Detriment* was perched on its five squat legs, with its retractable boarding ramp fully extended. Duggan walked around to the rear quarter of the spacecraft. The thirty-metre gouge in the armour plating had been plugged in the usual fashion. Quick-fix repairs were done by squirting molten alloy into the hole. The ship's engines could disperse the heat in minutes, leaving the alloy to cool and harden quickly, while the repair bots pressed the patch into shape when it was still malleable. It looked as ugly as Duggan had expected.

He approached the boarding ramp. Two men were stationed at the bottom, slender gauss rifles clutched diagonally across their chests, as if they'd been frozen in the middle of a parade ground exercise.

"Sir!" they exclaimed in unison.

"Turner, Jackson," Duggan greeted them. "Get yourselves to quarters. We're leaving at once."

"Sir?"

"I'm expecting three replacements. Have they shown up?"

"Sir, they came aboard less than an hour ago. Sergeant Ortiz is looking after them."

"I'm sure she is," Duggan replied, walking past the two men. They fell in behind him.

There was no reason to leave a guard here on the *Juniper*. Duggan had felt obliged – life as one of the fifteen infantry onboard a Vincent class was as perilous as could be imagined, so he made every effort to keep them occupied. Every Corps warship carried soldiers under the ultimate command of the vessel's captain. The Ghasts liked to get planetside and murder humans every now and again, particularly on the mining outposts where an aerial bombardment would accomplish little. The best way to combat a Ghast incursion was to get down there and shoot right back at them. The real downside for the infantry was that ship-to-ship contact involving something as small as a Vincent class almost invariably ended in the complete destruction of one vessel or the other, with the soldiers on board powerless to do anything other than await whatever would come. It could be a shitty job sometimes and Duggan knew all about it.

When he reached the bridge, Duggan checked and found the *Detriment*'s arsenal had already been restocked. A hull status update from the *Juniper* reported that the patched-up hole had cooled sufficiently for them to lift off. Duggan checked the crew roster to see if anyone had disembarked. He'd given no permission for anyone to leave and was pleased to see that he wouldn't have to go looking for AWOLs. The ship hadn't docked in weeks and it wasn't unreasonable for the crew to think they might get a bit of shore leave. There was more bad news to come for them.

"Where's Commander McGlashan?" he asked Breeze.

"Gym, of course." It was where she spent the majority of her spare time.

Duggan sent a message for her to attend the bridge and she appeared within minutes, sweat beading upon her bare shoulders and neck.

"We're going again already?" she asked. It was no secret, since the *Detriment*'s engines were already thrumming in readiness to depart. "I should have guessed when they sent every repair bot on the *Juniper* over to see us."

"You'd best get ready," he said, giving away nothing. McGlashan looked at him for a moment before shrugging. She wasn't in uniform yet, but Duggan didn't want to wait. He pointed at her seat and she took the hint.

On the view screens, Duggan watched as Hangar Bay One became flooded in a deep orange light, which cycled on and off. He knew there'd be sirens, which thankfully weren't piped through to the bridge. When the *Juniper*'s sensors had decided there was no one left in the bay, the four hangar doors slowly uncoupled and slid smoothly into recesses in the orbital's walls. There was another space beyond – an enormous airlock protected by reinforced doors.

On the bridge, everyone took their seats even though it wasn't strictly necessary. Space flight had been choppy in the dim and distant past. Now it was rarely more violent than a slight feeling of movement – akin to being in a lift and even that was something which the ship's life support systems fought to suppress. On the newest ships, there was nothing to betray whether the vessel was accelerating, slowing or not moving at all.

The image on the viewing screens began to move as the *Detriment* lifted. Duggan gave the autopilot instruction for it to rotate the nose towards the hangar doors. He didn't need to turn the ship at all – he was just programmed this way in some anachronistic acknowledgement that humans needed to feel like they were travelling forwards. When necessary the vessel could fly in any direction it chose.

The *Detriment* sailed out through the airlock, gathering speed steadily. There were limits on how much thrust the ship's pilot could utilise so close to the orbital and Duggan was careful not to exceed them. It was unlikely that such a small ship's gravity drive could knock the *Juniper* even a centimetre off its ellipsis, but there was no point in overstepping the mark so soon after the arrival which had pissed off the AI. Behind them, the airlock doors closed as quickly as they'd opened, leaving no visible seam to mark where they were. Even with the thrust limits, it wasn't long until Duggan could see the entirety of the *Juniper*, against the cold blue background of Kryptes-9. Soon, the orbital was little more than a speck as the *Detriment* gathered pace.

"Deep fission engines coming online, Captain," said Breeze. "The *Juniper*'s fed us the coordinates." He frowned as he saw where they were heading. Beneath their feet, there was the familiar rumbling shudder as the vessel prepared to begin the journey.

"Anderlechts *Delectable* and *Deeper* hailing us good voyage, Captain," said Chainer.

"What about the *Thunder*?" asked Duggan.

"There are only two ships within sensor range, Captain," said Chainer in puzzlement. "Are you expecting more?"

"There should be three," said Duggan.

"Captain, the *Thunder* was destroyed by Ghast forces in the Glimmer Nebula over ten months ago," said McGlashan, calling up the details on one of her screens. "She was carrying troops."

Duggan exhaled loudly. "How many?"

"Over seventeen thousand dead," said McGlashan.

"What a waste," was all he could think of to say. It didn't sound like enough.

"Aye, Captain. As it ever was."

"Deep fission engines ready," prompted Breeze.

"Let's be on our way," growled Duggan, steeling himself for the sensation of dislocation.

"Lightspeed-H attained," said Breeze a few moments later. "Holding steady."

"Please confirm all systems operational," said Duggan.

"Weapons systems online and at one hundred percent," said McGlashan. "Guidance systems, life support at ninety-nine point nine-nine. Propulsion systems at forty percent and climbing. Everything within expected parameters."

"Next stop, Karnius-12 system," announced Duggan.

"I'm seeing a ten week and three-day time to reach our destination," said Breeze. He didn't even try to hide the dismay.

McGlashan swore. She caught herself. "Sorry, Captain. I didn't know we were going that far out."

Duggan was sympathetic, but he couldn't let on. The crew would be pissed and he didn't blame them – many of them were due leave. They'd been properly stitched up. *That's the Space Corps for you*, he thought.

"What're we looking for, sir? If you don't mind me asking." said Chainer. "Is it something to do with that repair bot they've loaded into the hold?"

"I don't mind, Lieutenant," Duggan replied, unaware about the existence of the repair robot until that very moment. "We're hoping to find something that's been lost for fifty-three years. A ship. It's holding data that will let us know how much crap humanity is about to find itself in." The other three occupants of the bridge stared at him dumbly. He returned their looks for a time, before he continued. "If someone's going to put their life on the line, they should know what they're doing it for," he said. "Get everyone to the mess room. I'll fill you in with what I know."

Within ten minutes, the small contingent of crew and infantry were crowded into the mess room. The infantry didn't look happy and they stared at him expectantly. Duggan picked out the three new faces at once. They were younger than he'd expected. When everyone had arrived, Duggan stood up in order to address them.

"I know you're all wondering why we didn't stay long at the *Juniper*. We've been given an important mission and it's going to screw up any hope you might have of getting some time away from the *Detriment*." Across the room, voices were raised in barely-contained anger and frustration.

"I've not had any leave for nearly two years," said Nelson. He was medium height and wiry, with a scar running diagonally over his left eye.

Duggan looked back at Nelson, meeting the man's gaze evenly. "I understand that, Soldier. We've been sent to look for something. It's over ten weeks away in Karnius-12." The complaints were louder this time and Duggan was forced to wave the infantry to silence.

"What is it we're looking for, sir?" asked Corporal Baker.

"An old ship called the *Crimson*, that got lost fifty years ago.

It sent a signal to Monitoring Station Alpha, telling us to prepare for war."

"We know there's a war on," said Sergeant Ortiz. "We've been fighting it for long enough. Lost plenty of good men and women too."

"We all know that, but someone's decided this is important enough to send an experienced crew and a valuable warship to find out what's going on."

"Has it got new information on the Ghasts, sir?" asked West. She was hardly chest-high on most of the men, but not one of them would dare cross her.

"I really don't know, Soldier. All I've been told is that we need to recover the *Crimson* and fly it back to the *Juniper* for interrogation."

"They expect a ship that old to fly?" West said in disbelief, ignoring the fact that the *Detriment* was over thirty years old. "Do we even know if there's enough left of it to fly?"

"It cut off communications before the guys on the Alpha could get anything more out of it. It said the channel was no longer secure."

"That means trouble, doesn't it?" she asked.

"It could mean anything," said Duggan. "A passing Ghast ship, or the ship's core could have received false information from its sensors. We've tracked the *Crimson*'s signal back to a planet – it's a place so remote they've not even assigned it a number, let alone a name. We find it, the repair drone we're carrying does its business with the ship and then we fly it home. After that, it's back to the front for us all."

"Something about this stinks," said Monsey. She was tall, mouthy and popular.

"What do you mean by that?" asked Duggan.

"I mean that war is war. If someone tells you there's a war

coming, you listen to them. You don't send out a Gunner to investigate what's happening."

"Normally, I'd agree with you. The *Crimson*'s so old, I don't think anyone's really interested in what it has to say. If I had to guess, I'd say this is just a tick box exercise. The *Crimson* was part of a special project that cost a lot of money. There are probably people who want to know what happened to it."

"There are people still alive who worked on that ship?" asked Monsey.

That wasn't what Duggan had meant to say, but what Monsey said made him wonder if there was indeed anyone left alive who'd worked on the Hynus Project. They'd be pretty old now. It wasn't unknown for people to live a long time with the advancements in medical technology available to those willing to pursue the dream of life everlasting. He put the thought aside for the moment.

"On the plus side, it means that for once you soldiers will be seeing some action that doesn't involve sitting in the hull of a ship, waiting till you get blown to pieces."

"Or burned to a cinder," said Smith.

Duggan nodded his head in acknowledgement. "It's almost certain we'll have to get out of here and down to the surface to find out what state the *Crimson* is in."

None of them voiced an objection to that. Operations on hostile planets were what they were all paid to do. Duggan dismissed the crew and returned to the bridge, with McGlashan, Breeze and Chainer in tow.

CHAPTER FIVE

TEN WEEKS WAS a long time as far as military space flight went. The fastest warships could travel from one side of Confederation space to the other in fewer than five weeks, so it seemed that wherever the *Crimson* had ended up, it wasn't anywhere remotely close to the usual flight paths of Confederation vessels, bar the odd scout or mining ship.

Duggan tried to keep to the usual routines that kept him sane during long voyages. He rose early from his bed – as captain, he was granted the privilege of a habitable space big enough that he couldn't touch the side walls if he stretched his arms out. There wasn't much in it, yet it seemed somehow important to him. After rising, he would visit the small mess area to speak to the infantry and crew who came and went. The mess was a room about fifteen feet square with a few hard chairs and tables, all of them fixed to the bare metal floor. The military didn't go in for carpets and if you didn't like metal surfaces, you were screwed.

The mess had two food replicators. The word *replicator* was a common joke in the Corps. In reality, you pressed a button and the machine would deposit a tray of *something* in front of you, that more or less approximated what you'd asked for. The food wasn't replicated either – the ship's life support systems could produce a rudimentary selection of proteins, carbohydrates and fats. It could mix these together, add a quantity of colours and flavourings, and then compress the whole lot into something that a starving man might find appetising.

"This is carrots and beef?" said one of the soldiers in disbelief. It was standard practise to question the food replicator's output – it never got old.

"Better food than your mother ever made, Turner," called another of the soldiers. There were fifteen of them on the *Detriment* – the ship could carry more, but Duggan knew that fifteen was about the most you could fit on a Gunner before people started pissing each other off.

"If I live to be a thousand, I'll never know how they manage to get beef that tastes so much like chicken," said Turner, walking away in mock disgust.

"It's breakfast time anyway," called Davis. "Why don't you try one of these fine rashers of bacon? They don't taste much like chicken."

"No, they taste like shit," said Diaz, sitting himself down next to Davis.

Duggan watched the interplay between them. It reminded him of what he mentally referred to as *the good old days,* when he didn't have a care in the world. When all he had to worry about was himself and his squad. When he was too stupid – lacking in wisdom, he corrected himself - to worry about the possibility that he might get killed somewhere and never come home.

Now he was Captain John Duggan. *The* Captain John Duggan. The man who, as an infantry sergeant, had single-handedly overcome a fortified nest of Ghast warriors using only plasma grenades and his rifle. The man who'd fought his way across fifty kilometres of hostile terrain to save one of his rifle squad who'd been injured by enemy fire. The man who was known to put the lives of his men above his own. The man who'd lost over a dozen of his crew when a missile tube had exploded.

As he poked at a slice of blue-sheened 'ham' he recalled the time he'd spoken to the mother of one of the dead. She'd been grey-haired and old. Mary Geffen her name had been. She'd fixed Duggan with her pale, grey eyes and told him that it wasn't his fault and that even if it had been, she'd have forgiven him. Mrs Geffen had given him a hug and wept for her lost daughter. It had been almost more than Duggan could bear.

Commander McGlashan entered the room, caked in sweat from her morning workout in the gym. A couple of the soldiers called her out as unfit and suggested she might need another hour on the treadbike. She grinned and gave them the finger. Duggan smiled to himself – a rookie might have thought the discipline on the *Detriment* was lax, but he knew the crew trusted each other. Duggan waved McGlashan over. She nodded and pointed at the replicator, to indicate she'd be over in a moment.

McGlashan sat down opposite Duggan. She was lean and toned, with an air of competence that had earned her a lot of respect over the years. She was carrying a tray, which she put down in front of her. It had a grey paste on it, and something else that might have been an approximation of toast.

"Porridge," she explained, seeing his look. "At least that's what the readout said."

"I was on the *Archimedes* once," he said. "Long ago. Nothing but the best on there. If you wanted a steak, you better believe that what came out of the replicators looked, smelled and even tasted like a steak. There were rumours that they kept cows onboard somewhere in one of the lower decks." Just the mention of the steaks brought a memory of the scent to his nostrils.

She smiled. "Really? People thought they kept cows on there?"

"Some people will believe anything. The *Archimedes* is over nine kilometres long. You could keep a lot of livestock inside if you wanted to. Personally, I was happy to believe the ship's lead engineer when he told me that they get all the latest food replication tech installed as soon as the research labs produce an improved model."

"I've seen the *Archimedes* a few times," said McGlashan. "Always in the distance – too far to make out the details."

"I wonder where it is now. It's needed in the Axion sector from what Admiral Teron tells me."

"If they send it to the front, it'll make people realise that we aren't winning the war, in spite of what the news channels would have them believe." She wasn't easily fooled.

"There are thirty-five fully colonised planets in the Confederation. I don't know how they've managed to stop the questions."

"People believe what they want to believe. If you tell them their sons and daughters died as heroes, you can keep up the charade for a long time. It's only really been the last five years we've been in retreat. Before then, it was all glory. Join the Corps, shoot a few Ghasts a billion light years away and come back with a medal. That's what the abiding memories are. The glory of humanity."

"Except that it's been a lie and let them push through the cost-cutting even while we're losing major systems on the periphery. He shook his head bitterly. "I remember when we were making six Anderlechts and one Hadron class every two years. We weren't even trying. Now we're decommissioning the old ones quicker than the new ones are coming into service."

"There's not been a new Hadron in four years," McGlashan said. "I don't know if there's a yard big enough to make them in a single piece now."

"Teron says the enemy's got the edge. It's not looking good."

"We've known that for long enough, sir. I can remember my

first encounter with a Ghast light cruiser. They were so far behind us that hardly anyone wanted to cheer when we blew it into pieces. I was only on a Gunner at the time and the enemy had no hope against us. Now look at what they pack into their Kravens. Weapons that have come from nowhere. The Confederation's been standing still and they've just kept on running."

"There's got to be something we're missing," said Duggan. "No one can jump ahead as quickly as they've done, no matter how much they want to."

"Let's hope their infantry's carrying the same shit as they ever did, sir," said Davis from nearby. There was no such thing as a private conversation in the mess room.

"Yeah, we can get close enough to put a hole in *them* at least," added Turner.

"You might get a chance to put a hole in some of them when we get to where we're going," said Duggan.

"You think we'll see them when we go looking for the *Crimson*?" asked Davis, with the unmistakeable longing of a man who'd done too much fighting.

"We might. There are Ghasts where we're going. With any luck, we'll miss them. In, out and back home."

"I'll believe that when I see it, Captain," said Turner.

"Sometimes dreams come true," said McGlashan, the scepticism evident in her voice.

The days were boring and Duggan was on edge. Something was nagging away at him and he didn't know what. To occupy himself, he spent time tracking updates from the war. It wasn't looking good.

"Six Gunners missing in action. Axion Sector Nine," he said. "Anderlechts *Grimstone* and *Devoted* confirmed destroyed in combat against three Cadaverons."

"Damn," said Breeze, raising his head. "That's real bad."

"I served on the *Devoted* for two months," said Chainer.

"They were amongst the best I've seen. Taught me a thing or two."

"Sector Nine is only a short jump from Charistos, isn't it?" said McGlashan.

"Everything in Axion is only a short jump from Charistos," Duggan replied. "We need to get ships out there."

"Think they'll send the *Archimedes*? Or at least a pair of the Hadrons?"

Duggan shook his head to indicate he didn't know. "I've tried to call up the orders for our major ships. I'm denied access to see what's planned for them. I'd have been more surprised if I'd had the clearance."

"We're going to lose this, aren't we?" asked McGlashan. "What the hell do they even want from us?" It was a question that had been asked countless times by countless people.

"Sometimes you just have to accept that you're never going to understand your enemy," was all Duggan could think of to say.

The Human-Ghast war had started almost thirty-two years ago. There'd been no misunderstanding between two space-faring races. There was no initial friendship that had subsequently been lost. Rather, the first encounter had been between a Ghast heavy cruiser – which later become known as Cadaverons – and a small fleet of Confederation mining ships, far, far out from humanity's central planet of Earth. The Ghasts had simply destroyed the mining ships, killing all of the civilians on board. After that, there had been a number of minor skirmishes, during which it became apparent that the Ghasts were technologically less advanced than humans. Nevertheless, they began to actively hunt out Confederation spaceships until the ruling Council was reluctantly forced to describe the situation as 'war'. Unfortunately, they were complacent about it, thinking that the Ghasts' technological inferiority meant that they were little more than war-mongering upstarts.

After two decades of fighting, still perceived as a side-issue by the Confederation Council, the quantity and quality of the Ghast ships surged. Suddenly, their newest craft were almost a match for the Corps warships. The Confederated planets were populous and wealthy. Their shipyards could lay down dozens of armed vessels per year with the right level of funding. Confident in their assumed superiority, the ruling council continued to treat the Ghasts almost with disdain and neither side showed any determination to communicate. In fact, there was almost complete ignorance on both sides about who it was they were fighting. The difficulties of tracking a spacecraft through light-speed travel meant that casualties on both sides had mostly been confined to Space Corps personnel.

As Duggan searched through military databanks that were probably meant to be secured against him, the extent of the crisis began to emerge. Admiral Teron had indicated that the Ghasts had taken the advantage and if anything, he'd underplayed how far ahead they were. From what Duggan could see, they'd taken an incomprehensibly huge leap in technological advancement. It was almost unbelievable what they'd achieved. On top of this, one of Duggan's old contacts from his earlier days in the Corps sent him some classified documents that showed how the military had been trying to find a way to nail down the destination of a lightspeed spacecraft. The limitation continued to be the processing power of the AIs. If you networked enough of them, it became theoretically possible. Unfortunately, the theory hadn't yet been put into practise. The worst part of it was, recent data gathered from engagements with some of the newest Ghast vessels suggested that the alien species was years ahead of humanity in AI development.

"We're screwed," said Duggan to himself.

By the start of the tenth week, Duggan realised he'd had enough of being cooped up. Their destination wasn't far now, yet he couldn't help think that there was a long return trip to look forward to. He'd spent a lot of time trawling through archives and databanks looking for any information on the *Crimson*, in order to determine its maximum velocity and any other capabilities it might have. In the end, he'd turned up a blank. Whatever records there were of the vessel and the trillions of dollars it had taken to create it, they'd been thoroughly expunged. *Or classified so high that I don't have clearance to find out if they even exist,* he thought sourly. Not for the first time, he considered the possibility of sucking the contents of the *Crimson*'s onboard systems into the *Detriment*'s mainframes. If it was as much of a bucket as he thought it would be, it didn't seem likely that it could scrape past Lightspeed D or E. He knew he should have grilled Teron about it more than he had. In the end, there was no point in dwelling on the might have beens. While he was mulling over the possibilities, a red square flashed up on a display to his left, accompanied by a dull bleeping.

"What was that?" he asked.

"A Ghast ship," replied Chainer, his head roving across his instrument readouts. "Type unknown. Our sensors couldn't scan it in time. Looks like it picked us up as we came within range."

It wasn't unusual to be detected by enemy ships during light-speed travel. All it meant was that the Ghasts knew that a Corps ship had gone by. They wouldn't be able to plot their destination, nor follow them. They might have determined it was a Gunner, depending on how new the Ghast ship was and what technology it had onboard. It didn't really matter to Duggan. What was important was that he'd got confirmation of the enemy's presence so close to Karnius-12.

"Let's hope that's the only one," McGlashan remarked.

"Yeah," said Duggan. "Admiral Teron said the *Crimson* terminated its communication because it wasn't secure. Maybe the Ghasts picked it up."

"Would they spend any time looking?" asked McGlashan doubtfully.

"If I had nothing better to do with my time than patrol an uninhabited chunk of space and I received a signal from an enemy vessel, I'd go looking for it as well," said Duggan.

Two days later, the *Detriment*'s navigational sensors reported their imminent arrival in the Karnius-12 system, which was a series of fifteen planets orbiting a much larger than average sun.

"Twenty hours early," said Duggan, without much surprise. Calculating time across the vast distances involved was rarely an exact matter. The *Detriment*'s old mainframe had plenty of horsepower to run the ship, but it still ran out of steam when presented with certain problems. The AIs on a larger vessel could have nailed it down to within a few seconds. In the grand scheme of things, it wasn't important. On the positive side, the calculating error had brought them to their destination a day early instead of a day late.

"Do we know exactly where we need to come out of light-speed?" asked Breeze. "I'm sure we'd all prefer it if we landed on the nose, rather than six hours out."

"The Alpha locked the *Crimson*'s signal down to the fourth planet," said Duggan. "We have only basic data on it, since I don't think anyone's been out here in decades." He reached across to an indentation on the plasmetal console and brushed it with his finger until he located what he wanted. "It seems like the fourth planet is nothing other than a big old rock. Too far out to host life, not so far out that it's covered in ice."

"Could be any one of another thousand planets we've seen," said McGlashan.

"Nothing to get too excited over. If the *Crimson*'s there, we should be able to pick it up when we get close, even if it's keeping radio silence. A kilometre lump of metal can't hide for long."

"Did they bother to go looking for it when they first lost contact?"

"Teron said they did, without giving away too many details. Perhaps they were certain it had been lost in far space or destroyed. However long they bothered to search, they didn't find what they were looking for."

"It sounds like baloney to me," said Breeze. "If the *Crimson* was so valuable, why would they let it go without getting every tiny detail about it answered?"

"Yeah, something smells, that's for sure," added Chainer.

Duggan had already come to that conclusion. "It's a fifty-year-old mystery that may not even be a mystery. Whatever happened way back then doesn't concern us now. Let's find this piece of junk and be on our way home." He thought quietly for a few moments. "Let's keep ready. I don't like not knowing."

Less than an hour later, the *Detriment* grated judderingly into near space, exactly twenty-five minutes away from the fourth planet in the Karnius-12 system. Before Duggan could even catch his bearings, a priority communication came through on an encrypted military channel.

"Top secret," he muttered, his heart sinking as he read the details.

Planet Charistos discovered by Ghast fleet. Attempts at negotiation ignored. Military counterstrike failed. Hadron Supercruiser ES Ulterior destroyed. Surface of Charistos ignited by Ghast bombardment. Estimated civilian casualties: one-point-one billion.

"They've done it," said Duggan, putting his head in his hands. "The bastards. They've gone and done it."

43

CHAPTER SIX

FOR ALMOST TWO DAYS, the *Detriment* orbited the planet, her sensors constantly interrogating the surface for signs of an unnaturally heavy object. The planet was a barren rock with a diameter of a little over one hundred thousand kilometres. The surface was pocked and scarred from an ancient meteorite storm of unusual ferocity, which the ship's mainframe calculated to have occurred over three billion years previously. Without the presence of life to carpet the planet's surface, the undisguised craters looked fresh and jagged.

"Nothing showing, Captain," said Chainer. He'd exhausted himself with his efforts over the last forty hours and had found no sign at all of the missing *ESS Crimson*. They were all running on empty now, drained to enervation by the news of the massacre on Charistos. "I've covered every inch of the surface."

"Could it be hidden in one of those craters?" asked Duggan. His face was haggard and pale. He called up a magnified image of the surface of the main view screen. It was a mixture of greys and computer-enhanced blacks.

"If it was fifty metres long then it might have escaped notice.

It's a kilometre long and weighs well over a billion tonnes. I haven't missed it."

Duggan cursed. There'd been no sign of Ghast activity yet. Even so, he had the feeling that he was pushing his luck by staying out here. Everyone was getting edgy, like they knew the *Detriment* was a sitting duck.

"Should we contact Monitoring Station Alpha and get confirmation of coordinates from the source receptor?" asked McGlashan.

"It's a good idea, but they already fed the coordinates to the *Juniper* and the *Juniper* fed them straight to us. The *Crimson* is either here or it's been destroyed after sending the signal."

"What if it broke into pieces and the core somehow managed to survive with enough pieces to cobble together a transmitter?" asked Breeze. "It's happened before. There might only be parts on the surface instead of a whole."

"The sensors would have picked up anything big enough to transmit," said Chainer. "I can focus the search on smaller fragments if necessary. It'll take hours to scan for ten metre pieces or much longer if we want to scan for five metre chunks."

"I don't want to spend any more time here than is absolutely necessary. We're needed back where we should be, instead of out here looking for a phantom in the mist," said Duggan. He leaned across to have a look at the readouts, breathing in the bitter aroma of Chainer's thick, black coffee as he did so.

"Look here, Captain," said Chainer. "Here're the analyses. There's nothing that even remotely resembles what we're looking for."

"These crust scans over here. Iron ore?"

"Yes. Mostly hematite. It's nothing unusual. It wouldn't block our scanners."

"This is much denser. This area on the south pole."

"That's galena. Lead ore. Again, nothing unusual about it.

45

The *Crimson* should be much denser than that. It would stick out like a sore thumb."

"What about if the ship was underground?" asked Duggan. "Beneath all of this stuff?"

Chainer blinked. "I suppose it's possible it could hide if it was deep enough. A few hundred metres of lead would block even the *Archimedes'* scanners, let alone the ones we're working with. A kilometre worth of ship needs a pretty big hole."

"Are there any places that could hide a ship?" asked Duggan.

"Let me see." Chainer called up the detailed surface map which the ship's sensors had created during the two days' circuits of the planet. "You could hide the *Juniper* in some of these holes," he muttered, his eyes glancing over the results of his mainframe query.

"Anything?" prompted Duggan, impatient for an answer.

"There are at least a hundred fissures that might be wide enough to house a kilometre-long object," said Chainer.

"What about here where the ores are most thickly clustered?"

"That's an area nearly thirty million square kilometres. It looks like it took the brunt of the meteorite storm, which might explain the presence of so much ore. There must be fifty or sixty fractures in the rock that you could hide a ship in."

"Let's focus our efforts there," said Duggan.

"Aye, Captain," acknowledged Chainer.

Duggan changed their course towards the planet's south pole. "Which are the most likely places you'd hide a ship?" he asked.

Chainer called up a holographic view of the area, overlaid with the fissures in the planet's surface. The image hovered in the space of the bridge, tantalisingly realistic, yet impossible to touch. "We've got a couple here and another one here. I reckon you could fit a big ship into those ones."

"Anything in the data we've already collected from our scans that might help?" asked Duggan.

"I'd say we can rule this one out and this one. We flew directly over and got a pretty good view straight down. There's nothing at the bottom. And this one narrows almost immediately. You might squeeze something through."

"Not likely, though," mused Duggan.

Four minutes later, the *Detriment* reached a position where its scanners could gather additional data based on the new priorities which Chainer had given them. Duggan stood nearby watching the readouts, while McGlashan and Breeze didn't even try to feign disinterest. For another hour, the *Detriment* criss-crossed the crater-strewn south pole of the planet. In truth, the ship's sensors were advanced enough that they could pick up extraneous data even when they hadn't been instructed to do so. The mainframe wasn't quite aware, but it was well enough programmed to know that it was best to gather too much information when the opportunity arose, rather than too little.

"Nothing new," said Duggan, almost to himself.

"I reckon we've got seventeen possible locations," said Chainer. "Places where the surface metals are too thick to be certain they aren't hiding anything."

"Anything you can do to eliminate some of those? Seventeen is too many to search. It could take us weeks, especially if we have to get outside and use the tanks." Every gunner carried a total of four armed vehicles for surface work, which were affectionately known as tanks. They were technological anachronisms, but they were tough and packed a punch.

Chainer stared at his displays for a few moments, without speaking. Eventually, he gave Duggan the bad news. "I can't see any way of bringing the numbers down."

"Can you analyse the sites for any signs of surface disruption that might not have occurred naturally?" asked Duggan.

Chainer frowned. "I'm not sure I follow."

"I want signs of heat damage to the surrounding rocks.

ANTHONY JAMES

Anything hotter than a meteorite strike. Like something from a missile or a beam weapon. If the *Crimson* came in fast, it may have only had nanoseconds to pick its location."

"And if so, it might have blown an existing hole wider in order to get through," said Chainer in understanding.

"Exactly."

The results weren't long in coming. "This one, Captain. There are signs of something much hotter than expected. There's extensive fusing in the rocks in a big area near this crater over here."

"That's more like a cavern than a fissure," said Duggan, peering at the area. "Four hundred metres wide and three hundred tall. You could fit a ship in there."

"It would almost be touching the sides," said McGlashan. "Not something I'd fancy without guidance."

"That's our spot," said Duggan with a sudden certainty. "If anyone came looking for the ship they'd easily miss it if it were hidden in there."

"We're going down for a look?" asked McGlashan. She'd served her time as a foot soldier in the same way that he had, and Duggan suspected that she missed the days.

"I'm afraid not, Commander," said Duggan with a smile. "We'll allow Sergeant Ortiz and her men this one, shall we?"

McGlashan showed a flicker of disappointment. "Of course, Captain. It's their time to shine."

Duggan called up the ship's intercom. "Good news ladies and gentlemen. It's your chance for some action. Get suited up and report to the launch bay. Twenty minutes, please." He closed the channel and turned to the others on the bridge.

"I'll get down there and let Sergeant Ortiz know what's up." With that, he climbed out through the tight exit door from the bridge and navigated his way with a practised smoothness along the two hundred metres of corridors that took him through ultra-

48

dense engine matter towards the *Detriment*'s single, cramped launch bay. As he walked, Duggan could feel the immense, other-worldly power of the vessel's engines which surrounded him on all sides. Although the *Detriment* appeared huge to look at, there was hardly anything spare within its hull. Propulsion, weapons, guidance. All the important parts took up close to ninety-five percent of the interior. It left precious little room for a sizeable crew or cargo, not that the Gunners had ever been specifically designed to shuttle infantry into combat – their addition was more of an afterthought. Duggan had never asked what the production line cost of a Vincent class came to. He doubted it was a cheap way to carry four crew and fifteen soldiers.

The launch bay was an area at the lowest end of the ship and close to the rear. It was less than twenty metres square and six high, with only eight metres of alloy separating the contents from the oblivion of the vacuum outside. The four tanks took up the majority of the available space – they were angular and vaguely wedge-shaped, with stubby cannons mounted on turrets. They didn't need wheels and could hover over almost any surface. It was cramped and uncomfortable inside, with barely enough room to fit six infantry in their combat suits. Duggan had seen a dozen crammed into one before and it hadn't been a pretty sight.

The repair bot was sitting in the centre of the hold, between the four tanks. It was a matte grey cylindrical object, three metres long, squat and powered by a small gravity drive hidden some-where within. The robot's surface was utterly featureless to the naked eye and it was designed to operate in the most hostile envi-ronments imaginable. It appeared almost sullen as it waited in the hold.

In the remaining space of the *Detriment*'s bay, soldiers strug-gled into their combat gear, the sounds of their voices raised above the background noise of the engines. Duggan was experi-enced enough to pick up the nervous tension of men and women who were about to face the unknown. Soon, they were gathered in formation, with Sergeant Ortiz at their head. Their body suits were a dark grey, made of a flexible polymer and with an oversized alloy helmet that could support the suit's occupant for almost a month away from the ship. They looked strange and menacing.

"We'll not be setting the *Detriment* down," said Duggan. It wasn't usual practice to land, particularly in a potentially hostile situation like this one. The vessel would be an easy target if a Ghast warship dropped out of lightspeed close by. "We'll come to a height of two hundred klicks and then let you go. I've had the *Detriment*'s mainframe give the tanks and repair bot the instructions they need. You'll just sit back and enjoy the ride."

"Same as ever, Captain," said Ortiz, her voice imperfectly replicated by the suit's comms box.

"We think the *Crimson* piloted itself into a split in the surface over the planet's south pole. I want you to get in there, find the ship and point this repair bot in the right direction. Needless to say, you can't let anything happen to it, else we'll be trying to lift whatever's left of the *Crimson* into the hold that we're currently standing in. And I'm sure you can see there's not enough room to carry both tanks and spaceship fragments." The soldiers relied on the tanks for transport and firepower. They'd be loath to see them abandoned so that the *Detriment* could carry a semi-functioning computer core back to the *Juniper*.

"What happens when the *Crimson*'s fixed up, sir?" asked Ortiz.

"That depends on what state it's in and how fast it can fly. We have almost no data on its capabilities. The decision has not been made."

"Understood," she said.

With that, Duggan left the soldiers and returned to the bridge. He sat back in his seat and watched the internal readouts that told him the men and women had now boarded the tanks and were ready to disembark on his signal. Duggan gave McGlashan the nod to let her know she was in control for the drop.

"Bringing us in close, Captain. Thirty seconds," she said, tapping in a path to bring them near to the planet's surface.

"Thirty seconds and we'll be in place," echoed Duggan through his comms channel to Sergeant Ortiz.

"Roger that, Captain. Thirty seconds." Her voice was piped directly into the bridge and her words floated in the air.

"We're now one-hundred-and-ninety-five klicks up," said McGlashan. The viewscreen showed an image of a bleak, flawed surface. It was inhospitable by the standards of many planets, yet there were places that were much harsher than this one.

"Almost a walk in the park," said Duggan to himself. "Sergeant Ortiz, you're good to go."

"Roger," came the response.

"Cargo hold door open," said Breeze. "Tanks one, two and three on their way. Repair bot with them."

"Keep me updated, Sergeant."

Ortiz's voice came back at once. "Like you said, Captain. Just sitting back and enjoying the ride."

"We're pulling up to ten thousand klicks and we'll circle the landing zone. Keep the comms open unless I say otherwise."

"Roger. We'll leave a manned beacon up top at all times."

"Let me know when you're on the ground."

"Will do."

McGlashan brought the *Detriment* away from the planet's surface while they waited. The seconds passed until they became a few long minutes. The tanks could be dropped from twenty-five thousand kilometres in an emergency. They'd not have much power left by the time they landed, so Duggan had brought the *Detriment* in close so that the tanks' engines would have plenty of juice to spare. Once down, the armoured vehicles had no way of getting back up. Duggan planned to deal with that when it became an issue.

Ortiz's voice crackled into life, startling Duggan. "All tanks safely deployed, Captain, less than two klicks from the target. We've got the repair bot tagging along with us."

"Roger. Keep those updates coming."

Duggan found himself on his feet while he waited for further news. He wasn't sure why he felt so concerned, since he'd always thrived on taking risks. Something about this mission just didn't feel right. He wasn't given the time to reflect on the vagaries of fate or luck.

"Deep fission signature detected, Captain," said Chainer. "We've got a Cadaveron breaking out of lightspeed on the far side of the planet."

CHAPTER SEVEN

DUGGAN SWORE and then swore again. "Any chance they'll have detected us?"

"No chance at all."

"Sergeant Ortiz, we've got a Ghast heavy cruiser coming into orbit. We'll need to break off comms shortly. Keep your heads low."

"Roger that, Captain."

"Keep looking for the *Crimson* and we'll collect you when we're able."

"What now?" asked McGlashan. "Think it's here looking for us?"

Duggan ran his fingers through his short hair, feeling the sweat on his scalp. "I don't know what it's here for," he said. The implications if it *was* looking for them didn't bear thinking about. "Any further details, Lieutenant?" he asked.

"If I had to guess, I'd say they came in high," said Chainer.

"They'll probably circle the planet at fifty thousand klicks. It's how their big guns usually operate," said Duggan. "Any idea of how long till they pick us up?"

"No more than fourteen minutes until the risk becomes unacceptably high," said Chainer, looking at his screens. Pages and pages of possibilities scrolled before his eyes as the *Detriment*'s mainframe tried to nail down the likeliest course and trajectory of the enemy ship based on past recorded data.

"Let's give it nine minutes where we are and then we'll plot a course," Duggan said. He hoped they'd be able to orbit the planet a couple of times and avoid detection until the Ghast ship decided there was nothing here to bother about. "Sergeant Ortiz, do you copy?"

"I copy, Captain," she said.

"We're going to orbit the planet and we'll be out of comms range in approximately nine minutes. Keep the outbound channel closed and wait for us to contact you." There was a high chance that the Ghast warship would pick up a signal from the ground, especially if its own orbit brought it near enough.

"Roger that, Captain. Comms closed until we hear."

"Should we head into the fissure?" asked McGlashan. "If the *Crimson* got in there with seven times our mass, then we should be able to slide in real smooth."

"Negative, Commander. We don't know for sure what's down there. We'll be an easy target if we get anything wrong." He paused. "And we don't know for certain if the *Crimson* is there anyway. It's too much of a risk."

McGlashan didn't mention it again and in truth, Duggan was tempted to try a landing. The *Detriment*'s mainframe estimated they'd have an eighty-six percent chance of avoiding detection for two full circuits of the planet, with that number decaying at an increasing rate for subsequent circuits. The computer didn't have sufficient data to predict their chances if they decided on a landing. The surface fissure cut into the rock at an oblique and the sensors hadn't been able to penetrate far enough along to determine if there was enough room for a spaceship to navigate its length. All they had to go on was the evidence of an intense heat in the area. Duggan didn't like to rely on statistics if he could avoid it, but this time he was going to side with the mainframe.

"That's nine minutes, Captain," said McGlashan, when the time had elapsed.

"Sergeant Ortiz, this is the *Detriment* wishing you good luck."

"Make sure you come back for us," she said.

Duggan cut off the comms without replying. He wasn't a man to make promises he couldn't keep and the soldiers knew it well enough. They also knew that only death would stop him trying. "Take us away, Commander," he said.

"Already done."

"Listen out for anything," he said to Chainer.

The soldiers were out of comms range two minutes later. Duggan dropped back into his chair and shifted uncomfortably while he waited helplessly for this one to play itself out. To his left, McGlashan watched the weapons panels like a hawk, her fingers never straying more than a few inches from the deployment indentations on the alloy console. The air seemed even more stifling than usual.

The first circuit of the planet took eleven minutes and the next one nine. The *Detriment*'s hull temperature climbed as the gravity engines threw the spaceship in a tighter and faster orbit than the first.

"The next circuit will bring us back over Sergeant Ortiz's position," said McGlashan.

"Down to an eighty-three-point-two percent chance of escaping detection," Duggan said to himself. "How long till we're in comms range?"

"Just under a minute."

"Still no sign of the Cadaveron," said Chainer.

"What do they want?" asked Duggan. "Why here and why now?"

"Shit happens," said Breeze.

"Sergeant Ortiz, are you reading?"

"The sergeant's underground, Captain," came the voice of Turner. "She's left me up top."

"Anything to report?"

"We'll lose you in thirty seconds," interjected McGlashan.

"The going's rough, even for the tanks. A bit slower than we'd have liked. The squad is less than two kilometres along the fissure. You should see this place, Captain. Makes the Grand Canyon look like a knife cut in your steak."

"Understood, soldier. We're breaking off now. Keep low and quiet until you hear from us again."

"Will do."

Duggan closed the channel. He didn't want to give the Ghasts any more chance to detect their location than he had to. He got to his feet again, unable to settle. The readouts from the life support showed a sudden fluctuation in their power draw as they corrected the internal environment of the ship in order to protect the occupants from the gravity force of a series of sharp turns it was engaged in.

"How long till we're in comms range again?" he asked.

"Three more orbits and twenty-six minutes. Looks like we'll be hot at the end of this next one. A six-minute circuit, skipping just off the atmosphere."

"Seventy-nine-point-five chance of an unwanted interception," Duggan announced.

"I never liked the odds when they dropped below ninety-five percent," said Chainer. Before him, a hundred modulating bars danced to show the status of the engines. Advances in computing power had made the position of ship's engineer almost redundant. Regardless, Duggan liked the role to be filled, even though he knew that many Gunners flew with a crew of only three. He took comfort from the backup of having a fourth trained officer aboard.

At the end of the six-minute circuit, the *Detriment*'s nose glowed fiercely, the temperature at exactly one-hundred percent of its design tolerance. The mainframe would never push it beyond that unless it was overridden by the captain or the commander.

"The next one's a nine, then a ten-point-five," said McGlashan. "Twenty minutes until we see how the guys and gals are getting on."

"It needs to be good news," said Chainer.

"The only good news will be a fission signature from the Ghast ship," said Duggan. Before him, the chance of interception had fallen to seventy-four-point-nine. It would drop below seventy on the next orbit.

"What happens if they don't go?" asked McGlashan.

It wasn't a situation that Duggan wanted to contemplate. Nevertheless, he could feel the burden of the decision closing in on him, like an inescapable collision that he had no way to swerve around. "Why can't they just piss off?" he asked, not expecting an answer.

"Maybe the ship that pinged us on the approach read enough to be able to predict our destination," said Chainer. "The latest Cadaverons can almost outthink a Hadron class. If it managed to tally the presence of a Corps vessel way out of its expected arena with the signal from the *Crimson*, the ship's AI might just have put two and two together."

"How'd they manage to follow us, then?" asked McGlashan. "And if they knew of the *Crimson*'s signal, why didn't they know it was on this planet?"

"It's possible they intercepted the *Crimson*'s warning without knowing exactly where it came from. The further you get from a transmission's source, the harder it is to pin it down. I'll bet the Ghosts could have narrowed the source down to half a dozen systems in this galaxy. The Alpha's only designed to do comms and monitoring – the kit they're carrying could pick up the sound of a dog shitting on the pavement from half a trillion light years away."

"Nice example," said Breeze.

"So, it's down to luck," said Duggan, now sure that Chainer had guessed right. "Lucky for them and unlucky for us. It means they know we're here."

"Seems that way," said Chainer.

"Six minutes till comms range," McGlashan said.

"If the Ghosts know we're here, then they'll know that the *Crimson*'s here as well," said Breeze. "What if they came to the same conclusion as we did about where you could hide a ship?"

"The scanners on a heavy cruiser might be able to cut deeper through the surface opacity," Chainer added. "We don't know what their latest ships can do."

"Reckon they'll be able to pick up a single man on the surface standing with a communications beacon?" asked Duggan.

"I doubt it. Not easily. Unless they were actively looking, or at a comparatively low orbit."

"You've gone from an almost certain no, to an almost certain yes in the space of three sentences," Duggan admonished him.

"Sorry, Captain. I wouldn't want to rely on guesswork, so I'd probably assume they'll pick up Turner if they stay in the area long enough."

"One minute to comms range."

"Ghost ship just coming into the view of our sensors over the planet's curvature," said Chainer. "It's describing a tight circle over the south pole."

"Dropping us down to five hundred klicks," said McGlashan.

The external viewscreen showed them banking sharply and the planet's surface filled every inch of the space as they headed steeply downwards and away from the Ghast heavy cruiser, in the hope that they'd be able to hide low against the planet's surface.

"Did they see us?" asked Duggan.

"Unsure," said Chainer, leaning across to tap at an area of his console. "Yes, they saw us. I'm picking up the outline of a Cadaveron heading towards our position."

"Get us away," said Duggan.

"Already on it."

The life support systems surged again as the *Detriment* swung sharply about, wrenching the alloys of the superstructure almost to breaking point. The ship's sub-light drive shot from fifty percent to exactly one hundred percent as the *Detriment* accelerated at maximum power in the opposite direction to the approaching enemy. A screen to Duggan's right helpfully displayed the record bank image of a smoothly-rotating three-dimensional image of a Ghast Cadaveron – a three-point-five-kilometre-long mixture of wedge, cuboid and cylinder in dull silver, with twenty-eight banks of missile launchers, and an enormous front-mounted particle beam generator. It outgunned the *Detriment* by fifty to one. The only positive was that a Cadaveron carried so many weapons that they'd had to compromise on the engine mass. Out in deep space, it was faster than any Vincent class. Here in orbit the difference was much lower.

"How long till they get in weapons range?"

"I can't answer that for definite yet, Captain," replied McGlashan. "Their designs change all the time. This looks like a newer one than we've seen. There are a few structural differences that aren't in our records. It'll be a minute or two until we see how fast they can go while clinging so close to the surface."

"Let me know as soon as you know," said Duggan. Calm

settled over him and his mind ticked over methodically as it did its best to plot a course out of the predicament they found themselves in.

CHAPTER EIGHT

COMMANDER MCGLASHAN SPOKE the words that Duggan hadn't wanted to hear. "Looks like this is a fast one," she announced after less than a minute.

"How fast?" asked Duggan. It was just his luck to come across one of the Ghasts' new designs. Their ships seemed to change all the time and there was no way to rely on past experience to determine the capabilities of what another ship might be. Even to this day, the Confederation had precious little information on the extent of the Ghast resources, nor how populous they were. One thing was certain: the alien species had taken this war more seriously from the outset and now they were reaping the rewards.

"Three minutes twenty seconds until we're in range of their missiles. A maximum of fifty-five additional seconds for travel time at our current velocity."

Duggan didn't respond immediately. He was too busy thinking, with the familiar expression on his face that he always carried when the threat was at its greatest. None of the options were palatable and in the circumstances, he knew he'd have to pick the best one from a bad lot. The easiest option was to go to lightspeed. There was plenty of time to warm up the fission drive. Of course, that would necessitate abandoning both the soldiers on the ground and the mission itself. Duggan could accept failing the mission, but he could never accept failing the men and women on the planet's surface. The other option was to engage the Ghast ship and hope to somehow pull a lucky kill out of the bag. Duggan almost laughed out loud at the thought. There was no way in hell the *Detriment* could knock a Cadaveron out of the sky. That left one option, if only there was enough time to make it work. He grimaced. It was going to be like taking a kick in the balls.

"We need to reach the southern pole before they blow us to pieces," he said.

"That's going to stress the hull," said McGlashan almost absently as she input the new course and overrode the in-built safety parameters.

"I need a decaying orbit that will bring us into the planet's atmosphere at the last possible moment." The fourth planet's atmosphere was thin and comprised a mixture of carbon dioxide, nitrogen and a tiny amount of oxygen. Nevertheless, it would be enough to burn them up at the velocity they'd be travelling.

"What's the plan?" asked McGlashan.

"I'm going to tell the mainframe to take us over the point where we dropped off the soldiers. We're going to get in the last tank and try and get to the surface."

"They'll pick us up easily," said Chainer.

"Not if we drop a cloud of shock drones just before we leave," said Duggan. "With any luck they'll confuse the Ghast weapons systems."

"And then they'll either destroy the *Detriment* or watch it burn up as we drop too low in the atmosphere."

"Precisely."

McGlashan shrugged. She could see that Duggan was decided and if she disagreed with his choice she kept her own counsel. "I'll miss the old girl," was all she said.

"Lieutenants, make your way to the tank. You can suit up inside. I'm sure you'll not hang around to pick up your belongings."

Duggan didn't need to say anything further. Chainer and Breeze got to their feet and left the bridge with as much speed as they could manage.

"It's nearly set," said Duggan. "We'll remote jettison once we get to the tank. The ship will enter the atmosphere immediately over the landing site. At the speed we're going, she'll break apart almost at once."

"I hate having to do this, sir."

"Me too. Come on, let's get to the cargo bay," Duggan instructed, ushering his commander through the exit doorway. After she'd gone, he paused for one final look over the bridge of the spaceship he'd commanded for the better part of six years. It had been a true and faithful companion to him.

The air was cooler in the narrow corridor outside, yet not enough to dry the sweat that caked the pair of them as they hurried along in the peculiar half-crouch that you adopted after a while on a Vincent class. McGlashan called over her shoulder as she ran, her breathing hardly laboured at all.

"I've programmed in two small waves of shock drones to be jettisoned before the last big one. I thought it might keep the Ghasts guessing about what we're doing."

"Good idea."

"And the weapons systems will fire at anything which comes in range."

The newest Lambdas could outrange most Ghast missiles. The particle beam was more of a gamble. When they'd first appeared on the enemy warships, their range had been pathetically low. Over the course of only a few years, the weapon had been developed until its range was a match for most of what the Space Corps could field. It was academic – a few Lambdas weren't going to penetrate the Cadaveron's defences. Even if a couple got lucky, they didn't carry enough of a payload to cripple anything as large as the heavy cruiser. Still, it would feel good to know that the *Detriment*'s last throw of the dice caused the enemy at least a small amount of damage. It might be enough to send the Cadaveron crawling back to base for repairs. Duggan realised his mind was wandering and he forced it back to the present.

In the close quarters of the *Detriment*'s network of tight corridors, Duggan heard an occasional faint rumbling, sometimes accompanied by a shuddering beneath his feet. To a rookie, it would have felt like nothing more threatening than the expected operation of a spaceship. To Duggan, the sounds were indicative of the immense stresses that the *Detriment*s engines and structure were being placed under as the vessel fought to maintain a close orbit around the planet.

"It's going to be tight," said McGlashan, her voice almost conversational.

They burst out of the corridor and into the ship's cramped hold. The single remaining tank was in the farthest corner, the extra distance adding a precious couple of seconds to their journey. Lieutenant Breeze had his head and torso out of the top entrance hatch and waved them over, the gesture redundant, yet faintly reassuring.

"Your suits are inside," he called. He'd saved them the extra few moments it would have taken to haul the bulky cases of kit over to the tank.

Breeze vanished back within. McGlashan sprang up the angular nose of the tank and vaulted after him, dropping inside with the ease of a woman who'd done the same thing many times before. Duggan didn't hesitate and followed in the same smooth action, descending a shaft that dropped almost ten feet into the depths of the tank. There were rungs set in the grey metal walls and Duggan's hands snatched at them to slow his fall. He landed at the bottom, in a space that was hardly five feet high and wide. A grubby red light bathed him from the tank's interior and there was the strong smell of oil.

"Close it, quick!" urged Breeze, from somewhere deeper within.

His words were spoken in conjunction with Duggan's hand tapping out a fast combination of three buttons on a console adjacent to the hatch. A slab of metal almost a metre thick shot quietly across and sealed the interior. It was surprisingly cool inside – almost chilly.

"How long?" asked Duggan, his voice muffled by the thickness and solidity of the surrounding alloys.

"You only just made it, sir," said Breeze.

"Less than twenty seconds till we're in range of their missiles," added Chainer, watching a tiny display screen that showed an information feed from the *Detriment*'s main core.

The inner chamber of the tank was eleven feet long, six wide and slightly more than five high. There were three forward-facing seats to each side, all of them with tiny screens and cut-down control consoles. The central walkway was only two feet wide, with a smooth metal floor. The walls were a mess of pipes and wires, leading off to who knew where. The tanks were tough and reliable, yet disposable. If something went wrong, there was no expectation they'd undergo any sort of field repairs. If you found yourself stuck on one that broke down or suffered damage, all you could do was cross your fingers and hope someone would come and pick you up. In a way, they were the same as the Gunners – a mass of engines, weapons and armour, wrapped like a cocoon around the vulnerable human cargo. Duggan had always felt at home riding in one.

"The *Detriment*'s just taken a beam hit aft," said McGlashan coolly. She'd reached her seat only seconds before Duggan and patched herself immediately into the ship's computers.

"Damage?"

"Twenty percent of our engine capacity fried. That Cadaveron must be fresh out of the yard," said Breeze. "They shouldn't be able to hit us from so far out."

"How long till we're over our drop zone?" asked Duggan.

"One minute and eight seconds," said McGlashan.

"It's going to be a close one."

"They've launched missiles. I've got two waves of twelve. And here comes a third. Twenty of our own going back towards them."

"They're holding back," said McGlashan. "They must be expecting an easy kill. Normal recharge time on their particle beam is up in eight seconds. Our first wave of shock drones is gone."

"Missiles will impact in fifty seconds, ours in less than twenty."

"We've taken another beam hit. That one's burned out approximately thirty million tonnes of our engines," announced Breeze. "Bang goes anything above Lightspeed-A. That's if we can even get that online."

"At least their recharge is working exactly as expected," said Chainer. Everything else about this Ghost ship seemed to be more advanced than they'd expected.

Duggan wasn't paying attention to the consequences. He hadn't expected to get away on the *Detriment*. All he wanted was to escape to the planet's surface without the enemy ship detecting them. He paged through the updates and status reports on his own screen. "Second wave of shock drones away," he said. "And another twenty Lambdas."

"We need fifteen seconds lead time to make a clean launch for the tank," said McGlashan.

"I know, Commander. We're pushing it." Duggan laughed, the sound stark and without humour.

"None of our first wave of Lambdas got through, sir."

"Understood," said Duggan through gritted teeth. It looked like he was going to be denied even the modest satisfaction of giving them a bloody nose.

"We've got another two waves of twelve on the sensors," said Chainer. "They're spacing them out nicely."

The next few seconds tested Duggan's determination to the full. If they escaped the *Detriment* too early, they'd have a longer journey to make contact with Sergeant Ortiz, which would vastly increase the chance that the Ghast ship would detect them on the surface. If they waited for even a second too long, the hold of the *Detriment* would become their coffin. *How much longer till their particle beam recharges?* he asked himself.

"Yes!" shouted McGlashan. "We got a hit right on their nose!" Her words were strangely reminiscent of Duggan's own thoughts just a moment before. "Sending them another twenty Lambdas. Let's see how they like that."

"We might have knocked their particle cannon out," said Chainer, frantically looking through the sensor readouts for any sign of positrons leaking from the Cadaveron's hull. There was nothing, though the range was extreme.

"Their missiles have passed our first drones."

"How many'd we get?"

"Nine, six and one,"

"That leaves only twenty," said Breeze ruefully.

"Two, three and five of their missiles taken out by the second wave of drones."

"Initiating tank deployment," said Duggan, reaching forward to authorise the launch.

"What about our third wave of drones, sir?" asked McGlashan.

"Leave them to me," said Duggan. In his head, he counted down. *Twelve, eleven, ten, nine.*

"Bulwark cannons firing," said McGlashan.

"Come on," muttered Chainer under his breath.

Eight, seven. Duggan initiated the release of the final shock drones. A dozen launch tubes on the top of the *Detriment* spewed a glittering cloud of metal into the void above the ship.

The first Ghast missile impacted at the rear of the *Detriment*. It punctured halfway through the twenty-metre thick alloy armour, the warhead exploding and tearing out a huge chunk of the armour plating. Three more missiles struck in the vicinity of the first, shredding the super-dense materials of the ship's already ruined fission drive. The hull of the *Detriment* rocked and shuddered.

Four, three. In the *Detriment's* hold, sheltered for the moment from the worst of the explosions, a shaft opened beneath the tank. It was a perfect fit for the armoured vehicle. The tank's passengers got a sensation of movement. *Two, one.* The tank was sucked down the shaft and expelled into darkness, a little over one hundred kilometres above the planet's surface. Outside the tiny vehicle, dozens of kilometres away, four of the missiles from the Cadaveron's third wave detonated fruitlessly amongst the shock drones. The final two evaded the single Bulwark cannon that remained functional on the *Detriment* and plunged into the crippled vestiges of the spacecraft. The last Captain John Nathan Duggan saw of his ship was a crude, grainy image relayed onto his screen from the tank's feeble sensor array. In a flash of reds and intense blues, the *Detriment* was reduced to chunks of molten hot pieces and cast in a chaotic pattern across the planet's black sky.

The pain of the loss took hold of Duggan, much stronger than he'd expected it to be. He closed his eyes for a time. When he opened them, he was gripped with a determination he'd never felt before.

"Those bastards are going to pay for everything they've done," he said.

CHAPTER NINE

NO ONE SPOKE as the tank dropped from the sky towards the planet below. In the cramped interior, the occupants looked at the limited information from the vehicle's rudimental sensors and propulsion systems, as if the intensity of their study could somehow influence their helplessness.

"Any sign of the Cadaveron?" asked Duggan at last.

"There's something big way up there," said Chainer. "It's slowing."

"Try and keep the drones between us and the Ghasts," Duggan instructed McGlashan. "If we're lucky they'll either not bother looking or they'll see us as a piece of debris."

"Doing my best, sir," said McGlashan. The tanks were designed to fall and land safely. The pilot had only a limited amount of control over the direction since it was expected that the vehicles would be accurately dropped in the first place. The tanks were definitely not manoeuvrable.

"Eighty klicks and counting," said Duggan. It was peculiarly silent, ensconced in the tank's hull. There was a faint vibration and a humming from the machinery locked away behind the inner walls. Otherwise, the only sound was that of the people within. "On the bright side, it looks like we're coming in less than forty klicks from our target."

"The terrain's not perfect," said Chainer. He'd fed the results of the *Detriment*'s surface scans into the cores of each of the four tanks before the soldiers had left for the surface.

"Nothing this baby can't handle," said McGlashan.

Duggan called up the details. The ground was rugged and covered in loose rocks, gravel and dust. He asked the tank's guidance to plot the best route – forty-seven kilometres, taking into account a more circuitous route they had to take in order to avoid a mile-high vertical crag that the tank wouldn't be able to climb easily.

"A little under an hour to get where we're going," he said. "That Cadaveron's going to get plenty of opportunity to spot us on the way."

"It wasn't circling directly above where the soldiers came down," said Chainer. "Could be that they're hunting in the wrong place."

"That might buy us enough time," said Breeze.

"Yeah - it took us a while to find the right place."

"That's *if* we're at the right place," said McGlashan. "If the *Crimson* isn't there or if it's nothing but a lump of metals, we're a long way from rescue." The tank could send out a low-speed distress signal. This far out it would be hit and miss as to whether or not anyone could get to them before they ran out of power. That's if anyone even bothered to try. The risk versus reward wasn't high, particularly given how much the Ghasts had the Confederation on the run.

"They won't come for us," said Duggan. He didn't mean to sound fatalist and just wanted them to know what he felt was the truth. "They'd need a fleet of Anderlechts to ensure success.

They don't have the ships to spare and we're simply not important enough."

"We may not be, but perhaps the *Crimson* is," said Breeze.

"Don't overthink it. We're what they sent, not a fleet."

"Aye, that's right enough," said Chainer.

"Coming in to land," Duggan told them.

The vehicle's landing routines were almost entirely autonomous. Two kilometres above the surface, the tank's gravity engines slowed the hurtling descent towards the rocks below. On board, the occupants were given a ride that was rough in comparison to what they'd have felt on a spacecraft. The tank's life support systems were much more limited in their capabilities.

"A bit choppy," commented McGlashan. The tank's hull flexed and creaked to accompany the increasingly intrusive howl of the engines.

"I've not been on one of these since training," muttered Chainer. "I'd almost forgotten what it's like."

"Cheer up, Lieutenant. Soon we'll have landed on a hostile planet with no backup and no-one coming to our rescue."

"That's not what I wanted to hear, Commander."

The tank landed with a surprising smoothness. The vehicle's guidance system dropped them onto a clear area of the ground, hardly disturbing the gritty dust that was strewn thickly all around. The tank hovered for a second or two, a little more than a foot above the ground. Then, it rotated until its wedge-shaped nose was pointing towards the east and moved away on its pre-determined course. Its engines gave out little signature of their operation and the angular hull was designed to show an almost-invisible profile to hide it from sensor detection. It wasn't foolproof, but there again, nothing was.

"Might as well sit back and enjoy the trip, folks," said Duggan, sounding more cheerful than he felt. His chair crackled as he tried to get comfortable. It felt like it had been designed for a person with much shorter legs than his and Duggan found his knees pressed tightly against the console in front of him. He brought up the sensor feeds from the outside. The place was as bleak as any he'd seen. Some planets had atmospheres that were hostile beyond measure, where even the tanks couldn't stay for long. For some reason, Duggan had always loved the thrill of danger. Here it was barren and lifeless. Just another planet amongst countless others that had nothing of interest to bring anyone to visit. *Except that this one DOES have something,* spoke his inner voice.

Duggan watched the terrain pass by. The tank scooted over the undulations without any ceremony. There was the occasional sensation of ascending or descending, which was a similar feeling to that of being in a lift. The onboard computer showed a countdown of both time and distance to indicate how long till they'd arrive. With twenty minutes to go, Duggan succumbed to the inevitable and set to the task he'd been putting off.

"We should get into our suits," he said. "One at a time." They were bad enough to get into with plenty of space in which to operate. Inside the cramped cockpit of the tank, it would be an exercise in frustration and futility.

Duggan made his way to the locker where Breeze had stowed away four of the life-support suits. He pulled one free without much relish. It was cumbersome, though not as heavy as it looked.

"I never like wearing them either," said Breeze with a chuckle when he caught Duggan's expression.

After a short struggle, Duggan was enclosed in the dark grey polymer suit. It was about a centimetre thick all over and proof against a huge variety of atmospheric temperatures and conditions. Inside the gloves, his fingertips registered the feel of the material – it was somewhere between a plastic and a dense rubber. It resisted movement, but only slightly. After a few days in one, the wearer could usually operate almost like they weren't encumbered.

"Leave the helmets till we've arrived," he said. The helmets were oversized spheres filled with complex technologies and they were unpleasant to wear at the best of times, let alone in the bowels of a tank.

Duggan returned to his seat and left the others to don their own suits. He kept his gaze on the external sensors and watched as the vehicle entered the lee of a sheer cliff. To the other side, a flat plain of gravel and scree rolled away for what might have been a hundred miles.

"Want me to try and reach Sergeant Ortiz, sir?" asked Chainer.

"Maintain silence. We know where they are."

"Roger."

"If they broadcast a signal, shut them down fast."

"Will do."

On his screen, Duggan watched the cliff recede gradually into the distance. "Five minutes to go. We should start our descent any moment."

The tank's front sensors showed what looked like the lip of a cliff a short distance ahead. The edge appeared to be almost smooth, as if it had been filed down by three billion years of abrasion from wind-borne dust. The tank didn't slow and it glided easily over the edge. There wasn't a sharp fall - in fact, the lip was the edge of a crater. It was only because the *Detriment*'s sensors had told him it was a meteorite scar that Duggan knew as much. Before them lay a long slope that curved to the left and right, further than the eye could see. The meteorite had struck at an angle, leaving something between a furrow and a crater that was five kilometres wide and over twenty long. Their course had intersected the crater close to their destination. At the end of the furrow, the meteorite had smashed the rock into a huge cliff with a wide, vertical fracture running from the bottom to a point halfway up. It was here that Sergeant Ortiz had gone.

McGlashan gave a low whistle when she called up a view of the crater on her screen. "This must have been a big one. It looks painful even after all these years."

Duggan thought it a strange choice of words but didn't wonder about it. "We need to get underground as soon as we can. Turner said it was rough for the tanks so we might have to get out and walk sooner than we'd hoped. There should be room for us to get under cover before we have to ditch it." He planned to pilot the tank straight into the gap under the cliff, to minimise the chance that the Cadaveron would pick them up.

The tank cut down the slope at an angle. It made good speed and the ground soon levelled out. The cliff was visible in the distance – high, looming and rugged. It came inexorably closer and Duggan studied his viewscreen for a sight of their destination. The tank's sensors struggled to cope with the contrast between the shadows, so he wasn't able to get a clear view of the place he hoped to find the *Crimson*. They were still over three kilometres away when a voice scratched into being, piped into the tank's interior through a metal-grilled speaker.

"This is Infantryman Turner, hailing Detriment Tank Four. Do you copy?"

"Infantryman Turner, this is Lieutenant Frank Chainer. Shut down your broadcast immediately and await our arrival."

Turner didn't need to be told twice and the speaker fell silent.

Duggan swore at the unwanted communication. In his head, he willed the tank to move faster, cursing again at the thought that the Cadaveron might have detected their presence.

"I've got nothing incoming," said Chainer.

"Don't waste your time," Duggan told him. "If they send a

75

missile at us, we'll not get more than a couple of seconds' notice. These are surface vehicles."

"Definitely not equipped to pick up incoming missiles from space," added McGlashan.

"Fine, I get the message," said Chainer. He was used to working with equipment that was a lot more sophisticated than he had available to him now. The limitations were already bugging him.

"Best get your helmets on and break out the rifles," said Duggan. He clambered to the rear of the cockpit and picked up his own helmet. It was completely opaque from the outside – the computers within fed through all the details the wearer needed. Duggan crouched low and dropped it over his head. He felt a tightening around his neck where the tiny motors in the helmet forced a seal with the rest of the suit he was wearing. The feeling was disconcerting – like the suit could strangle him if it ever malfunctioned. There was a wraparound screen within the helmet, which automatically projected a copy of the outside world, enhanced to provide the most comfortable view for the human eye. There was the smell of decades-old stale sweat that every helmet Duggan had ever worn seemed to carry, as if the material was impregnated with it at the factory.

There was a second locker in the tank, set against the left-hand wall. Duggan gave the spoken command for it to unlock, his suit's comms unit relaying the detail to the tank's onboard computer. The locker door slid open with a faint hiss. Inside, there were six gauss rifles, resting horizontally on deep shelves. Duggan reached within and snapped the top one free of its mounting. He turned it over in his hand – a dull silver tube about three feet long and with a diameter of six inches. It had a hand grip at one end and another in the middle, with a recessed switch to fire. Duggan considered himself a good shot and he felt comfort from holding the weapon. Next to him,

McGlashan had put her helmet on and snapped out a second rifle.

"If feels good to hold one of these again," she said, her voice appearing inside Duggan's helmet. It carried the faintest of echoes as it reflected from the helmet's interior. It wasn't perfect, but you got used to it.

"Got a visual on Turner," said Chainer, still in his seat and awaiting his turn to get his helmet on.

"Where?" asked Duggan, squeezing back to his seat. In spite of his efforts, his helmet clanged off the ceiling of the tank's hold. A tiny readout appeared briefly to register the collision.

"He's just inside the fissure."

"Good man. That'll cut down the angle for the Ghasts to pick him up."

Duggan checked their distance. He'd left it late to finish dressing and the tank was almost at the cliff. When it got there, it was programmed to stop and await further instructions. Duggan didn't want any delay, so he overrode the autodrive and took the controls. The suit interfaced automatically with the tank and Duggan was able to control it using a series of hand gestures or his voice. It could be clumsy sometimes, but with practise it allowed the driver to direct the tank and perform other tasks at the same time.

"I've gone to manual," he said. "Taking us straight in."

The external sensors showed a clear image of the fissure now. It was several hundred metres wide at the bottom and streaked upwards, its jagged edges narrowing as it climbed. The planet had a long dusk and what little light arrived here from the distant sun was fading slowly. The tank's sensors struggled to enhance the interior of the fractured cliff face. They weren't able to read the path ahead perfectly, but Duggan could see enough to realise they were about to drop steeply.

"The cheeky bastard's waving," said McGlashan with a laugh

as the tank went past Turner at almost thirty kilometres per hour. The ground beneath sloped sharply downwards, before levelling out ahead.

"Looks like he's pulled the comms beacon further inside," said Breeze.

"He's got a nose for trouble," said Duggan.

"Are we going to stop and pick him up?" asked McGlashan.

"Shortly," said Duggan. By now, they'd left the soldier a couple of hundred metres behind. He'd shown no sign of following them since he'd been ordered to stay at his post. There again, he didn't know that the *Detriment* had been destroyed, though he would surely have guessed something was wrong.

When he judged that he'd taken them far enough into the fissure to block out their transmissions from the Ghast ship above, Duggan brought the tank to a halt. It hovered dutifully in the air as it awaited the next command.

"Turner, get yourself over here. Don't respond, you've got something listening out overhead."

A few moments later, the suited figure of Turner appeared on their screens. He ran with the peculiar gait of a man who'd worn a spacesuit more often than was good for him. To Duggan, the soldier looked like the old ocean sailors who rolled with the sea as they walked. The gravity on this planet was higher than normal, but Turner didn't seem to be bothered by it – that's what the gym work was good for. The soldier jumped up onto the tank's wedge nose. Everyone inside was suited, so Duggan sent the command for the hatch to open. The computer bleeped to warn that the interior airlock door was also open. He pressed a button sequence on his console to override it.

Moments later, Turner was inside. When he spoke, his voice betrayed an edge of excitement, the emotion exacerbated by his increased breathing from the recent sprint to the tank.

"They've found it," he said.

CHAPTER TEN

DUGGAN PUSHED the tank onwards into the deepening gloom. Its headlights and sidelights threw out a startling amount of illumination, which was just enough to catch the distant walls. "What condition is it in?" he asked.

"The hull is intact, that's all I know. Comms don't get through from the entrance and Sergeant Ortiz had to send someone halfway back to let me know that much. We'll be able to get about another klick along here and then it's on foot."

"Is the way blocked?" asked Duggan.

"There's a rock shelf. There'd be plenty of room to get the *Detriment* in over it." Turner frowned at the realisation that everyone on board was now on the planet's surface.

"The *Detriment*'s gone. We've got a Cadaveron circling above. It might not know we're here, but it certainly knows that *something* is here."

Turner was a good soldier and he didn't ask for more details about what had happened. There was no other conclusion for him to draw other than that they were effectively stranded on this planet. He couldn't change it, so he shrugged and got on with it.

After another twelve hundred metres, the floor rose sharply upwards as if it had been pushed from below, until it formed a high ledge across the entire width of the cave. Above the ledge was nothing but open space, vanishing ever higher into impenetrable darkness. In front, the *Detriment*'s other three tanks were arrayed in a neat line as if they'd been parked in a shopping mall.

"Over a hundred metres high," said Duggan. He was tempted to see if he could get the tank to climb it. They were made to fall and land safely, not to climb and he was sure it would be fruitless to try. Sergeant Ortiz knew her stuff. If she'd left the tanks here, it was for a good reason.

"How'd they get up?" asked McGlashan, flipping through different sensor images of the rocky ledge in front of them to see if she could find any sort of pathway.

"Don't ask me," said Turner. "There's been no time for chat."

"Let's get out and take a look," said Duggan. He shut down the tank's engines and pushed through towards the exit hatch. He keyed it open and hauled himself up the ladder, feeling his muscles strain under the additional weight of the suit and the planet's gravity. His breathing sounded loud in the enclosed space of his helmet and an amber warning light appeared to advise him politely that his oxygen consumption had increased by thirty percent. The hatch slid away into its recess and Duggan was able to exit the tank into the expanse of the cave. As he stood on the sloped front of the tank a feeling of contentment came to him. Some men feared the infinity of the universe, but not Duggan.

"Doesn't this make you feel alive?" he asked.

Behind him, Turner climbed through the hatch. "If you say so, sir," he said.

The tank's lights remained on and they provided sufficient illumination for Duggan to see the barrier in front. He jumped to the ground, landing with a heavy thud on the dark grey rock. The ground was fairly smooth around here and clear of visible grit or dust. The sensors in his helmet advised him that a wind of nine kilometres per hour blew from the entrance towards him. Duggan couldn't feel it at all in the protection of his suit. The rest of the crew emerged from the safety of the tank and hopped down one-by-one to join them.

"Can you see anything, sir?" asked McGlashan. Duggan's helmet readout helpfully outlined her body in a red light. Everyone looked the same in their suits.

"The light isn't good enough to see. I'll try and reach Sergeant Ortiz." Duggan opened a comms channel. "Sergeant Ortiz, do you copy?"

There was a delay of several seconds before a reply came. "I copy. We've found the *Crimson*, sir. She's a bit beat up, but I think you'll be able to get her to fly. The repair bot's busting a gut."

Duggan laughed. "I hope you're right, Sergeant. A Cadaveron arrived. We've lost the *Detriment*. The *Crimson*'s all we've got to get us home."

"Roger that, sir. You're on the surface, then?"

"That's right. We're parked up near the tanks. Which way to get up?"

"There's a place about a hundred metres to the left. It's a bit of a scramble, so you'll need to hold on tight."

"Thanks."

Duggan closed the comms channel to Sergeant Ortiz. "The good sergeant thinks the *Crimson* might fly," he said to the others nearby. Ortiz wasn't necessarily qualified to make the judgement but Duggan knew her well enough to give her the benefit of the doubt. She'd seen enough action over the years to recognize terminal damage to a ship's structure. "There's a path this way. Let's go."

With the other four in tow, Duggan set off across the cavern's floor. The shelf looked higher than a hundred metres when he stood at the base and it had a clean, smooth look. As he got further away from the tank, the computer within his helmet detected the reduction in light and it turned on the inbuilt torch, which danced ahead with the rhythm of his strides. It didn't take long to find what they were looking for. There was a deep, diagonal crack running up and away from them, with the lower edge jutting forward about three feet.

"She said it would be a bit of a scramble," said Duggan, staring at the ascent.

"She wasn't kidding," said Breeze.

Duggan led the way, keeping his chest close to the rock face as he sidled his way up. It wasn't something he'd anticipated taking part in and he found it a frustrating obstacle to reaching their goal. After a few minutes, he crawled over the top and breathed a sigh of relief. It wasn't that he was scared of heights – he was simply eager to be on his way. McGlashan came next and Duggan reached down to pull her up the last few feet. A couple of minutes later, they were all standing at the top of the ledge, looking downwards onto the gloom-shrouded outlines of the stationary tanks below.

"Let's hope we'll be flying on the way back," said Breeze.

"This place is huge," said McGlashan. "I don't think I've seen anything quite like it before."

Above them was only darkness. The light from their suit helmets was feeble compared to the space and it provided only a glimpse of the route along which the *Crimson* must once have flown. Ahead, the fracture sloped downward again, the floor littered with sharp-edged stones and boulders. They could have lain here for aeons. There was no wind, yet it evidently didn't carry enough dust particles to smooth off the raw edges of the stone.

"Another two kilometres, sir," said Turner. "Give or take."

"Let's get on," Duggan replied, aware that there might still be a Ghast heavy cruiser searching for them.

The straight-line distance wasn't relevant, since they had to veer around many obstacles and occasionally had to back-track for a short way. Some of the boulders were dozens of feet high and in places were piled upon each other. Duggan didn't spend much time pondering on the cataclysm that brought this about. He wasn't unaffected by it, but the time wasn't right to let his mind wander from the task before him.

The journey took almost half an hour and their arrival came almost as a surprise. The boulders were more thickly deposited this far into the cave and they entirely concealed the view ahead. Duggan pushed himself through a narrow gap and then his suit light reflected off something before him. It was something incomprehensibly massive, squatting menacingly on the floor of the cave, filling almost the entirety of the available space. Where his light contacted the surface of the object, Duggan could see that it was utterly smooth and without blemish. Ignoring the exclamations of the crew coming from behind, he jogged forward to see more of the spacecraft.

"That's the *Crimson*?" asked Chainer.

Duggan didn't answer at once. He'd already determined they were at the aft of the ship – the rear was rectangular and perhaps three hundred and fifty metres across, with a height of two hundred and fifty. The vessel's structure appeared to be suspended twenty metres from the ground and Duggan could just make out the rear four landing feet, each of them enormously thick in order to support the spaceship's immense weight. There were signs of damage on the underside – there was a black pattern across the silver, covering a hundred metres or more. It was impossible to tell what had caused the damage from here.

"Sergeant Ortiz, we're here. Give us some light," said Duggan.

"No can do, sir. The ship won't listen to me. It's above my station."

"Where are you?"

"We're all on board, sir. The ramp was down. It's a bit of a walk to get there."

"On our way."

They entered the shadow of the *Crimson*'s hull. It was one thing to see a ship the size of the *Detriment* from close up, but the *Crimson* was something else entirely. Where its landing feet were in contact with the ground, there were snaking patterns of stress fractures to indicate the incomprehensible weight of its engines and weapons systems. Duggan noticed that the hull tapered as they walked onwards and he imagined it might be slightly less than three hundred metres wide at the front. It was a classic wedge shape, yet somehow sleeker and more streamlined than most vessels in the Corps.

"It must have been something," said McGlashan, marvelling at the design.

"Admiral Teron said there were plans to build twenty. Maybe they shelved them because this one went missing, rather than through cutbacks."

"The brass only tell you what they want you to hear," said McGlashan, communicating through a private channel. She knew Duggan well enough to speak sedition when it was relevant.

"Maybe."

"Think the ship will accept your command, sir?" she asked.

"The command code algorithms are designed to be relevant in the past, the present and the future. Any Corps ship of my grade should accept mine." As he said this, he fervently hoped there'd be no problems. It didn't seem likely that he'd be sent out here if they knew he lacked the necessary authority for the *Crimson*'s mainframe to obey him.

"There's the plank," said Breeze.

The *Crimson*'s boarding ramp was about two-thirds of the way along the *Crimson*'s eleven hundred metre length. It was narrow and sharply inclined, with a surprisingly pristine surface made from a rubber compound to aid grip. You could always tell the expected number of crew on a ship by the width of its boarding ramp. On the *Crimson*, it was more of an afterthought.

"They weren't expecting many crew," said McGlashan.

Above them, a suited figure appeared. "Welcome aboard, sir," said Ortiz.

With a feeling of mixed apprehension and excitement, Captain John Nathan Duggan climbed upwards and onboard the *ESS Crimson*.

CHAPTER ELEVEN

DUGGAN FELT IMMEDIATELY AT HOME. The larger vessels in the Corps had wide, civilized corridors that would permit three people to walk abreast. They had cinemas, gyms, and open common rooms for the entertainment of the crew. Many of the officers had large rooms for their comfort, with the captain and senior officers provided with entire suites. The *Crimson* was different – it was just like a Gunner with its cramped corridors and peculiar smell of oil. Yet Duggan could immediately tell it was different. He didn't know how, but he knew this ship had been designed to win wars. *Even when we weren't fighting one.*

When he reached the top of the ramp, Duggan clapped Sergeant Ortiz on the shoulder. He dismissed her back to the other men and didn't delay himself in getting on with business. With his feet seeming to lead the way, Duggan found himself at the bridge. It was a little larger than the *Detriment's* had been, equipped with the same four seats. These ones were covered in soft leather, which had seen no sign of wear and tear. Duggan couldn't help but press his fingers into the covering on the captain's chair, wondering why the leather showed no signs of perishing. Around the room, there was the usual panoply of screens and status displays. A few of them displayed lines of digits and code in a dark green shade. The majority were dead. There was a metal wraparound console for each of the seats, covered in buttons and touch controls. It looked the same as the *Detriment*, yet with a strangeness to it that came from the years it had been waiting here in the darkness.

"Pipes!" exclaimed McGlashan, pointing at a row of three that entered through the bulkhead near the ceiling and exited through the side wall. "I've not seen a pipe on a spacecraft in years."

Duggan chuckled at her enthusiasm and sat himself down in the captain's chair. Even through the material of his suit he could feel it was comfortable. The console in front of him bore all the hallmarks of standard human design in the field of spacecraft controls. They'd been doing it the same way for a hundred years before the *Crimson*'s hull was laid down.

"Let's see what we can do," he said. Almost of their own volition, his fingers skittered across the controls, his suit relaying the tactile information through its material. The *Crimson*'s mainframe was online, with access currently denied. Duggan had a tiny chip buried into his forearm that contained an ever-changing chain of a billion numbers and symbols. In theory, it was meant to tally up with the exact same combination available to all Corps ships. The life support was off so there was no way Duggan was going to get out of his suit in order to make a direct skin connection with the ship's security plate. Instead, he used the suit's onboard processing unit to pull out the numbers and relay them directly to the *Crimson*'s mainframe. Immediately, a number of additional displays lit up around Duggan.

"I've got lights," said McGlashan as the commander's

displays flooded into life in front of her. She squinted at the sudden brightness.

"And here," said Chainer.

"Same," said Breeze.

"Right, let's see what we've got and what we can do," said Duggan.

For the next five minutes, he sat quietly as he interrogated the *Crimson*'s mainframe. The news wasn't what he'd been hoping for.

"The mainframe's showing an uptime of almost ninety-six weeks," he said. "Either it didn't send a signal straight away, or whoever sent us here sat on their hands for four months before deciding to act. On top of that, I've only been given clearance to activate and use the sensors, the life support and the propulsion systems. The rest of it is locked down - weapons and most of the databanks."

"Can you override?"

"I'm working on it. I'm denied access. Looks like the old girl is suspicious of newcomers."

McGlashan gave a shake of her head. "So, we've been sent all the way out here to bring the *Crimson* home, yet with no way to defend ourselves against attack?"

"Looks that way."

"What else have we got?" she asked.

Duggan poked around for a minute longer, giving out one or two low whistles of surprise, yet saying nothing.

"Don't you hate it when he does that?" complained Chainer.

"I've authorised all the consoles as much as I'm able. The life support is now online. It's already closed the boarding ramp and we'll have another five minutes till the atmosphere is hospitable. Admiral Teron wasn't lying when he said they'd spent a lot of money on this ship. If you believe this readout, the engines have one hundred-and-seventeen times the output of the *Detriment*'s. They're bigger and vastly more efficient."

"That can't be right," said Breeze. "That would make them far more advanced than the *Detriment*'s and we had a refit only four years ago to add on some extra power." He called up half a dozen readouts and positioned them side-by-side on his screen. "This thing's got more power than a Hadron class," he said, looking puzzled.

"That means we can just fly out and show that Cadaveron a clean pair of heels?" asked Chainer.

"Not likely," said McGlashan. "If it picks us up manoeuvring out of this hole, it'll blow us away long before the fission drives come online."

"The last record before the mainframe shut down shows that something fried a big chunk of the engines."

"It's had ninety-six weeks working at them," said Breeze. There were weapons that could disrupt the connections between the atoms that comprised the engines of a spaceship, in order to slow or stop them entirely. As long as the material remained in place, the vessel's mainframe could generally re-establish those connections or re-route as necessary. It wasn't a quick process. A missile strike was a different thing entirely, but the *Crimson* hadn't suffered any explosive damage that Duggan could see.

"Ninety-six weeks hasn't been long enough for it to repair everything. I'm reading a history of extensive damage," said McGlashan.

"We're not quite ready to fly out yet," Breeze replied. "We're at thirty-five percent."

Like a jigsaw puzzle of trillions of pieces, the earliest parts were the hardest to slot into place. The further along the repairs went, the easier they became. Thirty-five percent sounded low, but Duggan knew that meant the ship's core had completed the bulk of the work.

"That's much faster than I'd have expected. Perhaps the brain of this thing is quicker than it's letting on," mused Duggan. "Or maybe it was designed to be exceptionally good at specific tasks. Lieutenant Breeze, can you give me a prediction for when we'll be ready to fly at something close to peak efficiency?" He didn't need to spell out that he meant *with a chance to escape the Ghast heavy cruiser.*

"We'll be above ninety percent in approximately twenty hours, sir. A little longer if you want to go at a hundred percent."

As he talked, Duggan worked at the weapons systems. Without warning, the *Crimson* provided access to the locked-down sub-arrays. Several new options became accessible from his console and Duggan opened them up.

"It's let me into the weapons," he said.

"What're we carrying?" asked McGlashan.

"Wait on, I'm authorising you."

"Here we go," she said, excitement in her voice.

Duggan was ahead of her and he scrolled through the *Crimson*'s lists of arms and ammunition. "We've got eighteen banks of ancient Lambdas – big clusters. There're eight early-gen Bulwarks and a dozen nukes. Big ones. Really big ones."

"Nukes?" asked Chainer, blinking in amazement.

"Looks like it. Long range and slow."

"What're we carrying nukes for?"

"I don't know," said Duggan.

"Sometimes, when everything else has failed, there might be a time when you need to rely on a crude and filthy high explosive," announced Breeze. He sat back in his seat with an air of faint satisfaction.

"I wouldn't like to be within a hundred klicks when one of these things goes off," said McGlashan. "I didn't even think we made them anymore."

"We're carrying a lot of ordnance," said Duggan. "Teron

wasn't wrong when he said they'd put the good stuff onboard. This vessel must have been a flying juggernaut."

"Until they launched the first Hadron class, at least," said Breeze. "This ship would have been a match for anything. Even today they could refit it with the newest Lambdas and it would be worth sending to the front line."

"There's more," said McGlashan quietly. "Two more weapons systems. At first, I thought they were offline. Now I can see that the ship is preventing access."

Duggan picked up on it and tried to call up the details. He was blocked as well. "I wonder what they are," he said.

"Mines?" asked McGlashan.

"Nope, I can access the mines. They're under countermeasures for some reason. These are something different."

"Sounds interesting," said Chainer.

"I'll keep working on it," Duggan said. He looked at McGlashan. "See if you can find a back door."

"Will do. These things are normally locked down pretty tightly."

"Of course," said Duggan. "And how're our sensors and comms?"

"It looks like the repair bot's been busy," replied Chainer. "Unfortunately, it's had a lot to do. I've got onboard comms fully functional and nine of the thirty main sensor arrays are reporting themselves to be operational."

"No main comms?"

"None, sir. The ship sent its distress call through the emergency beacon. It must have known what a risk that was. It'll have lit up the receivers of everything between here and Monitoring Station Alpha."

"How'd it even get a signal out if our sensors couldn't find it?" asked McGlashan.

"It's been clever. From what I can see here, it waited until the tilt of the planet meant the cave mouth was pointing in the approximate direction of the Alpha. It fired the signal off and bounced it twice to achieve the angle it needed to reach space. The emergency beacons send out a much more robust signal than anything from a regular transmission system. You can do this sort of pissing about with them."

Duggan nodded to indicate his appreciation for Chainer's detective work. "How long till the main transmission systems are available? If we get out of this cave, I want to be able to speak to the *Juniper* immediately."

"I don't know. The repair bot is working on them now, but it isn't feeding a status update to the core. The comms are intricate," he finished.

"Keep me updated."

"I've got some bad news, sir," said McGlashan. "The autopilot and guidance systems aren't responding to my status requests."

"Broken?"

"I can't get into them to find out the extent of the damage. Maybe the *Crimson*'s landing wasn't so smooth and a few of the tertiary systems got knocked out."

"That's going to make things a little more difficult," said Duggan.

With those words, he climbed to his feet and stretched as he attempted to clear his mind. They'd found what they were looking for and against the odds, it appeared as if the *Crimson* wasn't the bucket of bolts he'd expected to find. There was still damage, but it could have been a lot worse than it was. *One-hundred-and-seventeen times the output.* The words echoed around in his mind as he wondered how fast the vessel would go. It wasn't an exact science, since the engines needed a super-powerful core to mould their output continuously through light-speed. Even the largest-engined vessel would be comparatively slow without the processing grunt to back it up. They wouldn't know how fast the *Crimson* was until they gave it a go.

Something boiled up inside. "Everywhere I look, there are secrets," he said angrily. "And I don't like it one little bit."

"What do you mean, sir?" asked McGlashan.

"Look at this spacecraft. Built for no reason and carrying enough weaponry to have knocked out half of the Ghast fleet if she'd been available at the start of the war. Old weapons, old defences, yet engines that we couldn't build even now. Other weapons that the captain isn't allowed to look at. I need to know what this shit is all about."

None of the crew had anything else to say and they stayed quiet. Duggan glowered angrily for a few moments until his spacesuit's helmet binged softly to let him know that the environment on the bridge was now adequate to support human life. He released the seal around his neck. It hissed softly and he put the helmet to one side, glad to see the back of it. He called up the onboard comms, which he patched directly through to Sergeant Ortiz's suit.

"Sergeant Ortiz. Let the soldiers know the life support systems are operational and they can take off their suits if they wish."

"Thank you, sir, we've already discovered that."

"Also advise them that the ship is armed and will soon be operational. I'll keep you posted on progress."

"Thank you, sir."

"And Ortiz?"

"Yes, sir?"

"How has Monsey been keeping up with her special skills?"

"Sir?"

"Hacking, Sergeant. Does she still practise?"

"I believe she might dabble when the opportunity presents itself."

"The opportunity is about to present itself now. Send her to the bridge at once."

"Will do, sir."

Duggan ended the communication and found the others looking at him quizzically. He smiled back. "Let's see if modern techniques can breach the defensive walls of a fifty-year-old warship's core," he said. "I'd rather fly with full knowledge of what's at our disposal."

Monsey arrived on the bridge five minutes later, stooping low through the entrance door. She carried a foot-square metallic cube, which had an old mechanical-style keyboard plugged into it and a separate grey-framed display screen balanced loosely on top.

"How's it going, soldier?" asked Duggan.

"I'm good, sir. I hear you need me to break into something."

"The *Crimson*'s mainframe. It's hiding something from me. I need access to the ship's databanks and weapons."

"That'll need time, sir," said Monsey, hiding her surprise. She put the cube down gently. "This baby's one of the latest boot-boxes. Updated with the latest military-grade boards when we were on the *Juniper* a couple of years ago. If this ship's as old as you say it is, I'll be able to crack it. They built the warship cores tough, so don't expect it to happen at once."

"I need something and soon," he said.

"I'll do what I can," she said. With that, she lifted the keyboard into her lap and began tapping away with a speed that indicated she'd had a lot of practise. Reams of text scrolled over the monitor's display, showing strings of encrypted numbers and letters. Her blue eyes stared unblinkingly at the screen, telling Duggan that she was already lost to the world.

Duggan picked up his helmet. "I'm going back outside," he said.

"Sir?" said McGlashan.

"If the autopilot's unavailable and most of our sensors are offline, I'll need to take another look at the cave - to see how much of a squeeze it'll be to get out of here if we have to make it without the guidance systems. The bulkhead viewscreen never seems quite good enough when things get really tight."

"Need company?" she asked.

"Wait here, Commander. I need you to keep working and see if there's anything else about this vessel that we need to be aware of."

She looked disappointed. "Understood."

Duggan put his helmet back on and made his way back down the boarding ramp at a half-jog. He needed to spend time on the *Crimson* to familiarise himself with the controls, but he also knew that there was no way he'd be able to pilot it out of the cave if he didn't have a mental image of what he was flying through. He was itching to test himself.

"Still a young man at heart," he muttered.

He pushed himself through the piles of rocks that covered the cave floor, with his helmet light set to maximum intensity. It wasn't bright enough to give him a perfect view of the walls and it certainly didn't illuminate the cavern's ceiling. What it did do was let him see enough to realise that he was going to have a fight on his hands to get the *Crimson* out of here without hitting something. Duggan got to the rock shelf and knew he'd come far enough. Beyond this point, the cavern opened up enough that it would be a piece of cake to get the *Crimson* out. He sat on his haunches for a minute, looking at the four parked tanks below. The increased gravity of the planet was starting to weigh down on him. Chainer's voice came through unexpectedly, a mixture of static and hiss to indicate the difficulty of communicating down here.

"Sir?" said Chainer. There was an urgency in his voice.

"What is it, Lieutenant?"

"We're too deep underground for our remaining sensors to detect anything in orbit. However, I've patched into the sensor array on one of the tanks and used that to piggyback to the beacon we left near to the entrance."

"And?"

"It's picked something up, sir. The same approximate dimensions and weight as a Ghast drop ship. I think they've found us."

"How far?"

"Three klicks from the cave entrance. Maybe less."

Duggan clenched his fists in anger and opened a channel to Sergeant Ortiz. "Sergeant. Get back in your suits and prepare for combat. We've got incoming." He killed his light, unslung his gauss rifle and lay low, with his suit helmet's sensors scanning ahead for movement.

CHAPTER TWELVE

"SIR, you should get back to the *Crimson*." McGlashan's voice was faint.

"Negative, Commander. I'm waiting here to find out what we're facing. They won't see me."

"Sir," she acknowledged. Even through the interference, her doubt was palpable.

"Sergeant Ortiz, I need your squad here at the shelf – on the double. Bring everything you've got."

Ortiz's voice crackled through to Duggan. "We're leaving the *Crimson* now. Good job we didn't take off those suits, huh? What've we got?" From the tone of her voice she was running, though it hardly sounded like she was labouring at all.

"Lieutenant Chainer's picked up what he believes to be a Ghast dropship coming to land less than three klicks from the entrance to this cave. We need time to get the *Crimson*'s engines up to peak efficiency."

"Any idea of their numbers?"

"None. I'm assuming they've sent a full complement." They

both knew that an enemy dropship could carry fifty of their soldiers, as well as several pieces of heavy equipment.

"Won't the Cadaveron just send missiles to blow this place apart when we've killed all of their soldiers?" she asked, confident as ever that she and her squad would come out on top.

"They may. We have to assume they don't know exactly where the *Crimson*'s landed. It'll take a heavy bombardment if they want to be sure they've got us. On top of that, they don't like to think we can beat them face to face. It could be that they send another dozen shuttles after the first one." Duggan also held a secret hope that the Ghasts would be interested in finding out what had brought the Corps out here. There was a chance they wouldn't necessarily try to destroy anything until they found out what it was they were dealing with.

"Shame about that beacon," Ortiz said. "They'll know we're here."

"Nothing we can do about that. We can't hide the tanks anyway."

"We'll reach you soon. Any movement?"

"It's quiet."

"Just the way I like it."

"Don't lie to me, Sergeant."

Ortiz laughed, a rich, throaty noise. "Wouldn't dream of it, sir."

The comms went quiet, giving Duggan a few moments to think. The soldiers had a long way to go and it would be a close-run thing for them to reach him before the Ghast forces arrived. He considered the idea of pulling everyone back and having them sit tight inside the *Crimson*. The trouble was, such a course would allow the Ghasts to reach the spacecraft without opposition. From there, they could report the ship's exact position underground and give the Cadaveron's captain an easy ride if he decided to launch a full broadside of his missiles towards the surface above. More importantly, it would also betray the fact that there was a Corps warship here. All-in-all, it seemed better to keep the enemy guessing.

His suit camera still hadn't picked anything up, so he took the opportunity to move to a new position on the edge of the shelf, where he could lie flat behind a raised area of rock. He kept his rifle braced against his shoulder and activated the head-up-display within the helmet. The results weren't perfect, though some of the areas of deepest darkness ahead were intensified into sharp relief.

As he waited, he made use of his CO's authority to connect with Ortiz's helmet feed. The soldiers were still finding their way through the rocks and they ran at an impressive pace. A speech-to-text overlay accompanied the feed, giving an update of the communications between the men and women. It was a useful facility when you needed to keep track of the action during an engagement without listening directly to what everyone was saying.

"Sir, I think you should reconsider," crackled the voice of McGlashan, trying again to get him to return to the *Crimson*. "You might get killed."

"Thank you for the concern, Commander. We need to keep the Ghasts from finding out what we're hiding here. At least until we can fly. Otherwise we run the risk of their captain bombarding the roof of the cave until it comes down on us."

"Aye, sir," she said, still not convinced.

"You can fly it out if anything happens to me," he said. McGlashan didn't bother to reply. She knew he was taking a pointless risk, as did he. *My decision to make,* he thought. His suit informed him that his heart rate and blood pressure were slightly elevated. *Not fear. Anticipation.*

There was movement behind him. The first of the soldiers arrived, dropping onto their stomachs and swarming along the ground towards the lip of the shelf, keeping their chests just high enough that their bandoliers of plasma grenades weren't dislodged.

"Spread out," said Ortiz, waving her hand to the left and right to indicate where the infantry should go. Amongst the men, Duggan saw the ship's medic, Corporal Blunt. He had a heavy pack of complicated healing kit fixed across his back that looked like it weighed seventy pounds.

Turner emerged last from the rocks, fifty yards back from the ridge. He'd been given the unenviable task of carrying the amplifier unit that would let them take remote control of the tanks. He dropped low and dragged it the remainder of the way to the edge.

The comms fizzed and hummed. "Captain Duggan, Sergeant Ortiz. This is Lieutenant Chainer. Something's just destroyed the cavemouth beacon."

"Roger," said Ortiz. "We're almost in position. Setting up remote connection to the tanks now." She was only ten yards from Duggan and flat on her stomach. Her helmeted head turned towards him and she raised her hand with first finger and thumb pressed together. "Shame we can't see the cave mouth," she said to him. The suit's sensors could only detect movement up to eight hundred metres, which was unfortunate since the gauss rifles could kill at two klicks or more.

"I'm taking command of this one, Sergeant," said Duggan over a private channel.

"Understood," came the instant reply. There was no rancour in her voice – she knew Duggan had earned his right to command.

"Stay down and keep your lights out," said Duggan across the open channel to the squad. "Switch on movement and heat sensors. The Ghast suits will mask their signature, but we might get warning of any ordnance. We'll try and surprise them with the tanks. I'll take tank one, Diaz you've got two, West three, Nelson four."

"Roger," came the responses almost at once.

Duggan instructed his helmet to tap into the amplification unit, which then relayed him to the onboard micro-core of tank one. "Tank one sensors seeing heat and movement," he said. The vehicles' sensor arrays were more sensitive than the tiny helmet arrays and they'd be relying on them to detect where the Ghast forces where and what kit they had with them.

"What do we have?" asked Ortiz.

"Ghast compact tank and troop movement," he said. "Tank one moving out. Tank two fall in behind. Three and four follow at three hundred metres. Activating weapons systems. Setting to auto detect and fire."

Under Duggan's instruction, the front tank glided smoothly ahead for three hundred metres towards the cave entrance. Suddenly, the sensor feed began to shudder, which told Duggan that its main armament was firing. The tanks could propel fist-sized chunks of depleted uranium at an incredible velocity and with reasonable accuracy over long distances. It was a crude method of waging war, yet it continued to be a cheap and effective way of destroying the opposition. You could track and intercept inbound missiles. You could deflect beam weapons with the right kind of armour. It was difficult to do anything about a heavy slug of dense metal coming towards you at fifteen klicks per second.

"What's it firing at?" muttered Duggan.

He accessed the tank's targeting system. It looked like Sergeant Ortiz had patched herself in for a look and had got there ahead of him. "Knocked out their tank, sir. That'll piss them off."

"Incoming," said Diaz, his voice calm.

"What is it?"

"No information at the moment, sir."

The feed from the Duggan's tank became an incandescent white, which faded quickly to static noise. In the distance, the floor and walls of the cave ahead of them glowed with the fierce light of the Ghast artillery attack. The white-hot burst vanished in a moment, leaving the first tank scorched, but apparently undamaged and still operational. The vehicles were made to absorb a lot of incoming fire, but Duggan knew that whatever had caused that blast, there'd be damage to the armour and probably to the equipment onboard. He checked and saw multiple failure reports from the onboard systems, including the forward sensors. Luckily, the engine hadn't stalled and the tank continued onwards at seventy-five percent speed.

"Computer-guided plasma launcher," said Diaz. His tank was the closest and its sensors had read enough to be sure what had struck the first vehicle.

"Tanks three and four under control," said Ortiz. "Heading after the others."

"We need to destroy that launcher before the Ghasts find out we're up here," said Duggan grimly. The plasma launchers were nasty against armour and nasty against ground troops. The splash damage could engulf even the most dug in of troops. Given the time, they could smash through almost anything, including a warship's heavy armour. The infantry was spread across a width of over one hundred metres, so they weren't clustered. Still, they'd become easy prey if all of the tanks were destroyed before they'd knocked out the Ghast artillery.

"Need me to take point, sir?" asked Diaz. Tank one was slowing the progress of the one behind.

"All yours, Soldier," said Duggan.

"Any sign of the plasma launcher?" asked Ortiz.

"Nothing yet, Sergeant," said Diaz.

There was another burst of light against the first tank. Its onboard warning alarms chimed urgently and fed through a number of deep red warning gauges showing that most of the onboard electronics had just burned out.

"Tank one out of action," said Duggan. "Tank two continue ahead. Three and four keep your distance."

With his tank going nowhere fast, Duggan spent a few seconds pulling up the details from the remaining functional array on the vehicle. He sent the data file through the suit's communicator to the *Crimson*, hoping that it wouldn't arrive corrupted.

"I need an enhance on that file. Immediately," he said. Even the *Crimson*'s old mainframe would have several hundred thousand times the processing power of the tank and it would be able to discern possibilities from the video that the tank's computer would not. The line hummed for a few seconds before McGlashan spoke.

"Captain Duggan, Sergeant Ortiz, I've got some bad news for you. There are two plasma launchers. One's in the cave mouth between two rocks to the far left. The muzzle is pointing through and into the cave. The other one is almost two klicks away. I can't get an exact location, only an approximation. They must have kept it with the dropship."

"Roger that. Diaz, West, Nelson. Target the rocks at the left-hand side of the cave entrance."

The soldiers in control of the tanks wasted no time. "Overriding auto targeting," said Diaz.

The short-barrelled gun of tank two clanked four times in succession, sending its ammunition at high velocity in the direction Duggan had indicated. The remaining two tanks followed suit, pumping out heavy metal slugs in short volleys. Their aim wasn't exact since it was hard to aim precisely through the remote control.

Before Duggan was able to confirm if the artillery piece at the entrance had been destroyed, another blast of plasma burst across the cave, the ferocity of it turning the exterior of tank two a molten orange. This time, Duggan's helmet picked up the spitting sound of the superheated air as it expanded at an immense speed, washing outwards for a hundred metres all around. Before the echo of the light had faded from Duggan's retinas, there was another plasma strike on the tank.

"Tank two out of action," said Diaz. "Two direct hits."

"Three and four taking evasive manoeuvres," said West. "Still firing."

Duggan continued to watched through tank one's remaining sensor and saw huge chunks of rock explode away from the boulders near the cave entrance over one thousand metres away. The barrage from tanks three and four continued, smashing the rock into pieces. Something metallic was hurled into the air, twisting and turning as its ruined mass arced fifty metres from where it had been positioned. There was other movement – shapes in powered armour scattered away, whilst others crept into the cave close to the side wall.

"Got the bastard!" said Nelson in triumph.

He'd spoken too soon. Another of the guided plasma strikes made a direct hit on tank four. Before the light of it had faded, Duggan was able to see a number of smaller explosions detonate against the vehicle's hull as the Ghast soldiers threw their grenades against it. For a moment, it looked as if the tank's armour might have shrugged off the attack, but then something else exploded against it in the muted colours of a conventional explosive launched in a low-oxygen atmosphere. Whatever it was, it stopped tank four immediately.

"Looks like it's down to me," said West.

"Ignore their soldiers and go straight for the second launcher," said Duggan, with utter calm. "I'll feed you the coordinates if I get anything exact," he told her. "You've got shock troops coming to the left."

"Roger. I'll hold fire until I see that plasma launcher," West replied.

"We can't give ourselves away - keep your movement to a minimum," Duggan told the squad. The suits were designed to give out hardly any heat and they could fool all but the most powerful infra-red sensors. It was all about the movement, which was easy to detect and hard to disguise. "I make it forty Ghost shock troops incoming. They're still out of helmet viewing range."

Duggan watched the Ghost soldiers advance through the sensor from tank one. They wore the powered alloy battle armour that he'd seen them wear ever since the first time he'd engaged in direct combat with them. The Ghosts were already much bigger than humans – seven feet tall humanoids that seemed almost as broad as they were tall, with dense bones structures and heavy musculature that made them as strong as they looked. Even so, they had no more ability to survive in a near-vacuum than a human and they ensconced themselves in servo-powered armoured suits, which were angular and ugly in design. The Ghosts looked slow and clumsy inside their suits and Duggan had always felt that the lighter suits of the Corps soldiers were better-suited to ground combat.

"Exiting the cave mouth now," said West. "Taking small arms fire and a couple of grenade strikes. Nothing to worry about."

Duggan patched himself into tank three for a few seconds. The landscape outside the cave was littered with rocks and indentations. The Ghost dropship could have hidden almost anywhere. The plasma launchers didn't need a perfect trajectory to score a hit, since their projectiles could veer through the air. Still, there were limitations to where the second artillery unit could be positioned in order to have scored a hit so deep within the cave. Wherever it was, random fire stood no chance of taking it out.

"Any news on the second launcher's position, sir?" asked Ortiz. "Those Ghast troops are going to realise we're here soon."

"Commander? We need something on the second launcher and soon. Got anything new for us?"

"Negative, sir. I've managed to connect to the tank through the amplifier but we're not receiving a consistent high-resolution feed. I'm transmitting the best data we have through to the tank's autofire systems."

"Keep at it," said Duggan.

"First Ghast squad coming to within eight hundred metres," said Ortiz.

"I'm taking fire, sir!" said Carter, with an edge of tension in his voice.

"Shit, I think they've got a couple of heavy repeaters with them," hissed Davis from his position nearby.

It looked like the Ghasts had come prepared for some real action. Duggan took a deep breath and prepared to give the order to respond. Before he could open his mouth, all hell broke loose - the rocks of the shelf and the boulders behind him seemed to explode into a million shards. The sharp fragments flew into the air, before skittering in every direction and bouncing away from the suits and helmets of Duggan's squad.

"Return fire," he said. "Kill those ugly bastards."

CHAPTER THIRTEEN

RETURNING fire was easier said than done. The Ghost heavy repeaters raked left and right along the edge of the shelf, keeping the soldiers pinned down. Duggan was able to see the weapons through tank one's sensors – they were little more than a chain gun mounted behind an alloy shield. The repeaters had tiny engines that let a single Ghost move them around easily, whilst also providing power to cycle the weapon. The enemy had moved four of them inside the cave mouth and they'd set up overlapping fire to ensure that Duggan's squad couldn't even lift their heads without the risk of having them blown off. All along the ridge, the soldiers occasionally looked over but there was little they could do to put the advancing Ghasts under pressure.

"Got one," said Jackson grimly, as a shot from his rifle smashed through the suit of an approaching Ghost warrior from over seven hundred metres.

"They're advancing in fives," said Ortiz. "Giving themselves plenty of cover." She ducked back down, just as two of the repeaters shattered a chunk of the ledge away nearby.

Duggan raised himself on his elbows and fired a couple of

ANTHONY JAMES

quick shots with his own rifle. The newest models had very little kickback, but he kept it braced against his shoulder out of habit. The gun hummed and whined, sending out its dense metal bullets towards the closest of the Ghast squads. One of the distant enemy was spun around and dropped to the floor. The Corps gauss rifles could punch through the Ghast armoured suits easily enough.

"I've been hit, I've been hit!" screamed Henderson. A way to his left, Duggan's suit magnified and enhanced a spray of blood as it was jettisoned from the soldier's body.

"Hold tight, I'm coming to get you," said Blunt, dashing across in a low crouch, his medical kit bouncing wildly on his back.

"How's that tank doing?" Duggan asked. "We could do with it back in here."

"The *Crimson*'s sent through its best guesses, sir. No luck yet. It's ridden one hit and there's been nothing else. I might be under the plasma launcher's firing arc," said West.

Duggan didn't say anything else and hoped that the soldier was right about the tank being too close for the plasma launcher to get off another shot. The Ghasts had them pinned down pretty well and it wasn't looking good. He fired off another three rounds in quick succession, unsure if he'd scored a hit.

"Is this quiet enough for you, Sergeant?" he asked.

Ortiz laughed in good humour as she fired a snap shot towards the enemy forces. "This is just perfect, sir," she said.

The heavy repeaters chewed up the rock face in front of him, forcing Duggan to stay low. He took advantage and connected with tank three's sensors. He could tell at once that it was firing and the main turret burned hot from the friction. Three bursts of four rounds bludgeoned the distant rocks into splinters. The tank fired another volley, this time shattering an overhanging shelf into pieces and sending a hundred tonnes of rock onto the ground beneath.

It appeared that West's opinion that tank three was too close to the launcher was wrong. The tank took another hit, though its evasive pattern was enough to ensure this next plasma burst deflected partially away from the angular front armour.

"Close," muttered Duggan. It was down to luck if the tank would find the launcher quickly enough. "I hate relying on luck," he growled.

"Don't we all, sir, don't we all." It was McGlashan, monitoring his comms output.

Tank three continued with its bombardment. Duggan caught sight of something and the sensor readouts confirmed a flash of hardened alloy, hidden fifteen hundred metres away behind a two-hundred-metre-wide bank of irregular rock.

"Got the dropship," he said in triumph.

"I've got the coordinates," said West. "Let's pray the launcher's with it."

Four heavy projectiles collided with the rock, each connecting within a few feet of each other. Another four followed and then another four, as the tank continued to trace an irregular pattern of movement towards the dropship's location. The final volley blew out an enormous chunk of the rock, leaving the Ghost dropship easily visible. It was an ugly design – blocky and functional.

"Say goodbye," said West. Duggan could picture her face as she directed the tank to fire.

The dropship was struck by a volley of depleted uranium rounds. It wasn't designed to withstand the punishment of high-calibre weaponry and its structure was crumpled and knocked over onto one side. Its hull split and the life-supporting gases of the interior were sucked out into the planet's atmosphere.

"There's the launcher," said Duggan.

The Ghasts' artillery piece had been placed to the rear of the dropship and was now fully visible. Its crew of four were gathered around it, their deaths assured. The tank took moments to reload and its projectiles took less than a second to cross the intervening space. The launcher and its crew were flung into the air, a mixture of metal and bodies thrown many metres by the unstoppable fusillade.

Duggan had almost no chance to feel satisfaction. Before he could give the instruction for the tank to return to the cave and take out the heavy repeaters, an explosion tore into the surface – this one much, much bigger than anything from the plasma launcher. The feed from tank three ended at once.

"The Cadaveron's just taken out the tank," Duggan said.

"That's not good news for us," said Ortiz. She was as matter-of-fact as ever.

Duggan took stock. The heavy repeaters continued their withering fire without cease. He didn't know how much ammunition they could hold and it didn't look as if they were going to run out before the advancing Ghast shock troops got close enough to do a suit-jump onto the ledge.

"We need to take out those repeaters," he said through gritted teeth. The destruction of the tank put them in real danger of losing this one.

"Their closest two squads have advanced to within four hundred metres, sir," said Ortiz. "We should be able to make it back to the rocks behind us if we stay low." The cave mouth was at a higher level than the floor beneath the shelf, but not quite high enough for the repeaters to fire directly onto the shelf. Duggan knew they should make a run for it.

"Dammit, we need more time for the *Crimson* to repair her engines!" he said.

"We're going to get slaughtered here, sir," said Ortiz.

"We've lost Henderson," said Blunt, patching a channel

straight into Duggan's suit.

Duggan swore loudly. He knew it was time to retreat. His head told him this one was a lost cause. The repeaters swept the shelf in front of him, sending a dozen serrated pieces of stone against his suit and helmet with a dull clatter.

"Sir, we should go, sir!" said Ortiz.

"Captain Duggan, you can't wait there any longer," said McGlashan, addressing him more formally than usual.

"If we have to fly out of this cave with the engines at thirty-five percent, that Cadaveron will blow us out of the air before we're fifty klicks from the cave!" he said. "We need more time!"

"There're too many of them!" shouted Collins across the open channel. He was close to panic.

A cold calm descended on Duggan as he considered his options. Just when he thought he'd have to concede this one as a lost cause, his brain came up with an idea. It was risky as hell, but once he'd thought it, he couldn't shake it off.

"Commander McGlashan. Are the *Crimson*'s aft Lambda batteries operational?"

"Yes sir, all eighteen clusters are functional."

"Good. I need you to fire two missiles at the cave mouth here. The repeaters are keeping us pinned down."

"Sir?"

"Do I need to repeat everything for you, Commander?"

"No. Sorry, sir. It's just that the cave mouth is far too close. The Lambda guidance systems don't kick in until they've gone more than twenty klicks. Otherwise the acceleration destroys the instrumentation."

"I am aware of this, Commander. You'll need to override and target them manually."

There was a pause on the other end of the line and he almost heard McGlashan gulp. "That's going to need a hell of a shot," she said.

"I trust you. Do it and do it now."

"Aye, sir. Working on the override now. You might want to tell the guys and gals to put their heads down."

"Listen up everyone. We're going to take out those heavy repeaters with the *Crimson*'s Lambdas. You'd best keep your heads down."

The squad's open channel became awash with a cacophony of shocked voices. Duggan shut them down at once and ordered silence. "And once those repeaters are destroyed, I want you to show any Ghost survivors that the Corps can be dirty bastards too."

"Amen to that," said Ortiz.

"Launching now, sir," said McGlashan.

Duggan flattened himself to the ground, willing himself to show as small a profile as possible. There was the tiniest of delays, during which two of the *Crimson*'s Lambda missiles shot away from their cluster, sleek tubes of single-burn gravity engines, guidance and payload. They followed an almost perfectly flat trajectory across the boulder-strewn cavern floor, racing over the huddled human soldiers, still accelerating at a colossal rate. The first warhead struck the cave wall a little over a hundred metres above the ground. The Lambdas were designed to pierce the thickest of armour and this one buried itself deeply into the rock face before its payload detonated, blowing out a ragged hole in the wall and incinerating the Ghosts and the heavy repeaters in a millisecond. The second missile shot out of the cave, its trajectory carrying it away from the planet's surface and out into space.

The heat from the blast washed down the cave, killing all of the advancing Ghosts and charring their bodies to ashes inside their suits. A cloud of blue-hot dying fire engulfed Duggan and his squad, roiling over and buffeting them. Each suit immediately shut down all non-essential power-draining subsystems as the life support system sucked all available power to keep the occupants alive. *Four hundred and ninety degrees*, Duggan saw the outside temperature peak at. *Can't resist that for long.*

To Duggan's relief, the temperature fell away rapidly as the Lambda blast receded. He crawled quickly forward towards the edge of the shelf and saw Ortiz doing the same. It was utterly dark below and his suit's comms and image enhancements were slow to reactivate. *Must have taken some damage.* After what seemed like an eternity, the suit's life support allowed the helmet sensors enough power to resolve the blackness below.

"No movement," said Ortiz. It looked like her suit was working a little better than his. "Damn, sir, that was crazy." Her voice carried a mixture of admiration and relief.

"Ghost forces eliminated. Well done, soldiers," said Duggan through the open channel.

Along the ledge, the rest of the squad pushed themselves to their feet. One or two of them looked distinctly shaky. A few half-garbled voices spoke at once, the men and women not quite recovered from what had happened.

"Sir? Is everything all right?" asked McGlashan. She sounded shaky too and Duggan realised he'd just told her to do something that could have killed them all.

"Your aim was good, Commander. Looks like you got them all."

McGlashan didn't say anything, but she didn't close the channel quickly enough to stop Duggan hearing her sharp exhalation of breath.

He stood up, feeling more elated than anything else. Then he saw the prone body of Henderson, with one arm torn off and a dinnerplate-sized exit hole through his back. Corporal Blunt had hooked the soldier up to one of his machines. It hadn't been enough. Duggan's feeling of victory evaporated at once. "Let's get back to the *Crimson*. Bring Henderson with us and we'll send him out into space. It's the least he deserves."

CHAPTER FOURTEEN

"SHOULD we leave anyone behind to keep watch, sir?" said Ortiz, as the squad of soldiers threaded their way through the boulders that led towards the *Crimson*.

"There's no point anymore. The Cadaveron can't fail to have picked up the Lambda blast. They'll know there's something big down here. The important thing is they don't know where the *Crimson* is, which denies them the opportunity to destroy it."

"Unless they bombard the surface and rely on luck, sir."

"There's always that, Sergeant. For the moment, I won't risk anyone else. The Cadaverons carry upwards of a thousand troops. We can be pretty sure that next time it won't be a single dropship that comes to investigate."

"At least these rocks should slow them up some," she said. "Might stop them getting their artillery close enough."

Duggan wasn't convinced but didn't say so. "You've got command again," he said, letting Ortiz know that she was giving orders to the squad again.

"Yes, sir," she acknowledged.

"I want these rocks to be riddled with grenades. To give the Ghasts something to think about when their foot soldiers come this way."

Ortiz unclipped one of the dull grey tubes from her bandolier. She gave the dial on top a twist, her fingers surprisingly nimble within the suit. Without a glance, she tossed it carelessly to one side, where it bounced twice before coming to rest. "It'll arm itself in five minutes. Anything comes within twenty feet and it's boom time. We'll not be able to come this way again."

"We shouldn't need to, Sergeant."

Sergeant Ortiz passed on the instruction and soon all of the soldiers were arming the grenades they carried with them and flicking them away between the rocks with a practised nonchalance, as if they were throwing away something of no concern at all.

"How're the quarters on the *Crimson?*" Duggan asked her, partly to pass the time and partly because he wanted to know.

"We might as well be back on the *Detriment,*" said Ortiz, her voice betraying the faintest hint of amusement. "The food replicator's a sight to behold."

"The *Crimson*'s internal layout is practically identical to a Gunner, going by what I've seen," said Duggan. "They must have hired the same designers. We're packing a lot more weaponry than we had on the *Detriment.*"

"Enough to beat that Cadaveron?" asked Ortiz. There was hope in her words. For all her toughness, she didn't want to die out here.

"We'll be trying to outrun it, not shoot it down," said Duggan. "The *Crimson* looks like it's a real killer, but it's still over fifty years old."

They got back to the *Crimson* much more slowly than Duggan would have liked. Carrying the body of Henderson slowed them down significantly, though there was no way Duggan was going to leave the man behind. At the bottom of the boarding ramp, he thanked the squad and dismissed them to their quarters. Duggan made his way towards the bridge – it had felt good to be out there with a rifle in his hand, but it was a relief to be back on a spaceship again.

"Welcome back, sir," said McGlashan. She looked almost gaunt. They already knew about the loss of Henderson and it was clear from the haggard faces on the bridge that the man's death didn't sit easily with them.

"What's our status?" he asked. "I doubt we've got more than another couple of hours before we have Ghast troops knocking on our door."

"Twelve hours until ninety percent on the engines," said Breeze.

Duggan frowned. "Going quicker than expected?"

"Yes sir, much quicker. It's going like we're packing a modern AI, rather than a bunch of silicon."

"Could it be highly optimised?"

Breeze looked pained, as if he didn't want to commit to an answer. "Could be, sir."

Duggan turned to Monsey. "Any progress, soldier?"

"They've locked the core down pretty well, sir. Or should I say *cores*. It's the strangest arrangement I've seen."

"What do you mean?" asked Duggan.

"It's like they've got an old mainframe piggybacked on top of another back-end core. I don't know how to explain it better than that. It's not something I've come across before. The front end is a design I recognize. I'm only getting glimpses of what the back end is doing. It's fast, sir. *Really* fast."

"Some sort of push-pull system?" he asked. "Or done to improve the redundancy?"

"Unlikely, sir. The term *mainframe* on warships like this

always encompasses a dozen layers of redundancy anyway. This is something different. I can't get a proper go at the second core at all."

Duggan was intrigued, but didn't know what to make of the soldier's words. He left her to it and considered his other options. The Ghasts were certainly not going to leave them alone now that they'd seen their dropship destroyed and picked up the launch of two Lambdas. They'd either send an overwhelming force of their troops to the cave, or they'd pound the surface above. Given that their ground troops had been killed before they could discover any worthwhile information about what was hiding here, Duggan had to assume the Ghast commander would send more of his soldiers.

Another two hours passed in a tense near-silence. The clacking of Monsey's keyboard was louder than the air conditioning and the faint humming sound that was prevalent throughout the entirety of the ship. There was something about it which made Duggan think that the *Crimson* was eager to see action. He shook the feeling away.

"Engines at forty-five percent," announced Breeze. "Whatever the core is doing, it's flying through it."

"Not quickly enough," said Duggan.

"I've got movement on the sensors," said Chainer. "I'd say it's ground troops coming towards our position."

"They can't get anything big enough to hurt us through those rocks," McGlashan replied. "They're not going to damage anything throwing grenades and firing their rifles at us."

"Of course, they aren't," said Duggan. "However, their plasma launchers might be able to land a few shots on us if they can get them far enough into the cave."

"Do they have the firepower to pierce the *Crimson*'s armour?" she asked with a frown.

"Who knows? I can't recall a time when a piece of Ghast artillery was given the opportunity to fire upon a Corps vessel."

"Probably best we don't find out," said Breeze, without lifting his head from the instrument panel.

"Here they come," said Chainer.

All five on the bridge watched on the viewscreen as a dozen Ghast soldiers came into view from the cover of the rocks. They took a defensive position, spreading themselves widely amongst the outcrops and loose boulders.

"There're more behind these ones," Chainer said. "I'd guess at least three hundred. I'm picking up their attempts to transmit."

"Can you read what they're saying?" asked Duggan. It made no difference – it didn't take a genius to imagine what details their message contained.

"Negative, sir. The *Crimson* was build long before their latest encryption methods. It'll take the mainframe a while until it learns how to decrypt what they're sending."

"Fine," said Duggan, waving the matter away. "See what it can come up with. Don't divert from other tasks."

The Ghasts didn't take any hostile action immediately. They set up position and watched from within their alloy space suits.

"What are they up to?" wondered McGlashan.

"They probably can't get a message to their ship's captain," said Duggan. "I'll bet they're having to send some of their soldiers back towards the cave entrance so they can act as a relay for the message. It'll buy us some time. Not much, but better than none."

Another thirty minutes passed until, without warning, the Ghast troops disappeared into the rocks as if they'd never existed.

"Got plasma rounds incoming, sir," said McGlashan, five minutes later. "Lots of them."

"At least we've got our answer," said Duggan. "It doesn't look as if the Ghasts are curious enough about the *Crimson* to bother trying to capture it." On one of his screens, he watched at least a dozen red dots which came in a wavering line towards the *Crimson*. Each of the dots represented an incoming plasma shell. "Let's see what damage ground artillery can do to the armour of the Hynus project's pride and joy."

CHAPTER FIFTEEN

THE CLUSTER of dots came closer and closer, until one by one, they winked out. A damage readout plotted a variety of graphs, charts and tables to indicate where the impacts had occurred and the extent of the damage. Deep as they were in the structure of the ship, none of the occupants felt even the slightest indication that anything was amiss. The plasma launchers were designed to take out armoured vehicles like the *Detriment's* tanks. Against an eleven-hundred-metre warship, they were rather less effective.

"They're going to need something bigger," said McGlashan with a grin. "They hardly scratched us."

"They've got plenty of time," said Duggan. Sure enough, a second cluster of the red dots appeared on his screen, drifting silently towards the *Crimson*.

"The bastards got our range pretty easily," said Breeze.

"Their soldiers will have planted a tracking beacon beneath us, or somewhere nearby," Duggan told him. "All they'll need to do is point their launchers this way and let their guidance systems do the rest."

"Second rounds have impacted. The surface of our aft armour plating has melted to a depth of nearly a metre."

"Dammit!" said Duggan. "I don't want them whittling us away before we've even taken off."

"Engines at forty six percent," said Breeze. It had only been a few minutes since his last announcement.

"Third wave incoming," said Duggan under his breath. He turned his attention to Breeze. "If we forget lightspeed, how long until you can get the gravity drives functioning?"

"They'll work now, sir. I just don't have enough data to predict how fast we'll be able to go with them."

"Divert the mainframe until it's working fully on the gravity drive."

"I'm on it," Breeze replied.

"How're you coming on with the core, soldier?" asked Duggan.

"Still at it, sir," replied Monsey noncommittally. "Don't rely on me getting it unlocked before you need it," she said.

"Do your best," he replied. In truth, he didn't know if whatever was held in the locked-down core was going to be of any use to them. Regardless, he had no intention of letting up in his efforts to find out. It appeared as if the *Crimson* had secrets and he was determined to find out what they were, before he got back to the *Juniper*. *Assuming the Cadaveron doesn't blow us to shit first.*

The third barrage struck the *Crimson* and it wasn't long until a fourth appeared on the spaceship's detection screens. Duggan breathed deeply, feeling the warm air of the bridge fill his nostrils with its comforting odours.

"I'm taking direct control of the first rear Lambda battery," he said.

"You don't have the angle, sir," said McGlashan. "I think they've learned from the last missile strike they took from us. Our sensors won't reach outside, but we can plot back to the Ghost position by analysing the trajectory of the incoming rounds. Even if you fire as flat as the Lambdas will go, you're going to overshoot."

"I think you're right," he said with a humourless laugh. "Maybe it'll give them something to think about though."

"Just don't bring the ceiling down and block our way out," she replied.

The fourth wave of plasma fire scoured the *Crimson*'s outer hull. Before a fifth was launched, Duggan triggered the release of another of the *Crimson*'s arsenal of Lambdas. A concealed opening at the rear of the spaceship slid open for the briefest of moments. A ten-metre-long alloy tube screamed away, accelerating at a rate quicker than any local space warship could manage. The missile's guidance system remained inoperative as the Lambda exited the cave at a speed that made it difficult for a biological eye to detect. It flew low and fast over the clustered Ghost artillery. At last, the guidance computer came online, too late to prevent the missile from detonating against a steep escarpment, almost eighty kilometres beyond the Ghost positions.

"Missed," said McGlashan on the *Crimson*'s bridge. "Got another wave of plasma rounds incoming. Same number as before."

"Did we get anything from the Lambda's transmit log?" asked Duggan.

"Nothing. The signal got blocked by all these rocks."

It wasn't unexpected, but nor was it what Duggan had hoped to hear. Without the transmit log, he had no way of determining whether or not his first launch had been at all close.

"How're the piloting systems?" he asked suddenly.

"Still down, sir," said McGlashan. "I had them on a low priority until we got closer to launch. The repair bot's working on the sensor arrays."

"Never mind," Duggan told her. He turned to Lieutenant Breeze. "Start the gravity drive."

"Sir? It'll slow down the repairs," said Breeze.

"Do it."

"Whatever you say," said Breeze. "We're only at fifty percent."

"I understand. Bring them up."

"Coming online now."

A feeling of excitement ran through the people on the bridge. Even Monsey felt it and she looked away from her efforts to hack into the *Crimson*'s core in order that she could see what was happening.

"Ladies and gentlemen, we're starting her up," said Duggan over the internal comms. "Since we have no idea what to expect, I'd suggest you prepare for a bumpy ride."

A grumbling vibration coursed through the floor, scraping like two pieces of indescribably heavy metal rubbing against each other. There was a humming, whining sound which rose in pitch. The noise became louder and higher in frequency, yet it somehow faded rapidly into the background until it was detected only at the extremes of human hearing.

"What the hell is this?" asked Breeze. "I've not heard a ship that sounds like this one and I've been on a hundred. I was standing less than twenty metres above the *Archimedes'* fission drive on one of her earliest flights and it was nothing like this."

Duggan knew what Breeze meant. The *Crimson* sounded rough – harsh even, but there was something about it that raised the hairs on his neck. Not even the *Detriment* had come close and that was as seat-of-the-pants as any warship built in the last fifty years. He reached over the buttons and indentations on his console, their arrangement as familiar as any Corps ship.

"Let's see how easy this bird is to fly," he said.

"What're you planning, sir?" asked McGlashan. She looked dazed.

Another barrage from the Ghast artillery washed over the ship's hull, leaving the surface glowing briefly white before the armour dissipated the heat and the white faded to a dull orange. Duggan cleared his mind of the distraction and looked at the two horizontal black metal bars in front of him. They were set in a comfortable position for him to reach when he was reclined in the captain's chair. The control levers had buttons embedded into them and there were a series of sliders and more red buttons adjacent. He stared at them for a few seconds. It was so long since he'd needed to use manual controls that his eyes hardly even noticed their existence these days. *Going soft,* he reprimanded himself. He stretched out his left hand and rested it on one of the control levers. The metal was cool and smooth. His other hand reached for the second control lever, his thumb taking a natural position between two of the buttons.

"We're leaving this place. Right now."

Chainer, Breeze and McGlashan exchanged glances. "There's not a lot of room, sir," said McGlashan at last. "You can't get a ship this big out of here without the guidance systems."

"You've got less than seventy metres spare at the narrowest point," said Chainer. He looked worried – very worried.

"And you'll be coming out backwards," added McGlashan.

"With reduced engine capacity and a Ghast heavy cruiser circling over our position."

"We'd best not hang about, then," Duggan told them. His face lit up in a broad smile and he felt completely calm. Without giving the matter any more thought, he pulled gently at the left-hand control lever. The *Crimson* lurched fractionally as it rose a few feet from the ground. Duggan corrected the tilt. The action came to him automatically, even after so long of relying on autopilot systems to get his ships to where he wanted them. He stabbed at a button on the console and a flashing light indicated that the landing gear had retracted into the hull.

"Piece of cake," muttered Chainer anxiously.

The pilot's displays threw up reams of information, which flashed onto Duggan's primary and secondary screens. A head-up-display shimmered in the air before him, feeding through the details from the warship's external sensors. Many of the arrays were still not functional and Duggan found he had to patch together a mental image of the *Crimson*'s surroundings based on the details he gathered from those of the sensors which were operational, and from his recent trip outside.

"Up we go," he said to himself. Proximity alerts flashed to warn him that the *Crimson* had come within ten metres of the left-hand wall of the cave. In a hovercar it would have been ample room. When you were piloting more than a thousand metres of warship, the distance suddenly seemed tiny. As if it had decided that lights alone were insufficient warning, the *Crimson*'s warning systems played an insistent buzzing sound through a speaker on the bridge. The sound instantly set Duggan's teeth on edge.

"That last artillery barrage scraped underneath us," said McGlashan. "It just missed."

Duggan only half listened. Although he was calm, it was taking the utmost concentration to keep the *Crimson* steady. The control sticks were sensitive and the designers hadn't expected the pilot to ever need to handle the ship in such a confined space. They'd probably been thought of as redundant anyway now that the mainframes and AIs were relied on to pilot Corps vessels. There'd been more than one captain who'd suffered the indignity of having their command stripped because they'd decided to show off by taking direct control of a spaceship. Either way, Duggan was glad the option was still available on the *Crimson*.

With a deep breath, Duggan steadied the ship and brought it

another ten metres away from the wall. He doubted that a low-speed collision would do much damage, but he didn't really want to find out what would happen if almost two billion tonnes of ultra-dense metal struck several billion tonnes of heavy ore. Slowly, he raised the ship until it hovered above the highest of the boulders that littered the cave floor. He pulled at the right control stick and the *Crimson* began a steady movement backwards. Duggan scarcely noticed that the vibration of the hull had smoothed off as the spacecraft glided through the thin atmosphere.

"Another artillery strike, sir," said McGlashan. "Ten hits and four misses. They've recalibrated their aim."

"I wonder if their crew realise we're coming," Duggan replied.

"We'll need every second we can get if we're to escape that Cadaveron."

Duggan had most of his focus on keeping the ship level, but he had a sudden idea. "How're you with aiming the Bulwarks manually?" he asked. "We've got two out of eight at the rear?"

"I'll give it a go, sir," said McGlashan, picking up his meaning at once. There was still no room for the Lambdas to target the artillery. The Bulwarks, on the other hand, might be a better bet once they could get a line of sight along the cave. If McGlashan could manage it, things would become messy for the Ghast artillery and their crew.

"Looks like we're coming close to the ledge now, sir," said Chainer. Duggan was surprised that it had taken so little time. There again, two klicks was almost nothing to a spacecraft, even one being piloted as gingerly as the *Crimson*.

"I see them!" said McGlashan. The excitement in her voice was clear. "The cocky bastards must have thought we were grounded. They're spread across the cave mouth."

Duggan couldn't take his eyes away from what he was doing

in order to look across at the commander's console. He felt the faintest change in the *Crimson*'s structure as it absorbed the recoil from the two rear Bulwarks. The early models of these cannons had suffered from enormous amounts of kick, such that it had taken many iterations before they could mount more than a single one on practically any vessel. In his mind, he could picture them spewing out their depleted uranium projectiles. The modern versions could burst up to twenty thousand rounds a minute as a last-ditch defence against incoming missiles. He didn't know what the *Crimson*'s versions could do, but he could imagine them shredding the rock floor of the cave like it was nothing more than paper. The Bulwarks bore similarities to the main armaments on the tanks, only they were much, much bigger and vastly more destructive.

The Bulwarks fired again, and this time Duggan was able to glance at an external feed from the cavern outside. He saw a hundred deep rents across the stone and something that might have been the mangled remains of ground artillery. Chunks of rock fountained into the air once more and he saw a couple of silvery shapes thrown violently into the distance.

"That's the last of them," said McGlashan. "Not much they could do about that."

Duggan didn't hang around. Gaining in confidence, he increased the speed of the *Crimson*, feeling the ship's gravity drive respond eagerly as its output rose to a tenth of one percent. For the first time in over fifty years, the ESS *Crimson* emerged from its hiding place and into the bleak darkness of the unnamed planet's night.

CHAPTER SIXTEEN

ALMOST AT ONCE, the warnings came. Chainer's station chimed a multitude of updates, which mirrored themselves onto Duggan's tertiary console screen. McGlashan's hands moved rapidly across buttons and touch panels, as her brow furrowed in concentration.

"I've picked up the Ghost ship," said Chainer. "It's high and circling towards us."

"Has it detected us?" asked Duggan.

"No way to tell, sir. Too many of our own sensors are damaged."

Duggan didn't respond immediately. He pushed at the spaceship's control levers to bring its enormous bulk to a halt. With a twist of one lever, he swung the nose around and lifted the vessel away from the planet's surface. A wave of giddiness threatened to swamp him and he saw McGlashan stumble forwards against her own console. The *Crimson*'s outdated life support systems caught up with the crushing effects of the acceleration and the feeling subsided almost at once. Duggan took a deep breath and rammed the left-hand lever as far along its slot as it would go. The feeling of giddiness returned, much stronger than before, but this time the life support was able to counteract the tremendous stresses within a second. For all its size, the *Crimson* wasn't at all ponderous. There was a vibration deep enough to set Duggan's jaw aching and then the warship rocketed away, eleven hundred metres of engines and weapons.

"Nose temperature already at thirty-five percent of design tolerance," said Breeze. "You'll need to take us higher and soon."

"The Cadaveron's changed course," Chainer said. "It's coming to see what we are."

"Can't get a lock on with the Lambdas," McGlashan added. "We're at the extremes of range and the sensors I need are out of action."

Duggan checked their speed. Even with its gravity engines at little more than half power they were approaching ninety percent of the *Detriment*'s maximum speed. It wasn't going to be much good if they burned up because he was keeping so low to the surface.

"Bringing us up," he said. "I don't think we can outrun them yet."

"I think they've launched, sir," McGlashan told him. "Can't be certain."

"Release shock drones."

"It doesn't look like they're shock drones as we know them," said McGlashan. "They're some sort of metal globe with a transmitter in. They're away now. Not sure what good they'll do." She looked at the countermeasures readouts. "We're carrying plenty of them," she said with grudging admiration. "We must have dropped about ten thousand just there."

Duggan thought fast. He had to assume the Cadveron had launched at least four waves of missiles at them and given their previous encounter with it, they might have a little over fifty seconds until impact. Maybe as much as a minute. The *Crimson* was now at the extremes of the planet's atmosphere and the hull temperature had steadied. The Cadaveron was at least five thousand klicks higher and an uncertain distance behind. It showed no signs that it wanted to drop into a lower orbit. Whoever the Ghast captain was, he or she wasn't stupid. All the heavy cruiser needed to do was to keep up the pursuit and launch missiles until the *Crimson* was eventually knocked out of the sky. Duggan checked his velocity. Incredibly, the *Crimson* had reached one hundred and five percent of the *Detriment*'s maximum gravity drive speed.

"We might outrun these bastards," he said. "If we can live long enough."

"There'll be no deep fission engines for hours, sir. The core is working entirely on the gravity drive."

"Understood, Lieutenant. Keep focus on the gravity drives for now."

"Ghast missiles within range of some of our working sensors," said McGlashan. "We've got four waves of twelve. Uncertain if there are others coming after. Impact with our drone cloud in eight seconds."

"Are the Bulwarks getting enough information to target them?"

He got his answer soon enough. The deep vibration of the *Crimson*'s engines was suddenly accompanied by a low thrumming.

"The six we can bring to bear are firing on auto, sir." She paused. "The drones have destroyed twenty-three of the incoming."

"Release more."

"Looks like we don't need to," McGlashan replied after a few seconds of staring at one of her screens.

"We've got them all?" asked Duggan in surprise.

"We've been on the *Detriment* too long, sir. The *Crimson*'s got near Hadron-class cannons. They're old, but fast and they've destroyed the rest of the missiles."

Duggan blinked. "The *Crimson*'s not *that* big," he said. "We're carrying eight supercruiser-sized Bulwarks?"

"I'm only telling you what I see, sir."

"She's right, Captain," Breeze told him. "This ship is far denser than the *Detriment*." He called up the schematics for an old Anderlecht cruiser. The *Crimson* didn't have the schematics for anything newer in its databanks. "From memory, I'd say we're easily the heaviest spacecraft per meter cubed that the Confederation navy has."

"What the hell is going on here?" asked Duggan. "The *Crimson*'s ancient. The Corps engineers have been trying to improve engine density for decades. They've hardly moved on since the war started. A percent or two every year."

"Yet here we are," said Breeze lamely.

"They've launched more missiles," said McGlashan. "I can't see how many. Drones away."

"We're losing them," said Duggan with a low whistle. The distance pings showed that the *Crimson* was creeping away from the Cadaveron. "We'll be out of missile range in less than a minute."

"More cat and mouse till the deep fissions are up."

"Something I'll happily accept," Duggan replied.

A minute later, the second waves of Ghast missiles encountered the same fate as the third. More than half collided with the drone cloud, while the remainder were shot down by the *Crimson*'s Bulwark cannons. Duggan reflected that for the first time, the Cadaveron's captain had slipped up by underestimating what he'd faced. Some of the Ghast heavy cruisers could launch more than a dozen waves of twelve missiles at a time. If Duggan had been piloting an Anderlecht cruiser, that's how fast they'd have come. *Maybe their factories are having problems keeping up with missile production,* Duggan thought. It was some consolation, though he realised that a lucky Lambda hit from the *Detriment* had taken out the Cadaveron's particle beam. Things might not have gone so well if the *Crimson* had taken a few hits from that.

"We're out of missile range," said McGlashan.

"We're quicker than they are, even with this damage," Duggan replied. He looked at Monsey. "Any news, soldier?" His internal alarm bells had begun to ring with increasing urgency. Somebody in the Corps had been keeping secrets when they'd sent him out here and he was desperate to find out what was going on. The *Crimson*'s data banks might just hold the information he wanted.

"I'll let you know, sir," she said, not even lifting her face to look over.

"The Ghost ship's veered away on a new course, sir," said Chainer.

It had been inevitable. Once it became clear that the *Crimson* was the faster vessel, the Cadaveron would be forced into plotting an AI-determined semi-random course that would have the greatest chance of intercepting them. Duggan had nothing to rely on but himself with the autopilot non-functional and he didn't like the idea of trying to beat an AI at a task they were perfectly designed to excel at. He could buy them some time by heading directly out into space. On paper, it sounded like a good idea. In reality, as soon as the planet stopped becoming an impediment to the Cadaveron's sensors, they'd be able to do a short-range lightspeed jump to bring them out near to the *Crimson*. It wasn't something that would have been possible even ten or fifteen years ago, but the processing power available to a larger ship made this new tactic viable. Duggan had almost been caught out by it the first time it had been used against him.

"Put everything onto the deep fission drive repairs," he said as soon as the Cadaveron broke off the direct pursuit.

"Doing it now, sir," said Breeze. "I reckon we'll be able to break into a low lightspeed in under three hours."

"Low enough that they'll be able to follow us?" Duggan asked.

"I'd have to go with 'yes' on that one. Everything about this Ghast ship suggests that they're carrying the latest and greatest."

"At least they didn't shut us down like the light cruiser did to the *Detriment*."

"Maybe we didn't get close enough for them to try," said Duggan. "We have to stay ahead."

"Our chance drops with every circuit," said Chainer. If there was a pessimist amongst the crew, it was Chainer.

"Someone once told me that a computer can never truly produce randomness," said Duggan. "Even the most powerful of AIs rely on an algorithm to generate something that looks random, but when you boil it down, it's only part of an infinitely long string of numbers. Let's see how the Cadaveron's AI works against the randomness of a Corps captain's brain." With that, he swung the *Crimson* about and pushed the nose downwards towards the surface.

For the next hour, Duggan changed course and speed at regular intervals, hoping that his approach would somehow allow them to elude the pursuing Cadaveron long enough for the *Crimson*'s fission drives to become available. The heat on the bridge was stifling and Duggan felt the sweat beading across his forehead. When he looked at Chainer, he saw the lieutenant was feeling it worse than he was, and the man had to wipe his face regularly with the sleeve of his uniform. He'd found himself a coffee from somewhere and steam rose from the tarlike surface of the liquid.

As the minutes wore on, Duggan found himself more and

more impressed with the *Crimson*. There were spacecraft which were difficult to control manually – generally the larger they were, the more cumbersome they became. Even a Vincent class was sluggish to respond to commands from the control console, though Duggan vaguely remembered that their hulls had initially been designed for civilian craft. It was only later they'd been adopted by the military for use in their smallest and most numerous warships. The *Crimson* was different – it was as if it had been designed from the ground up to be a pure-blooded hunter-killer. McGlashan had picked up on it too.

"If we had twenty more of these we'd kick them out of the Axion sector," she said. "Even without refitting the Lambdas."

"It's something all right," said Duggan. "Set three of these on a Cadaveron and the Ghasts would soon find out what a real challenge is."

In reality, the Space Corps databanks held records of at least thirty-five known Cadaverons which had been detected but not destroyed. The intel guys had tried to extrapolate the total numbers of Ghast heavy cruisers from the known quantity. The number they'd come up with was exactly fifty-eight. It had stuck in Duggan's head for some reason. *Fifty-eight. There's someone being paid a lot of money to be so precise. I hope they've over-estimated.* The Ghasts had bigger ships than the Cadaverons – some of them almost as large as the five-kilometre Hadron supercruisers, of which the Corps had only seven with the destruction of the *ES Ulterior*. So far, there'd been no direct engagement between a Hadron and a Ghast Oblivion, at least not that Duggan was aware of. He had no idea what happened around Charistos before the planet's population was wiped out.

"The repair bot's brought two more sensor arrays back to functionality," said Chainer.

"Eleven out of thirty?" asked Duggan.

"Aye, sir." Chainer went quiet for a moment. It usually meant he was concentrating hard. "None-too-soon, it looks. Got a ghost of something at four thousand klicks above us, twenty degrees offset, coming on a near-intercept path."

Chainer fed the projected path of the Cadaveron through to Duggan's tertiary display. Duggan hauled the *Crimson*'s nose around and pointed it upwards. He increased their speed to maximum and the almost impossibly heavy spacecraft accelerated hard out of the planet's atmosphere, her nose already beginning to glow.

"No sign of a launch yet, sir," said McGlashan.

"What's our range?"

"Borderline missile range, I'd guess. If they've not fired yet, I'd say we've made it."

"We've just had something sweep through our aft quarter engines," said Breeze. "Efficiency down eleven percent. Looks like they got their particle beam working again."

It wasn't news that Duggan wanted to hear. He checked the *Crimson*'s speed and did a quick calculation. With the reduced efficiency, they were still going much faster than the *Detriment*'s maximum velocity. That meant they should be able to outrun the Cadaveron, assuming the Ghasts weren't able to fire the particle beam again.

"Programme set: particle beam recharge twenty-five seconds. Begin," he instructed the *Crimson*'s mainframe. Instantly, a timer began on his display, mirrored across onto McGlashan's. The spaceship's core was intelligent enough to account for the delay between the weapon strike and Duggan's instruction, so when he looked at it, the countdown was already at eighteen seconds. From their earlier encounter with the Cadaveron, they'd learned that its particle beam had a much longer range than they'd expected. The problem was, he didn't know exactly how far that range was. It would make all the difference. His brain raced through the possibilities. Although the *Crimson* was pulling away, he had to assume that it wouldn't be enough and they'd take another beam hit.

Duggan had one of those minds that could instantly evaluate the possibilities of a battlefield. As a foot soldier, he'd been able to imagine the players in combat as the pieces on a gameboard. When he'd finally pushed himself to a promotion and joined the crew of a spaceship, he'd carried the skill with him. *We should be able to ride a second hit before our speed drops too low. Can we hide behind the planet's curvature?* was his first thought. He pictured the distances between the two vessels. Even if he dropped to within five klicks of the surface, he didn't think it'd be enough. The Cadaveron was too high to be caught out by such a move.

"Got something new coming, sir. A fission signature. Big. Very big."

"They've sent a Hadron to look for us?" asked McGlashan.

The words had hardly left Chainer's mouth when the *Crimson*'s damage displays showed a number of spikes to indicate a second particle beam hit in the same place as the first.

"That one's only cost us six percent," announced Breeze.

"Sorry to piss on your good news, but it's not a Hadron. We've just had an Oblivion battleship drop into far orbit."

CHAPTER SEVENTEEN

"HAVE we got every damned Ghost warship in this sector looking for us?" said Duggan, his voice loud with anger. "Things must be worse than we've been told if they can spare a battleship way out here!"

"Double the fun," said Chainer to himself.

"I think we're beyond the range of their particle beam now," said McGlashan.

"Two Ghost warships hunting us in orbit cuts our chances right down," said Duggan. "It's only a matter of time."

"How fast are the Oblivions?" asked Chainer. "I've never seen one outside of a holoscreen before."

"They're plenty fast," said Breeze. "One of our scouts pinged one at Light-N a few years ago. There were no complaints about funding cuts in the fission drive engineering division after that. Money can't buy you time, though. Never could and it's come far too late for us to catch up anytime soon."

"Yeah, the story of mankind's destruction," said Chainer with a snort.

"I want no more talk of that, Lieutenant!" barked Duggan.

"We can't allow ourselves to give in to fear. We'll beat these bastards, no matter what it takes!"

"Aye, sir," said Chainer quietly.

Duggan continued to stare at his HUD. "We need to do something about that Cadaveron," he said. "It's the weakest of the two enemy warships."

"They'll be out of sensor range in a few seconds, sir," said Chainer.

"Can you read what the enemy vessel did when it reached the cloud of shock drones?" he asked.

"Yes, sir. They did what they normally do and crashed right through the middle of them. They'll have picked up a few dents, but they'll have saved a few seconds by not changing course."

"And they know they're shock drones and not hull mines because the drones actively transmit, while the mines do not."

"Yes, and the mines fly at a known speed. They're not sophisticated enough to fool the Ghasts' sensors."

"Indeed," said Duggan. He called up his weapon's panel. "Twelve nukes onboard. Big ones, like you said."

"Long range and slow."

"With big old, programmable boosters," Duggan added. He activated two of the missiles and created a speed and trajectory for them. "We need to keep that Cadaveron on our heels," he said.

"They're still following," said Chainer. "They'll break off once we get too far ahead."

Duggan pulled back on the control stick, reducing the Crimson's speed gradually until it was travelling fractionally slower than the Cadaveron. "Let's keep them interested," he said.

"What's the plan? You're up to something," said McGlashan. "I know when you're up to something."

Duggan didn't respond at once. His mind worked feverishly as he calculated a course that would keep the Cadaveron in a straight line behind them. He made a subtle change to their trajectory that would let the enemy close the distance between them. "On my word, I want you to release the drones," he said.

"Understood," said McGlashan, staring at him with wide eyes. She'd guessed what was coming.

"Release," said Duggan. A moment later, he confirmed with the *Crimson*'s mainframe that he really did want it to fire two additional weapons from the ship's arsenal.

"They're gone. Two nuclear missiles right behind." McGlashan looked up in admiration. "Keeping a perfect pace with the drones."

"I don't know if it's possible to catch an AI napping. Pray that it is," he said.

"Those drones might confuse their scanners long enough," McGlashan replied. "As long as they don't spend too long wondering why we scattered our countermeasures without any inbound missiles."

Duggan found his grip tightening on the control levers, until his knuckles showed white through his skin. "Not long," he said.

"They didn't go through the drone cloud, sir," said Chainer. "They missed it by a whisker."

"Did they take evasive measures?"

"Can't tell you for definite."

"We're back in particle beam range," said McGlashan. The words hardly left her mouth before the *Crimson* took another hit to the rear.

"Another four percent gone, sir," said Breeze. "We're pretty resistant to whatever they're firing. The *Detriment* would have been floating adrift after a third hit."

"They'll burn us out eventually," said Duggan. "How long till our speed is cut to below theirs?"

"We're almost there, I'd say."

"Fire drones on my command," Duggan said calmly.

"Sir," acknowledged McGlashan. "We'll be within missile range in less than one minute. I don't think they'll hold back this time."

"Still waiting," said Duggan, his eyes darting across a dozen readouts in front of him.

"Their particle beam will be ready in ten seconds."

"Release," he said.

"Drones away. Nukes with them."

"Keep your fingers crossed, ladies and gentlemen. This is our last chance to surprise them before we have to slug it out with missiles."

"Their particle beam got us again," Breeze said.

Duggan checked over his console. The *Crimson*'s speed had dropped below the Cadaveron's maximum sub-light velocity. They'd soon be a sitting duck. The tension built. None of the four said anything as they waited for fate to roll its dice.

"Not long till they can launch missiles," said McGlashan. "They're approaching the cloud."

Duggan clenched his jaw. "Come on you bastards," he said.

"I'm detecting gamma rays at the extremes of our sensor range, sir," said Chainer. "Lots of gamma rays."

"The Cadaveron?"

"Can't see. No, wait, it's changed course and speed. It's heading away at an oblique and slowing down."

Duggan jumped up and punched the air. "How'd you alien murderers like that?" he bellowed. "Two gigatons of the Space Corps' finest." He recovered his composure and dropped back into his seat. "Bringing us around. I want every Lambda cluster ready to go!"

"Aye, sir."

With a twist of the control stick, Duggan brought the *Crimson*'s nose about, bringing the vessel in a tight curve, a few hundred klicks above the barren planet. The giddiness from the life-support delay hit him and he shook it off. The spaceship had taken significant damage to its gravity drive but it was still fast. Soon, they'd closed in enough for Chainer to determine more details about the Ghost ship and he brought up a zoomed image on the bulkhead screen. The Cadaveron was travelling at reduced speed, and it rotated slowly as it hurtled through the atmosphere. The dull silver of its exterior was blackened and rippled near to the cone-shaped nose.

"I was expecting more damage," said Chainer, hints of disappointment in his voice.

"There's not enough oxygen for it to have taken much blast damage," said Duggan. "I'll bet it's shielded to hell against gamma rays as well." He smiled. "Just not enough to block out two gigatons detonating off its armour." In truth, Duggan didn't know if the nuclear blasts had knocked out all of the Cadaveron's weapons systems. Its engines were clearly offline, but other than that, he could only guess at the extent of the damage. He turned to McGlashan. "Fire."

The Crimson could bring twelve of its eighteen Lambda batteries to bear. "Full broadside on its way," she said, her voice tight. The missile tracker became a sea of red dots, which rocketed away through space. One hundred and forty-four Lambda missiles cut through the vacuum at an awe-inspiring velocity. The missiles had been built decades before and the engines failed on three, leaving the warheads to drift slowly behind the others. The remainder of the weapons functioned as intended, their guidance systems sending them on an intentionally uneven path to their goal. Around the Ghost ship, star-bright bursts of white appeared and blue tracers appeared from the ten port-side Vule cannons.

"They're not completely helpless," said McGlashan.

"Fire," said Duggan, his voice crisp and clear.

The Crimson sprayed out its second broadside and this time all of the Lambdas activated. The first wave met the withering storm of Vule fire and the concussive bursts of the Cadaveron's plasma flares. Dozens of the missiles were shredded, but four of them penetrated the enemy countermeasures, setting off a row of thumping white explosions along the spaceship's flank.

"We're locked and loaded, sir," said McGlashan.

Duggan didn't look away from the viewscreen. "Fire."

Another six missiles impacted with the Cadaveron. The heavy cruiser had a vast array of countermeasures, but it would normally have been accompanied by a number of much smaller Hunter spacecraft to act as a buffer between itself and incoming fire. Out here in the depths of uncontested space, it had no such outriders. When the light faded from the detonations of the second wave, the huge rip in its hull was clear to see. Still its Vule cannons continued to fire and the plasma flares scattered all around without cease.

"Fire," said Duggan, his face set with determination.

The third wave crashed into the stricken Ghast vessel, two of the Lambdas plunging into the tear in its hull. This time the blasts almost ripped the spacecraft in two and Duggan realised that he should have conserved his ammunition. He watched the fourth wave of missiles land all across the three-kilometre length of the heavy cruiser. As white faded to black, the Crimson's sensors showed a scene of twisted hunks of alloy drifting without purpose across the star-strewn sky. The crew stared at the image for a while. Even in a war as ruthless as this one, it was sobering to imagine the death they'd just wrought amongst the enemy.

"I've been told the Ghasts have fifty-eight such vessels," said Duggan. "And now they have only fifty-seven." He reached down and ran his fingers along the edge of his console. "It's my wish that we get the chance to destroy each and every one of them."

"Amen to that," said Chainer.

"We've still got an Oblivion battleship somewhere in orbit looking for us, sir," said McGlashan.

"We have, Commander. At least we've given ourselves a chance to evade it for long enough until our fission engines are ready to go."

"To hell with that, sir!" she replied with a grin. "I say we go hunting for them!"

Duggan grinned in return and sat in his seat. He took the control sticks and chose a course and speed at random. He looked at Monsey. She'd put her keyboard to one side and her eyes were still on the image of the disintegrating Ghast ship. "What do you think, soldier?"

"Let's get them, sir."

Chainer breathed out noisily, the sound of a hundred tensions being released at once. "One kill and everybody goes crazy." He shook his head and hunkered down over his screen.

CHAPTER EIGHTEEN

FOR ALL HIS WORDS, Duggan had no intention of looking for the Oblivion battleship. They'd just pulled off a good win, but he wasn't stupid or foolhardy enough to throw his ship and his crew against one of the prides of the Ghast fleet. Instead, he crossed his fingers and hoped that the *Crimson*'s mainframe could repair the fission drives before they caught sight of the battleship.

"Think we should divert our repairs back to the gravity drive, sir?" asked Breeze. "It'll give us extra flexibility if the Oblivion finds us."

"We could be damned if we do and damned if we don't," said Duggan. "We'll either get lucky or we won't."

"I thought you didn't believe in luck, sir?" asked McGlashan.

Duggan snorted. "I don't, Commander. However, as captain of this vessel, I'm required to give due consideration to everything."

McGlashan laughed. "Whatever you say, sir."

Over the course of the next six hours, Duggan sat almost unmoving as he directed the *Crimson* in an unpredictable orbit around the planet. Most of the time he kept the vessel low to the surface in the hope that the curvature would act as an additional barrier against detection. Although the atmosphere was thin, it was sufficient to keep the hull of the spacecraft constantly at the upper end of its design tolerances. As time progressed, Duggan became increasingly aware that he was pushing himself to his own physical limits. He'd not slept since the *Detriment* had been destroyed and even then, he'd only been able to snatch an hour or two of fitful rest. The crew suffered as well and all of their heads had begun to droop. Monsey had taken herself back to her quarters for some shuteye.

"Here you go, sir. Another cup of the finest in-flight coffee you're ever likely to taste." It was Lieutenant Breeze. The man leaned down to put a cup of the dark, steaming liquid next to Duggan, balancing the cup precariously next to a touch panel. A half-eaten plate of brown mush was left forgotten nearby.

Duggan neither knew nor cared if the panel was waterproof and he took a sip of the coffee. His mouth was so bored with the taste that he could no longer decide if it was good or bad – only the memory of his first few mouthfuls hours ago told him that it was criminally poor.

"Drink much more of that and you'll not be able to sleep no matter how badly your body wants to," said McGlashan.

"It feels like I'm immune to the caffeine," he replied. He turned his head towards Breeze. The lieutenant had just about made himself comfortable in his seat. "How are the fission drives coming along?" Duggan asked.

"Three hours and I reckon we might be ready to pull off another great escape."

"They'll call me Lucky John Duggan if we last that long."

"That's got a ring to it," McGlashan said. "Lucky Captain Duggan."

"Don't push it, Commander," he replied.

"What's going to happen to us when we get back?" she asked, changing the subject abruptly.

Duggan shrugged. "All I can go on is what I was told. There's information somewhere buried in the ship's core that we need access to. Whether it's useful or not, I don't know."

"Think Monsey can crack it? She doesn't seem to have made much progress."

"Don't be fooled by her appearance. I've checked her files – she's had an interesting past to say the least. She's got form when it comes to cracking military hardware. And don't forget – this is a Space Corps warship. There won't be easy backdoors into the core that any kid with a keyboard could play guessing games to get through."

McGlashan raised an eyebrow. "Sounds like our soldier has an intriguing background."

"She's as well-qualified as anyone to do what I've asked her to do," said Duggan.

"It seems a bit hush-hush to me. The *Crimson*, I mean," said Breeze. "We all feel it. Are you sure what you're looking for isn't better off staying hidden, sir?"

"I'd rather be punished for knowing too much than for knowing too little."

"What will happen to the ship once they've interrogated it?" asked McGlashan. "I've already grown fond of her."

"If they've got a spare shipyard they'll probably re-fit the Lambdas and the Bulwarks, then send it out to join the rest of the fleet."

"With a new captain and crew?"

"Yes, Commander. With a new captain and crew. Even without my current unpopularity amongst certain factions within the Space Corps, they couldn't justify having us sitting on our behinds while they refit the *Crimson*. We'll be put onto whatever

Gunner they have going spare and told to go kill some Ghasts in the Axion sector."

"At least that'll be an improvement over what we've been doing up till recently. You were wasted when they had the *Detriment* searching through the fringes of Confederation space."

"I don't think anything will be good from now on, folks. Charistos is gone. They Ghasts have opened the gates. It's only a matter of time until they find Angax. Even if they don't, their advances in AI cores means it'll be two or three years until they can follow us through low lightspeed. Humanity is pretty much screwed unless something changes and soon."

"Is it really so bad, sir?" asked McGlashan.

"I don't know, Commander. Probably. Maybe. I'm tired. I've never met a man or woman who could look on the bright side when they've been deprived of sleep."

"Yeah," she said, unconvinced.

"I wish we had some long-range comms to pick up what's happening," said Chainer. "It seems like the repair bot's been given a long priority list and the main comms are somewhere in the middle. I don't know which shit-for-brains thought that the comms for a stranded ship were a medium priority, but I'd like to punch him in the face. The autopilot's right at the bottom of the list."

"It'll take longer to sort out the bot than it will be to let it get on with what it's doing," said Duggan. "And we can't spare anyone to re-programme it. The *Crimson*'s core doesn't recognize all of the repair routines and technologies on the bot either, so we can't get the ship to do our dirty work."

"I understand that, sir. It's just frustrating, you know? I don't like being blind. It feels like we're facing half the Ghast fleet with both arms tied behind our backs."

"One way or the other it won't be too much longer now, Lieutenant. Keep focused and we'll get out of here in one piece."

Chainer nodded vigorously, like a man desperate to convince himself that something was true. "You can count on me, sir."

"This the moment when our sensors pick up the Oblivion," said McGlashan, her eyes glittering with mischief.

"Ha ha. Not this time, Commander," said Chainer. "We're clear all across the board."

"Have you ever come up against an Oblivion, sir?" asked Breeze. "I've heard about them and read up on the files. Sometimes you just need to see one in the flesh to know what you're up against."

"I saw one of their first prototypes. Maybe eighteen years ago, when the Ghasts started to build bigger to try and match us. That one wasn't much larger than a modern Cadaveron. The Hadron *Devastator* destroyed it way out in a place nobody's heard of. It was one-sided, but the Oblivion soaked up a hell of a lot of missile fire before it broke apart. I think it would be a close-run thing between the *Devastator* and one of the newer Oblivions. The latest two Ghast battleships the Corps is aware of were calculated to be similar in volume to the Hadrons."

"How many Oblivions are there?"

"Last I heard, we know of twelve. Three of them are more than ten years old, the other nine are newer and larger. We have to assume they're carrying the latest weaponry."

"With seven Hadrons and the *Archimedes* left to face them," said Breeze. "And a few dozen Anderlechts."

"They're building faster than we are, Lieutenant. We had our chance to go after them more aggressively years ago. We might have blown the opportunity to finish the war on the winning side."

Monsey returned to the bridge. She offered a smart salute and sat cross-legged on the floor with her keyboard. She looked hardly more refreshed than when she'd left five hours ago.

"Not get much sleep, soldier?" asked Duggan.

"Not really, sir. It always happens when I've got a hard nut to crack. The numbers and possibilities spin around in my head and won't give me peace." She grinned. "Makes it a bastard to get any sleep."

"I'll leave you to it," said Duggan. "I'd recommend a few cups of this fine coffee to overcome any fatigue."

Monsey grunted in response, clearly not buying it. Moments later, she was lost to the world once more, her keyboard clattering as she continued her game of cat and mouse with the mainframe's anti-ingress codes.

Duggan concentrated once more on keeping the *Crimson*'s course as erratic as possible. Two hours passed and he found that tiredness was lulling him into a state of relaxation. The danger of the situation hadn't gone away, but he knew he was close to falling asleep.

"Getting a ping," said Chainer. "High and wide – something much bigger than us."

"That's not what I wanted to hear, Lieutenant," snapped Duggan, reading the coordinates that Chainer sent through to him.

"Just telling it like it is, sir."

"I know, Lieutenant. I'm just tired is all."

"No worries, sir. It's definitely the Oblivion. It knows we're here and it's coming around."

"Can you get a scan of it?" asked Duggan, changing course to point the *Crimson* directly away.

"Size and approximate mass only. Over four thousand metres long. Nearly a billion and a half cubic metres. I wouldn't like to drop it on my foot, sir."

"Lieutenant Breeze, give me some good news."

"Wish I had some, sir. Fission engines at seventy-eight percent. Another fifty minutes till we're able to do anything other than crawl away."

"We don't have fifty minutes," said Chainer. "We've got another fast one. The Ghasts are closing on us."

"Not enough data on their vessel to determine when they'll be able to fire," said McGlashan.

"I wonder how we'd fare with full sub-lights," mused Duggan aloud.

"We'd piss all over them, I reckon," said Breeze.

Duggan had a thought, one he realised he should have had several hours ago. "Lieutenant Breeze, what are you basing your calculations on for when we'll be able to reach sufficient velocity to escape?"

"Standard metrics, sir. We'll be able to hit high Light-A. Low Light-B in five minutes. Even a Cadaveron would have a good shot at reading our trail at that speed. I would hate to guess what the Oblivion could manage. We don't want to lead it to the *Juniper*."

"Indeed not, Lieutenant. On the other hand, there's nothing that's particularly *usual* about this spacecraft, is there?"

"I suppose not," said Breeze. "It's old military tech though. The parameters are easy enough to predict."

"Military tech," repeated Duggan, without elaborating.

Without warning, the lights on the bridge dimmed, their intensity dropping until the crew were almost in complete darkness. Before any of them could say a word, the lights strengthened and were at their normal brightness less than a second later.

"They've tried to shut us down, sir. We're not even in missile range yet."

"They must have the same weapons systems that the Kraven light cruiser we destroyed a few weeks ago used against the *Detriment*," said Duggan. He cursed loudly.

"With a much better range on it as well," said McGlashan.

"They'll have at least one particle beam to add to the fun," said Duggan. "They'll rip us apart if they get close enough to use

150

it." Without turning from his own screens, he spoke to Lieutenant Breeze. "Point us at an offset somewhere between here and the *Juniper* and power up the fission drive."

"Aye, sir. Bringing them up."

"Estimated time?"

"Calculating it now. Only thirty seconds. Colour me impressed."

Duggan activated a channel to the infantry quarters. "Alert. We're going to attempt lightspeed in less than thirty seconds." There was no time to fill them in on the details. They'd be scrambling for something solid to hold onto – most of them had served long enough to remember a bumpy ride from fission drive activation.

Monsey spoke up, catching Duggan by surprise. "There's some proper grunt to this backend core, sir. Whatever it is, it's *not* fifty years old. It's modern and real fast. I mean like nothing I've seen before fast. Its utilisation went up to nearly one hundred percent just as the Ghasts tried to cut our power."

"Questions with no answers," muttered Duggan.

"They're lighting up their fission drives as well, sir," said Breeze. "I wonder if they're going to try and follow us."

"Another power surge," said McGlashan. "Coming now."

Once again, the lights dimmed. This time they didn't go nearly as low and came back almost at once.

"Another utilisation spike," said Monsey.

"They've launched something, sir," said McGlashan. "A single warhead from the looks of it."

"Anything to add, Lieutenant Chainer?" asked Duggan.

"I see it, sir. It must have a greater range than their usual missiles. Assuming it reaches us."

"I think we can safely assume that it's going to blow the crap out of us if it gets here in time. Another piece of something new."

"It's coming at us incredibly fast. Fifteen seconds to impact."

Breeze laughed, the sound without any humour. "Fifteen seconds till we can go."

"The Bulwarks aren't targeting the missile. They're not even registering it as an incoming object," said McGlashan. She breathed out. "Life can be interesting around here."

"Ten, nine..." said Breeze.

"Come on," said Duggan.

"Dropping countermeasures," said McGlashan. "Something makes me think they're not going to work."

"Seven, six..."

"More countermeasures away."

"Five, four..."

"It's already through the first drone cloud."

"Three, two..."

"Damn them to hell!"

"One, impact..."

The impact didn't come. There was a howling sound and the spacecraft shuddered. Duggan felt something clutch at his innards and twist them hard. His chest tightened and he struggled against the violent urge to throw up whatever was in his stomach. He was faintly aware of someone retching and he saw McGlashan with her head bowed and her hands to her face. The physical stresses on his body built and Duggan thought he might pass out. Moments before he lost consciousness, the sensation receded, though not as quickly as he wanted.

"Are we hit?" asked Chainer, his voice thick as if he'd bitten his tongue.

"Hull integrity at near maximum," said Breeze a few seconds later. "Fission drives down to thirty percent and climbing."

"We made it," said McGlashan. "Just barely. I can't believe the Bulwarks couldn't see that missile. They're definitely all online and operational."

The *Crimson*'s life support systems caught up and Duggan

shook his head to clear away the fog. Something caught his eye. "Lieutenant Breeze, can you confirm my velocity readout?"

"This can't be right. I'm getting us at Light-P. With a quarter of the drive awaiting re-routing."

"Lieutenant Chainer, do you have enough sensors to get an accurate reading from the surrounding stars?"

"Not accurate, sir, but I should be able to get something close enough. Let's see what we have." Chainer's voice was stronger and he looked alert as he worked out an approximation of their speed. "Light-P it is. Give or take."

Breeze whistled with the appreciation of a man who lived and breathed engines. "We'll be at the *Juniper* in ten days at this rate. Except I've programmed us to drop back onto the gravity drive three days from here, in case we were followed."

"Great, we'll have to go through that dislocation again," said Chainer. "Remind me not to eat anything beforehand."

"That Oblivion won't be following us at this speed," said Duggan. "Re-route and point us straight at the *Juniper*."

"On it now, sir."

"Ten weeks out and here was I thinking it would take us six months to get back," said Duggan. "Instead it's only ten days. I would kill for some answers."

"Working on it, sir," volunteered Monsey. She'd recovered quickly from the burst into lightspeed and had resumed typing as if nothing had happened.

Duggan opened a comms channel to the soldiers' quarters. "Sergeant Ortiz, please report."

There was a pause for a few moments. "This is Sergeant Ortiz. We got a bit shook up. The pride of a couple of the guys got hurt. Otherwise, no injuries." Another pause. "A bit of a rough ride, that one, sir."

"My apologies, Sergeant. I'll try and give you more notice

next time. No guarantees – you know how it is. Let your squad know we're on our way back to the *Juniper*. Ten days."

"Aye, sir. Ten days sounds good to me."

Duggan cut the channel and looked over at the people on the bridge. "I'm going for some sleep. Don't break anything while I'm away."

CHAPTER NINETEEN

SIX HOURS LATER, the alarm bleeped a discordant sound that was perfectly engineered to ensure it was impossible to sleep through.

"Off!" Duggan commanded and the alarm fell silent. He lay still for a few minutes to give his head time to clear. His body needed more than the six hours he'd allowed it, but there'd be time to catch up later. As long as he could function without making any stupid errors, it would be sufficient.

The Captain's Quarters on the *Crimson* were just about what he'd expected them to be – cramped and barely comfortable. Duggan was used to it and didn't need anything more, though it would sometimes be nice to stay in a place a little bit more luxurious.

"When I get some vacation," he grunted, rolling off the narrow bed.

A few minutes later, he reached the bridge. McGlashan and Chainer were nowhere to be seen.

"They left a few minutes after you," said Breeze. He looked utterly exhausted. "My turn when they get back."

"Go on now, Lieutenant. Get some rest – you deserve it. There's no risk of interception at the speed we're going."

Breeze pushed himself to his feet. "I won't argue with you." He mumbled. With a yawn, he half-stumbled away from the bridge to his bed, leaving Duggan and Monsey on the bridge.

"Any developments, soldier?" he asked.

"Getting there, sir." She hesitated, as if she wanted to say something more.

"What is it?"

"The more I see of the backend core, the more I'm left wondering about it."

"What do you mean?"

"I don't really know. I haven't cracked it yet, but I've seen enough to think that it's designed completely differently to any other core I've encountered." She chewed on her lip. "It's as if the front-end mainframe and the back core are speaking different languages. Similar, but not quite the same. They've been cobbled together and are getting along just nicely, yet there's a problem with understanding."

"The *Crimson* was the result of the Hynus project. It had a lot of money thrown at it. And I mean a *lot*. Could the *Crimson* have a new type of core resulting from that?"

"It's possible, I guess. I can't understand why they didn't develop it further, since it's brutally fast at almost every task. I can see a few weaknesses to how it approaches some calculations. Otherwise, it has few downsides."

"Maybe it's got a trillion dollars' worth of rare metals in it," he said.

"Yeah, maybe."

"Perhaps we'll find out a bit more when you crack it. I need to know about those weapons systems, soldier."

Duggan sat down in his chair and ran through the *Crimson*'s status reports. Everything was as expected, with the fission drive still at seventy-eight percent. Repairs couldn't proceed on the fission drive or sub-lights either while the ship was travelling at lightspeed. They just needed a break from action for a few days to bring everything to a level Duggan would be happy with.

"Always playing catch up," he muttered.

An hour later, McGlashan returned to the bridge. She looked sharp and fresh – she was one of those people who could steal an hour here and there and keep on going. Chainer arrived after another hour, looking shabby and dishevelled. He had a cup of coffee in one hand and a can of generic hi-stim in the other.

"I never grew out of my youth," he said, smacking his mouth. "If I didn't lie in till eleven, I always felt like crap."

"Hi-stim overdose," McGlashan told him. "I don't touch that stuff."

"Some of us never learned how to powernap," he replied without irritation. "There was nothing to report for the last few hours sir. No recorded pings, no sign of anything trying to sniff us out. The bot's got three more sensor arrays online. We'll be at full sensor strength before we hit the *Juniper* and with any luck the long-range comms will either be fixed or near as damnit."

"Good. I want us to be as ship-shape as possible before we see any more action."

"Sir?"

"Yes Commander?"

"While you were sleeping, I had a chance to do some calculations. Based on our known volume, ship dimensions, quantity of Lambda batteries and so on, I figure that whatever the two unknown weapons systems are, they're taking up a big chunk of space. Much bigger than anything I've seen on a ship before."

"An early beam weapon?" asked Duggan. "I know the Space Corps had a functioning unit long before we started seeing them on the Ghast warships. I don't know if the research was completely abandoned, but I think we only have two vessels that carry one owing to their size and expense. The *Archimedes* has one and the Hadron *Maximilian*."

"Maybe that's what they are. We could be carrying two. That would be interesting."

"If we ever get a chance to unlock them," Duggan replied with a shake of his head.

The following nine and a half days crept by. Duggan wondered if he should be grateful for the break, but all he could think about was the deaths of a billion people on Charistos and the secrets that the *Crimson*'s core kept locked up tight. Monsey kept at it, pushing herself for as long as twenty hours on some days, while she tried to find a way through the ship's defences. Even though she didn't say it outright, it was clear she was becoming increasingly frustrated at her failure to defeat the core's protective layers.

"I once took control of an old Gunner in under five hours," she said. "That was when the military police came knocking on the door. Didn't matter much to me then – I'd beaten the best minds in the Corps and took one of their ships out if its bay. Remotely, of course."

"I know all about it, soldier," Duggan told her. "I still don't know how you didn't get twenty years for that one."

"I got five and that was enough," she said with a smile. "I never got a shot at anything bigger than a Vincent class. I told myself that something as old as the *Crimson* would be a piece of cake. Except it's orders of magnitude harder than a thirty-year-old Gunner."

"Still sure you'll get there in the end?"

"The bravado in me wants to say 'hell yes'. The part of me that's older and wiser tells me to keep my damn mouth shut and not make any more predictions."

Duggan was disappointed and it was hard to keep it from his face. "We've been through too much to go without answers. We get back to the *Juniper* and they'll take this ship off me."

At the beginning of the tenth day of their escape from the Ghast Oblivion, the *Crimson* came within near space range of the *Juniper*.

"Well what do you know?" said Breeze. "The old mainframe predicted the flight time bang on the nose. We'll be coming out of lightspeed in ten minutes time."

Duggan connected through to Sergeant Ortiz. "Sergeant? I promised you advance warning of any possible turbulence, so here it is. Ten minutes and we'll arrive in local space close to the *Juniper*."

"Thank you, sir. Some of the guys reckon they're due a bit of leave. Any chance you can put in a good word for us when we dock?"

"I'll do my best. No promises. You know what the Corps is like."

She laughed with a complete lack of bitterness. "Understood, sir. We've been living on hope not certainty for long enough now. I'm pretty sure they know how it is."

"Kryptes-9 in five minutes," announced Breeze a short while after. "We'll arrive in near space an easy seventy minutes ride out from the *Juniper*."

"We can't wait seventy minutes, Lieutenant. I want us to come in closer."

"Yes sir!" said Breeze. "Fifty minutes?"

"Let's try for thirty minutes, shall we?"

McGlashan stifled a laugh. "You're really going to piss someone off."

"Time is of the essence, Commander. And I'm not in the mood for waiting."

"Coming out of lightspeed should be easier than going in, right?" asked Chainer.

"Who knows, Lieutenant. Is your stomach empty?"

"I just ate, sir. Waffles, they were meant to be."

"Make sure you point your face away from me when we arrive."

"Yes, sir." Chainer looked green already.

The *Crimson*'s near space arrival was more serene than its entry. The ship grated and juddered, producing a scraping sound from somewhere deep within that almost had Duggan worried. There were a few moments of nausea which passed quickly.

"Orbital Station *Juniper* hailing us on short-range comms," said Chainer. "The AI isn't happy to see us."

"Obtain landing permission. Say it's an emergency and we're coming in without autopilot."

"Permission denied, sir."

Duggan laughed. He was much happier dealing with a truculent AI than he was trying to escape from a Ghast battle-ship with half of his weapons systems unavailable. "It must know what this spacecraft is. Tell it to speak to Admiral Teron."

"I've relayed the message sir. It's warned us to keep our distance."

"Setting a course directly towards Hangar Bay One," said Duggan.

"He's enjoying this a bit too much," observed McGlashan.

"*ES Deeper* hailing us, sir. Telling us to keep our distance or they'll be forced to engage."

"Where are they?"

"I'm picking them up leaving high orbit around Kryptes-9. It's good to have the sensors back."

Before Duggan could push things any further, the *Juniper*'s AI provided clearance for landing in Hangar Bay One.

"It's holding off from any further criticism, sir. Someone must have told it to keep quiet."

"Let's get docked and see what we've missed since we've been away," Duggan said, realising how desperate he was to find out. He pushed the gravity drive to maximum and the *Crimson* rocketed onwards at such a speed that he had to quickly back off for fear of making the AI do something they'd all regret. "We'll have near twice the sub-light speed of the *Detriment* when the re-routing's completed."

"Shame we'd burn up if we tried to go so fast in orbit," said McGlashan. "It'll be nice to know what she can do with a fully functioning gravity drive though."

Thirty minutes later, they were docked. The *Juniper*'s bays could hold larger spacecraft than the *Crimson* and Duggan found it easy to pilot the ship in and land it smoothly. It was the kind of stuff they drummed into you in training, even when they knew the automatic guidance systems would do the work most of the time. Duggan had always possessed a talent for it, which came from a lack of fear about the consequences of getting it wrong.

"Nicely done, sir," said McGlashan.

"Stay here," he warned, getting up from his seat. "Keep everyone onboard until you're ordered to leave. When we get the chance, I'll let you take our next assigned spaceship out without the autopilot."

"Thanks – I'll look forward to it," she said.

Duggan marched off the *Crimson* and took the lift to the 17th floor of the Military CU. He strode across to the reception desk, where the same man who'd greeted him weeks ago was sitting.

"Déjà vu," Duggan muttered to himself.

"I didn't catch that, sir," said the man.

"I'm here to see Admiral Teron."

"Yes, sir, he's expecting you."

"Thanks, I know the way," Duggan growled, walking past.

Minutes later, he was at Teron's door. It slid open at once, and Duggan stepped inside.

Teron was inside, leaning forward intently on his battered leather chair. "Captain Duggan," he said. "I hear you've found what you were looking for."

CHAPTER TWENTY

"WHAT THE HELL did you send us to recover, sir?" asked Duggan.

"Like I told you, Captain. Old military tech that sent us a warning about a coming war," Teron responded smoothly.

"You're hiding something! I know you are! I lost one of my men finding that ship, damnit! Then I find it's faster than anything else in the fleet and it's got some kind of advanced core that can ride an attack from a Ghast disruptor. On top of that, half of the Ghast fleet were out there with us. There was an Oblivion battleship, sir. A new model. What was it doing so far away from anywhere?"

Teron had the good grace to look pained. "The *Crimson* is important. Not just for the information it holds, but for what it's carrying."

Duggan took a deep breath. "What exactly *is* it carrying, sir? Why did we spend so much on that ship and then not follow through with the tech? If we had the *Crimson*'s engines on every ship in the fleet, we'd already have a big advantage on the Ghasts.

We'd be able to outmanoeuvre them in every dogfight. Outrange their missiles. It could be all the difference."

"I know, Captain Duggan. I've looked through the design specifications. It was damn fast when it left the shipyard."

"I tried to look it up. Access denied. Why is the information buried so deep? We should have an army of engineers digging up the files and building on the research."

"We can't," said Teron quietly. "There are no records of the design."

"What do you mean, no records? How'd they build the damn thing in the first place? Are you telling me that someone's lost the files? Or they've been destroyed? How could you lose all that? There must have been exabytes of data!"

"They're neither lost nor destroyed."

"What are you telling me, sir? Why aren't you talking straight?"

"Because I'm not allowed to, John." The two men stared at each other for a time. Eventually, Teron looked away towards one of the banks of screens on his office wall. "Charistos finally drove the message home to the Confederation Council," he said. "There've been riots on Earth, New Earth, Hope, Pioneer. Every habited planet in the Confederation has seen some sort of unrest. The people realise they've been fooled and that the Ghasts really might wipe us out. We've gone to total war. Everything from now on will be geared towards destroying our enemy. Before you left to find the *Crimson*, the military was already receiving more funding than we could easily deal with. Imagine that - our infrastructure was so badly cut, we could hardly spend the money quickly enough. Now the investment is *pouring* in."

"What about the shipyards, sir? The factories? The research labs? We can't just revive them and expect everything to work at full speed again."

"I understand your cynicism, Captain – it's something I've

been accused of myself on more than one occasion." Teron gave a glimpse of a smile. "However, someone in the Space Corps had enough clout to ensure that many of our facilities were moth-balled, rather than dismantled. It'll take time to bring them up to speed, but I assure you it'll take a lot less time than it would to build them from scratch."

"Where do you get the people to work them? We must have lost the skills and the expertise."

"The Confederation has implemented National Service. *Interplanetary Service* would be a more appropriate term, of course. There was no resistance to the proposal at all. Even now, we're commandeering the scientists and engineers we need. Just think of it – we have access to tens of millions of people across the Confederated planets who have skills we can put to good use. We'll not go wanting for lack of suitable personnel."

Duggan ran his fingers across his stubbled chin. He hadn't had the chance to shave yet. "I'm almost impressed. Why didn't we do this five years ago when it might have meant something?"

"We are all guided by the whims of our superiors. This is the hand we've been given and we have to play it to the best of our ability. We've already begun work on two new Hadrons. There will also be eighteen new Anderlechts, on top of those partway through construction. The Hadrons will take five years before they come into service. The first Anderlecht will be ready in two. There'll be another flagship when we can build a big enough yard. We're designing a whole new class of heavy cruisers to match their Cadaverons. It's a gap in our fleet we've put up with for too long."

Duggan's mind raced at this cascade of new information. "It's good to hear we're doing everything we can, sir. We're totally outgunned at the moment. We're going to need a lot more than two Hadrons and we'll need them a lot sooner than five years from now."

"Indeed, but it's a start. As I said – we have unlimited funding. When the facilities become available we'll have the money and resources to lay down another five Hadrons. And another five after that. We are going to have so many light cruisers that the skies will be filled with them." Teron's eyes glittered angrily. "We're going to beat these bastards, even if I have to take charge of a spacecraft myself!"

"Tell me about the *Crimson*, sir," Duggan said.

Teron leaned towards him. "I can't. This is top-top secret. Even I only have partial access to the files." He sat back again and steepled his thick fingers in front of his face. "The *Crimson* is carrying several things we need, that we thought we'd lost for good until we received its signal. We have to break the ship up and take the pieces to the labs. I am not a man prone to melodrama, so you must believe me when I tell you that the *Crimson* is the greatest hope for humanity's salvation."

"I had guessed there was more to it than the need for a simple databank interrogation."

"I didn't lie to you, John."

"Does partial truth count as the truth or a lie?"

Teron exhaled loudly. He didn't look comfortable. "We received the *Detriment*'s death code. I know you loved that ship."

"We were surprised by a Cadaveron. We didn't stand a chance."

"There's a Vincent class parked in Hangar Bay Two. Its captain got killed in a Ghost ambush on the surface of an outlying mining planet. *ES Brawler*. Fitted with new Lambdas and the same engine mods as you had on the *Detriment*. You've been assigned to it."

"What about my crew? And the soldiers?"

"The *Brawler*'s already got a crew. I hear some of yours are overdue vacation."

"I don't want a new crew, sir! I want the crew I've got!"

"I'm sorry, Captain Duggan. I need them here on the *Juniper* where I can keep an eye on them. I'm sure they know little of importance about the *Crimson*, but I can't have them going around spreading rumours and gossip. I've given you more information than I should have done, out of respect for who you are."

"I understand, sir. I don't like it and I don't agree with it, but I understand."

"I'll see what I can do to reunite you with the same crew when you return from your next assignment. By then, the need for secrecy may well have diminished. For now, you're dismissed, Captain, and the men and women on the *Crimson* will have some much-deserved rest and relaxation here on the *Juniper*. You'll be reporting for duty first thing in the morning. Things are difficult for us in Axion and we need every spare ship to keep the Ghasts from finding Angax."

"Yes, sir," said Duggan through gritted teeth. "Permission to tell them myself?"

"That will be fine. Don't take too long. I have a team of engineers preparing to board the *Crimson*. I don't want them having to contend with ill-will from any crew who might have overstayed their permission to remain."

Duggan rose to leave.

"Oh, and Captain Duggan?"

"Sir?"

"Good work bringing the *Crimson* back."

Duggan didn't say anything more and left Admiral Teron's office. A few minutes later, he was in the lift again, alone as it climbed silently through the *Juniper*'s immense interior. The overly-chilled air should have been a welcome change after weeks in the hot and claustrophobic confines of the *Crimson*'s bridge. Instead, it made him crave to be back in the heat and oil-scented humidity. His earpiece bleeped and a voice came through. It was Commander McGlashan. She sounded excited.

"Sir? Monsey's found something."

"What is it?"

"I'm not sure yet. She's breached one of the databanks. There's reams of stuff in there, much of it still encrypted." She paused. "I didn't want to start looking until you got back."

"Start looking now, Commander. Get Lieutenants Chainer and Breeze on it as well. Tell Monsey to keep up with her efforts."

"What are we looking for?"

"I don't know. Anything that looks interesting. Something that tells us about the *Crimson*."

"We're on it, sir."

"Commander? I'm heading back to the ship now. I'd planned to wait so that I could tell everyone face to face. There doesn't seem like much point now. We've run out of time. Find out what you can, but we'll need to leave the *Crimson* soon."

McGlashan didn't answer at once and Duggan was sure she'd guessed the implications of what he'd said. "Understood. See you when you get here, sir."

The lift ride took a few minutes, though it felt much longer. A voice came from a tiny wall speaker to announce the arrival at Hangar Bay One and Duggan stepped out into the vast, open space. The *Crimson* was still there, low, sleek and menacing in the artificial light of the *Juniper*'s interior. Duggan could see pocks and scalding across the rear of the vessel where it had taken hits from the Ghast plasma launchers. There were areas of a darker grey, which he recognized as damage from the Cadaveron's beam weapon. The bay was much busier than Duggan had ever seen it, with groups of men and women clumped everywhere, dressed in a variety of uniforms. The area around the *Crimson*'s boarding ramp was crowded and there was a lot of shouting coming from the middle. Duggan pushed his way through, uncaring if he ruffled any feathers as he did so. Sergeant

Ortiz was standing at the bottom of the ramp, accompanied by Turner, Jackson and Nelson. They held their gauss rifles threateningly and Ortiz was talking loudly to someone. Duggan elbowed his way to the front.

"Captain Duggan!" she said, giving him a salute. She looked unruffled.

"What seems to be the trouble, Sergeant?"

"Sir, these people are attempting to board the *Crimson*. We have not been told that they are permitted to enter, therefore I have been obliged to assume that they have no authority to do so. Not until the captain of this vessel advises otherwise."

"Thank you, Sergeant, you've done the right thing. I'll handle this."

"Aye, sir!"

Duggan turned to face the tall man who had been shouting the loudest at Sergeant Ortiz. He had an off-white uniform and a badge that indicated he was one of the *Juniper*'s leading engineers. The man opened his mouth to speak, but Duggan cut him off with a hard stare.

"Who are you?"

"I'm Engineering Captain Newt Miller, deputy head of engineering on the *Juniper*. We've got a lot to do, Captain and your soldiers are preventing us from getting on with it."

"These soldiers are doing their duty, Captain Miller, as I'm sure you're aware. If they had let you board without direct orders from me, they would have been open to a court martial. This is a vessel of war and you are in no position to order them to stand aside."

Miller swallowed, but didn't lower his gaze. When he spoke, his voice was conciliatory. "Captain, I've been instructed to get working on this spacecraft as soon as possible. I have nearly a thousand men ready to begin."

Duggan doubted that Miller knew any more than he did

about the secrets of the *Crimson*. The man had a job to do and he just wanted to get on with it. "To begin on what, exactly, Captain Miller?"

Miller hesitated as he considered whether or not Duggan had any right to know. "We're to set up an interface between the ship and the *Juniper* to expedite an extraction of data. Some of the vessel is to be dismantled in preparation for delivery to New Earth. What they plan to do with the pieces when they get there, I have no idea. After that, I believe we're to fit replacement engines and upgrade the weapons systems."

Duggan outranked Miller, but he wasn't in a good position to instruct the man to stand down. Nor did he have any justification to do so, given that he'd been technically removed from command of the *Crimson*. Before the conversation could progress to its inevitable conclusion, the blue-white light in the hangar bay turned abruptly to a deep, sickly red. At the same time, a siren began to wail. Captain Miller and his technical leads looked about them in confusion.

The impersonal, androgynous tones of one of the *Juniper*'s AIs spoke calmly over the blaring siren. "All personnel to station, all personnel to station. Attack imminent. Repeat: all personnel to station, all personnel to station."

There was admirable purpose amongst the hundreds of men and women and Duggan could see them hurrying off towards the many exits from the hangar bay. Captain Miller turned away and started giving out instructions to the people next to him.

Duggan forced open a channel to the *Crimson*'s bridge. "Commander, what's happening?"

"The *Juniper*'s sensors have picked up a Ghost Cadaveron breaking out of light speed, sir. Right at the extremes of detection range." She swore. "Make that two Cadaverons. Looks like they've got lucky and found us."

CHAPTER TWENTY-ONE

THE CROWD at the end of the boarding ramp had almost dispersed. Duggan turned to Sergeant Ortiz. "Get onboard and fast!"

She didn't need telling twice and ran up the ramp, with the other three soldiers close behind. Duggan followed at once and shouted through an order for the ship to be sealed. There was a hiss as the ramp began to close, cutting out the red light from outside and leaving Duggan to race along the dimly-lit corridors of the spacecraft. Before he was halfway to the bridge, he felt the familiar vibration of the *Crimson*'s engines coming online.

When he arrived, he found McGlashan, Chainer and Breeze at their stations, each of them looking ready for action. There was no sign of Monsey.

"What're your orders, sir?" McGlashan asked at once.

"We need to defend the *Juniper*. It's too valuable to lose."

"Sub-lights are ready to rock and roll, sir," said Breeze.

"Lieutenant Chainer, get us clearance to leave. The *Deeper* and *Delectable* can't beat two Cadaverons."

"On it."

"Find out what's in Hangar Bay Two. We'll need everything we can muster."

"I already checked," said McGlashan. "One Gunner. The *ES Brawler*."

"There's no captain assigned to it. That's the ship I'm meant to command."

"They must have found someone, sir. From what I can tell, the *Brawler*'s in the process of leaving its bay."

"Sir, the *Juniper*'s denying our request to leave," said Chainer.

"For what reason?"

"It says that you're no longer in command of the *Crimson* and the ship has been placed under quarantine."

"Ask it again. Make it clear we have sufficient firepower to provide worthwhile assistance to the ships already out there."

"Okay, I'm trying."

"Tell the stubborn bastard that it has insufficient authority to approve its own inevitable destruction."

McGlashan laughed. "Like that's going to work."

"It's come back with a negative again. Doesn't look like we're going anywhere soon."

"Patch me through to Admiral Teron."

"His channel is blocked, sir."

"All warships above Vincent class can override channel blocking. I'll bet the *Crimson* could get through to the Confederation Council weekly congress meeting if it wanted. Get me the Admiral."

"Yes, sir. Here we go. Got him."

A voice crackled through to Duggan's earpiece. It was Admiral Teron - he sounded surprised at the interruption. There were other voices in the background to suggest he was attending an emergency meeting.

"Who is this? What are you doing?"

"Duggan, sir. You need to overrule the *Juniper*'s AI so that the *Crimson* can assist the *Deeper* and *Delectable*."

"Captain Duggan, I can't allow that vessel to leave. I'll be strung up if it gets destroyed."

"We can't do anything sitting in the hangar, sir. Two Anderlechts don't stand a chance against those Cadaverons. I know the *Juniper* packs a punch, but it's an easy target."

Teron paused before he spoke again. "There's only the *Deeper* out there, Captain Duggan. The *Delectable*'s been ordered elsewhere. Very well. Give me a moment and I'll authorise your departure."

It happened quickly. "The *Juniper*'s provided approval, sir," said Chainer. "It won't open the doors until the hangar's cleared. From what I can see on the external sensors, it looks as if that won't be too long."

Teron spoke again. "Captain Duggan, will that be all? My attention is needed here."

Duggan wasn't done yet. "Sir, the unlock codes for the *Crimson*'s weapons systems, please."

"I am not permitted to give you those."

"You know what we're carrying."

"Of course I know!"

"The codes please. If it'll give us a fighting chance, you owe it to us to provide those codes."

"I only have the authorisation for the disruptors, Captain." He sighed audibly. "Very well. I'll transmit the unlock codes. They should come online in the next few minutes."

"Thank you, sir."

"I'll have your balls for this, Duggan."

Duggan smiled. "I'm sure you will, sir."

"Good luck out there. We don't want to lose the *Juniper*. The Corps has big plans for it." Teron's concern sounded far more for the orbital than for his own life.

Duggan closed the connection. "Have you received anything?" he asked McGlashan. The others on the bridge had only been party to Duggan's half of the conversation with Teron. They'd gathered enough that they didn't need to ask for details.

McGlashan didn't look up from her console. "We've got something coming through now." She raised an eyebrow. "The unlock codes are fourteen trillion characters in length. There are thirty of them in total. No wonder Monsey was taking so long to crack them."

"Let me know when we have access to the disruptors."

"Will do, sir. These are the same disruptors as the Ghasts have been using against us?"

"I hope so, Commander."

"Captain, the hangar doors are opening."

Duggan reached for the control bars and pulled gently back. It already felt completely natural and his instrumentation told him that the *Crimson* was hovering thirty feet above the hangar floor. The nose of the ship was pointing away from the doors and it would take precious seconds to rotate it in order to fly out forwards.

"I came out of a cave backwards, this hangar should be easy," he muttered. The pilot's viewscreen showed the floor of Hangar Bay One speeding by underneath the spacecraft. Moments later, the cold alloy was replaced by the unending blackness of space, against which the icy blue of Kryptes-9 was sharply contrasted. When the *Crimson* had completely emerged, Duggan wrenched hard on the controls to spin it around, simultaneously feeding in enough power to thrust the craft away from the *Juniper*. The tail of the warship came within a hundred metres of the orbital's wall. The AI would be pissed again. Duggan didn't care – there were more important things to be concerned with.

"The gravity drive repairs were completed while we were docked," said Breeze. "They're at one hundred percent."

"I'll have a picture for you in a moment, sir," said Chainer. "Right, got them. The first enemy vessel is engaged with the *Deeper*. Looks as if they're trying to lure the enemy away to the other side of Kryptes-9. I can't tell if it's working or not. The *Brawler*'s moving to intercept."

"What about the second Cadaveron?"

"Heading straight for the *Juniper*. Four hundred thousand klicks and closing."

"Let's cut them off," said Duggan. He pushed the gravity drive to maximum output and the giddiness came. It lasted a second or two until the life support negated the effects of the acceleration.

"I'm getting a fission signature, sir," Breeze announced. "An absolutely enormous one."

"Another Oblivion?" asked Duggan sharply.

"Not this time. It's coming from the *Juniper*. They're getting ready to hit lightspeed."

Duggan shook his head at his own stupidity. Naturally the orbital wasn't going to hang around. Even if the Ghast attack was repulsed, the enemy would have certainly relayed the *Juniper*'s position on to the rest of their fleet. There'd be twenty Ghast warships heading at full lightspeed towards their location already.

"Any idea how long?" he asked.

"I'm sorry, sir – I have no idea. It'll be nothing like as quickly as a warship can do it. I mean, have you seen the size of the thing?" Breeze sounded breathless with excitement.

"The disruptors are online, sir! We're carrying two of them!"

"Give me the details, Commander."

"Range almost two hundred and fifty thousand klicks. They'll pull juice from the fission engines. The power draw is *huge*."

"Can we use them yet?"

"No, sir. Their status tells me they're still warming up. They'll be ready in less than a minute."

"If they draw from the fission engines, that must be why the Ghasts haven't been firing them at will," said Breeze, studying the disruptor feeds. "My top of the head calculation tells me the *Detriment* couldn't provide enough power to use the disruptors at anything more than ten or fifteen thousand klicks."

"*Two hundred and fifty thousand* klicks, Commander? That's far more than the range of the newest Lambda prototypes. What's the longest range we've taken a hit from a Ghast disruptor?"

"One hundred and thirty-two thousand klicks from that last Cadaveron we escaped."

"Incoming enemy warship at three hundred and forty thousand klicks," said Chainer.

"Can you give me anything on the *ES Deeper*'s situation, Lieutenant?"

"Negative, sir. They've gone behind Kryptes-9. We'd pick up a fission signature. Anything else? Not a hope."

"Want me to hit the bastards as soon as the disruptors are ready?" asked McGlashan.

"Hold till I say."

"Aye, sir." She looked disappointed.

"Three hundred thousand klicks."

"Fifteen seconds for the disruptors."

"Two hundred and sixty thousand klicks."

"Disruptors ready when you say the word, sir."

"Fire as soon as they come in range, Commander."

"They've launched something, sir," said Chainer.

"Firing the disruptors."

The lights on the bridge dimmed low. There was a high-pitched whine, almost beyond the scope of hearing. A thumping sound shook the entire hull of the spacecraft.

"Fission engines down to ten percent. Enemy vessel no longer emitting positrons," said Breeze. "We just used enough power to light the biggest city on New Earth for a month!"

"Enemy missile on its way. At our combined speed it's closing at six thousand klicks per second. I'm picking up the same readings as I got from the missile the Oblivion sent after us," said Chainer.

Duggan frowned. "They can't target us from so far out, can they? Neither our missiles or theirs will target until they're within a range threshold."

"Another piece of new tech for us to deal with," said McGlashan. "This could be a game-changer if they can launch from so far."

"We're still closing with the enemy vessel at three thousand klicks per second, sir," said Chainer.

"We'll be in Lambda range in approximately thirty seconds," said McGlashan.

"Fission drive at twenty percent. Climbing fast."

"Their missile will reach us in a little over twenty seconds."

"Recommend evasive manoeuvres, sir," said McGlashan. "The Bulwarks aren't targeting again."

"We don't know the range of that missile, Commander. It might follow us across half the galaxy. We've only got a minute before the Cadaveron's power comes back."

"Fission drives at twenty-eight percent."

"Target that missile, Commander. Hit it with the disruptors."

"We've not got the power to hit it from far out, sir."

"Fire them, Commander. Do it soon."

"Five seconds to impact."

"Firing disruptors."

The whining sound was repeated and the walls of the bridge shuddered at the outpouring of energy. Duggan hauled the *Crimson* away to one side and off the path of the inbound missile.

Chainer blew out a lungful of pent-up air and McGlashan clenched her fist. "Got it," she said.

"Fission engines at three percent and climbing."

"The enemy missile has gone by, sir," said Chainer. "Negative strike."

"I want every Lambda locked onto that Cadaveron as soon as you're able, Commander. Give those bastards hell."

Less than twenty seconds later, the combined velocities of the two ships brought the Cadaveron into Lambda range.

"Twelve clusters away, awaiting reload," said McGlashan.

"Bringing us round. Give them the other side."

"Remaining six clusters have launched sir."

"Fire again when ready," Duggan said, altering the trajectory of the spaceship in order that the first twelve clusters could launch again as soon as they were ready.

"Off they go," she said.

The four of them watched soberly as three hundred and sixty Lambda missiles sped across the intervening space towards the disabled Cadaveron.

"First wave impacts in ten seconds," McGlashan said. "We've not got enough missiles to keep this up all day."

"Pulling us away to one hundred and forty thousand klicks," said Duggan. "I don't want them firing at us when their power comes back."

"Will it happen in time?" asked Chainer. "I've lost count of the seconds."

"We've gone past one minute already," Duggan replied.

"I'm detecting Vule traces from their port side," said McGlashan. She looked up. "One hundred and five successful Lambda strikes from the first wave."

"Shit," said Chainer. "That's got to be enough to knock out three Cadaverons."

"Sixty more confirmed strikes."

"There's going to be nothing left for the next ones to hit," said Breeze quietly.

By the time the remaining missiles reached the position of the enemy vessel, their guidance systems were reduced to chasing ever-smaller fragments of the Cadaveron. As Duggan swung the *Crimson* towards Kryptes-9, all that remained of the heavy cruiser was a cloud of metal shards and white-hot dust.

"Let's get over here and see what's happened to the *Deeper*," he said.

As the spaceship accelerated across the vacuum, Duggan found questions jumping unbidden to his mind. If *Admiral* Teron only had partial access to the systems onboard the *Crimson*, what sort of rank would be needed for full access? Outside of the Confederation Council, he could only think of one name and it wasn't somebody he wanted to hear from again – a name that would bring him only trouble. The man who had condemned him to life in the backwaters of the Space Corps. He put the thoughts aside and concentrated on the current situation.

CHAPTER TWENTY-TWO

THERE WAS no sign of the *ES Deeper*. The *Brawler* was heading towards the planet with a trajectory that indicated her captain was intending to take a random orbit in the hope of intercepting the Ghast heavy cruiser. The destruction of the second Cadaveron had taken hardly any time and the *Crimson* rapidly gained on the much slower Gunner.

"Do we have any data at all on the *Deeper's* position?" asked Duggan. "I don't want to end up chasing around Kryptes-9 for a day in the hope that we stumble across an engagement."

"We've got no details on their flight path at all, sir," Chainer replied. "I've just enquired with the *Juniper* and her AI can only provide a flight path until the *Deeper* went behind the planet. The *Juniper's* got the best sensor arrays this side of Monitoring Station Theta, but they still can't see through two hundred thousand kilometres of rock and ice."

"We should be grateful the enemy captain took the bait, sir," said McGlashan.

"The stupid warlike bastards," snorted Breeze. "They'd have had a shot at the *Juniper* if they'd acted together."

"I've seen them behave like this before," said Duggan. "It's as if they get a medal for every Confederation ship they shoot down."

"Or a promotion," offered McGlashan. "It makes you realise how little we know about them."

"We can guess their motivations by their actions. Today they've screwed up badly and given us the opportunity to capitalise on it."

Chainer called over. "Sir, I've got a priority request from the *Juniper*. It's Admiral Teron."

"Don't hang around man, patch him through."

"Coming through now."

Teron's voice spoke into Duggan's private channel. "Good work, Captain. The *Juniper*'s preparing to jump. I want you to take the *Crimson* and get out of there as soon as you can."

"Sir, what about the *Deeper*? A single Anderlecht is going to have a tough time against that heavy cruiser."

"I know, Captain. I've been there myself and come home with the scars. The *Crimson*'s too valuable to lose. As soon as the *Juniper* departs, you will set a course at maximum speed. You are to rendezvous with the *Archimedes*."

"Sir, with the disruptors we can help the *Deeper*."

"I gave you an order, Captain. As soon as the *Juniper* leaves, you're to break off any attempt at engagement and make for the *Archimedes*."

"Our fission drives have gone cold since we fired the disruptors." Duggan looked across at Breeze with a stare that told him not to say anything that might be overheard. "I don't know how long till they'll be ready."

"I know how they work, Captain. I've read the files," said Teron with a dangerous edge to his voice. He sighed and spoke again. "Captain Duggan, those are the only working disruptors that the Confederation possesses. If the *Crimson* is destroyed, we lose access to a weapon that might bring us back onto an even footing with our enemy."

"I understand, sir. The Ghasts have a new long-range missile. We'll do our best to keep them at bay until the *Juniper* goes to lightspeed. Over." Duggan cut the channel before Teron could order the *Crimson* to withdraw to a position closer to the space station. He looked at Chainer. "I don't want him getting through again, Lieutenant. Block any further communications from the *Juniper*. Make it look like a technical issue."

"Aye, sir," said Chainer.

"Lieutenant Breeze, any clue as to when the *Juniper* will leave us?"

"They've been holding at peak output for nearly four minutes, sir."

"That's not an answer."

"No sir, it wasn't. I don't know when they'll be ready. There's a good chance they don't either."

Duggan guided the *Crimson* into a high orbit and continued to close in on the much slower Gunner ahead of them. "Get me a channel to the *Brawler*."

"Short range comms channel coming through, sir."

"*ES Brawler*, this is Captain John Duggan, please acknowledge."

"Captain Duggan, this is Commander Emily Smith."

"You left the hangar ahead of us. Did you pick up the enemy's orbit?"

"Negative, sir. We're approaching this one blind in the hope we can help out."

"Don't engage the Cadaveron without assistance. You can't beat it."

"Understood. Want us to ride with you, sir?"

"Negative. I don't think you'll be able to keep up."

The *Crimson* flew past the *Brawler* at a distance of three hundred klicks and almost double the velocity. "So I see, Captain. Good luck."

"She sounds nervous," said McGlashan once the communication channel was closed.

"Can't say I blame her," muttered Chainer, a sheen of sweat visible across his forehead.

"Fission drive back up to sixty percent," said Breeze. "At least we'll be able to shut them down."

Duggan remembered something McGlashan had said a few minutes ago during the fight with the second Cadaveron. "How many missiles do we have left, Commander?"

"Three hundred and twenty-one. Enough for one and a half full-cluster launches."

"Normal procedure is to carry enough for twelve launches from each tube," said Duggan with a frown. "The *Crimson* should have been loaded with over two and a half thousand missiles. We should have more than fifteen hundred left."

"Maybe they sent her out with a half-load for her trials."

"The *Crimson* wasn't on a trial. It had entered active service. Somewhere along the lines it's fired well over a thousand missiles from its payload. When things calm down I want you to find the audit logs."

"Will do sir. Ten to one they're in the locked-down databanks."

"I'll not put a dollar on it, even at ten to one, Commander."

Lieutenant Chainer cut into the conversation. "The *Juniper*'s accelerated to Lightspeed-G, sir."

Breeze had been monitoring it too, and his eyes were wide. "The biggest fission output I've ever seen."

"Could run a couple of pocket calculators from it, then?" asked McGlashan.

"I'm picking up another signature from the far side of Kryptes-9," said Chainer. "Too small to be a Cadaveron."

"The *Deeper's*, getting ready to haul out," said Duggan. "No point in them sticking around here to get themselves blown up now that the *Juniper's* gone. "Looks like our work here is done for now. Lieutenant Breeze, get us ready to leave as well. Set a course for the *Archimedes*."

"Winding them up as we speak, sir. There's not been time to get them to re-route to one hundred percent, but they're near enough. Let's see what she can do this time. Thirty seconds till we're ready. I've sent a warning through to the quarters below. They'll be at a shade over ninety percent when we go and should climb to ninety-nine post-jump."

"Want me to speak to the *Brawler*, sir?" asked Chainer. "They can't have missed it either."

"Tell them to leave the vicinity at the earliest opportunity. I doubt Commander Smith has any orders, so she can pick the New Earth military base or she can head over to Angax if that's where her gut takes her."

"Commander Smith sends her regards, Captain. They'll take a look at what's happening around Angax."

Duggan smiled. There were plenty of brave men and women in the Space Corps.

"Sir?" It was Chainer. "The fission signature's died."

The smile drained away. Duggan knew the answer, but had to ask the question. "Without departure?"

"Yes sir. The *Deeper* hasn't gone anywhere."

"Want me to cut the engines?" asked Breeze.

Duggan shook his head, certain that the *Deeper* had been destroyed. He clenched his teeth, suppressing the urge to try and force an engagement with the enemy vessel. He remembered Teron's words that the *Crimson* had the only disruptors available to the Confederation. He knew himself that the engines were something special, even if Teron hadn't mentioned it. There were many other secrets to the warship, he was sure. Layer upon layer of them, hidden away from him, yet tantalisingly close. He didn't want to be known as the man who threw away humanity's chance of settling the score for the destruction of Charistos. Over a billion dead, with tens of billions more hoping for something to come that might improve the odds of victory. Against that, a lone Cadaveron was an insignificant prize, which only a madman would chase in the circumstances.

"We go for the *Archimedes*. Best speed."

The words had scarcely left his mouth when the entirety of the *Crimson*'s eleven hundred metre length was shaken by a vibration that rolled through the bodies of the men and women on board. Dizziness and nausea crashed into Duggan, battering him with increasing intensity until he felt consciousness begin to fade. Before the merciful relief of the darkness claimed him, Duggan had enough time to give thanks that the ship's engines were only at ninety percent when they made the jump.

CHAPTER TWENTY-THREE

CAPTAIN JOHN DUGGAN cracked an eye open. He was in his chair on the bridge. A few feet away, McGlashan groaned slightly, beginning to stir. Breeze and Chainer were out for the count. It looked like Chainer might have caught his forehead on the edge of his console and there was a bump already beginning to form. Duggan tested his body and found that his strength was returning quickly. Regardless, he was in no hurry to test it out.

"It's like being back in the academy gravity acclimatiser," said McGlashan, her words slurred. "The one you can't beat, where they turn it up until everyone blacks out."

Duggan grunted a response, not ready to make light conversation. "Lieutenant Breeze? Lieutenant Chainer?"

Breeze jerked at the sound of the voice. He was a strong man and would be angry with himself for falling unconscious. "Sir?"

"What's our status?"

As Breeze brought himself round, Duggan pushed himself upright and half-stumbled towards Chainer. He checked his pulse – it was beating strongly. The bump on his forehead looked like it might need some attention from Corporal Blunt.

"Sir, we're going at a tiny fraction below Light-T and still climbing. They're going to have to invent a new scale." Breeze looked dazed and Duggan wasn't sure if it was because of the effects of the acceleration or because of the speed they'd attained.

"Sergeant Ortiz, please report," he said.

Ortiz spoke, her voice notably weaker than normal. "Damn, sir." She cleared her throat loudly and apologised for it, like she wasn't thinking straight. "We've got cuts and bruises. Corporal Blunt's checking Diaz out for concussion."

"Send the corporal here as soon as he's finished with Diaz. Lieutenant Chainer's taken a knock to the head. Send Monsey as well. I need her plugged in to the core as soon as she can. The *Juniper*'s escaped and we downed one enemy Cadaveron. Next stop, the *Archimedes*."

"Good news about the enemy vessel, sir. I hear there's real steak on the *Archimedes*. A herd of cattle in the hold, just waiting to be turned into the best cuts of beef."

In spite of the circumstances, Duggan couldn't help but laugh. "I don't want to rain on your parade, Sergeant - I doubt there's ever been a cow within a thousand klicks of the *Archimedes*."

"Until I see otherwise, I'll continue to believe, sir."

Duggan closed the comms channel and turned his focus back to the bridge. His head had cleared and his strength had just about come back. Chainer moaned quietly and his lips moved slightly.

"Think he's okay?" asked McGlashan, concern on her face.

"Just a knock on the head, Commander. I'm sure Corporal Blunt will have him right as rain in a few minutes." Duggan peered in closely – Chainer was paler than usual and his face was dripping with sweat. It was hot, but not that hot.

"The fission drives have climbed up to full," said Breeze. "Ninety-nine percent available and we've topped out at dead-on

Light-V. That officially puts us as easily the fastest ship known to man, woman, or Ghast."

"I like those figures, Lieutenant. Feels like we're setting a new Confederation record for speed. We're the trailblazers of the Corps," said McGlashan.

"Five days and eight hours until we rendezvous with the *Archimedes*. Assuming she doesn't change course or speed in the meantime. Or decide to make a lightspeed jump somewhere."

"The *Juniper* should have sent a message on ahead. If not, we might be following the *Archimedes* around like a lost dog until we find it."

"Five days?" asked Duggan. "Which sector's she in?"

"Garon sector, according to our path and ETA."

"What the hell is the fleet's capital ship doing out there?" asked Duggan. "That's about as far from Axion as you can get."

Neither McGlashan nor Breeze offered an answer. Breeze shrugged and looked uncomfortable at the possibilities.

"Who commands it now?" asked McGlashan.

"It should still be Admiral Johnson," said Duggan. "The man's not known for his reluctance to face danger head-on. I wonder why he's taken the flagship so far away from it."

Corporal Blunt arrived, bringing his box of tricks with him. Duggan pointed to Chainer and the medic nodded his acknowledgement. He unslung his medical pack and crouched down to start poking at the half-conscious Lieutenant Chainer. Within seconds, he had several wires attached to Chainer's flesh.

"Nothing to worry about, sir. He has a mild concussion, but nothing to keep him off duty. He's going to feel like crap when he comes round. Want me to give him a shot of something?"

"I need him at his best," said Duggan.

"Right you are. One dose of synthetic adrenaline it is. We call it adrenaline, but that's just so people think it's something nice and friendly we're sticking into their arm." He held up a large needle, filled with a clear fluid. "The list of drugs in this is so long it'd take a med-student a week just to write them down." With that, he jabbed the needle unceremoniously into Chainer's arm. There was a quiet hiss as the syringe's onboard micro-brain squirted the fluid into the lieutenant's vein. The result was immediate. Chainer practically jumped upright, his eyes sharp and bright.

"What?" he gasped.

Corporal Blunt was familiar with the reaction and continued to speak to Duggan as if his patient didn't exist. "He might become nauseous in a few hours when that wears off. If he needs any more, let me know." Blunt turned to Chainer as if only just realising he was there, before clapping him on the shoulder in a familiar manner. Every field medic Duggan had ever worked with had some sort of oddness about them and Blunt was no exception. It was probably how they coped.

"Thank you, Corporal. I'll speak to you if I need anything further."

"Right you are, sir." Blunt gave a half-smile and turned to leave. The arrival of Monsey with her own kit meant it was a squeeze for him to get through the door.

"I need you to continue as you left off, soldier."

"Will do, sir."

"Commander McGlashan tells me you've unlocked one of the databanks?"

"I have, sir. Even that felt like breaking through a brick wall with a toffee hammer. There was no chance to index any of the data. I didn't access it via the expected method of entry."

"That's fine," said Duggan. There'd been no time for any of them to start sifting through what they'd found. He indicated to Monsey that she should get on it and she nodded. He looked at Chainer to see how the man was doing. The lieutenant had recovered from his shock awakening and was hunched over his console, his hands blurring as they called up data feeds from the ship's sensors.

"How're we doing, how're we doing?" said Chainer to himself. His voice carried an almost frantic note. Duggan recognized the effects of a high dose of battlefield adrenaline.

"Lieutenant Chainer, how long till our long-range comms are functional? I'd like to get a message through to the *Archimedes* as soon as we come out of lightspeed."

"They're next on the list, sir. The repair bot should be on it later today. Yes, that's it, today. They should be fixed soon. Do I make it six days till we reach the *Archimedes*? No, five days. It's closer to five days. They'll be ready before we dock. I've got to get on, sir."

McGlashan was familiar with field medication as well and Duggan caught her grinning at Chainer's babbling speech.

"We've got five days ahead of us, Commander," Duggan said. "That gives us plenty of time to find out what we can."

"I'm already on it, sir," she replied.

They spent the next few hours hunting through the huge quantities of uncategorised data that Monsey had unlocked for them. If they'd accessed it through the usual front-end it would have been easy to find anything of interest. As it was, the work was slow and tedious. Duggan found his frustration growing as he picked through a seemingly endless array of schematics for the *Crimson*'s hull.

"Admiral Teron told me there are no design plans on record for this ship," he said. "Yet that's all I can find here. I find it hard to believe that they sent all the technical drawings and specifications out with the ship and didn't keep any of them on the lab mainframe. From what I gather there aren't even a few damned print outs available to look at."

"I see hull composition, Lambda mountings, life support,"

said McGlashan. "Even something about the replicators. There are more than two hundred drawings for the boarding ramp."

"Nothing about the engines or the disruptors," mused Duggan. "Or the last unknown weapons system either."

"The Ghasts have disruptors, sir. They've only started to use them recently. Could they have stolen the designs from us?" She hesitated. "Or could someone have sold the details to them?"

"I don't know, Commander. None of it's making any sense at the moment. If the Space Corps had this technology fifty years ago, why didn't we use it? Teron talked about funding. I can almost believe that, but why would the records vanish?"

"Do we know for definite there are no records?"

"I believed him when he told me," said Duggan. "It's why they're so desperate to have the *Crimson* back now. I saw it in Teron's eyes and I can see it with my own eyes. This warship is a game-changer."

"You don't think there was a traitor who sold the plans to the Ghasts?"

"There'd be no logic to it. What would such a traitor gain? Money? I can't imagine there's anyone who had access to not only steal all the data, but to completely expunge it from every place it was stored and backed up. It can't have happened."

"There are a few people who could pull it off though?"

"One or two people in the Space Corps, perhaps. A dozen members on the Confederation Council. It wouldn't be at all easy and I can't imagine there'd be enough gain to make it worthwhile. Is there really someone out there who hates the human race enough that they'd assist an enemy which gives every impression that they want to make us extinct? For nothing more than money?" He shook his head at the thought. The same name that had come into his head earlier paid him another visit. He kept it quiet.

"What, then?"

"The answers have to lie here somewhere, Commander. In the *Crimson*'s databanks. This was a top-grade warship. You can be sure that every snippet of information pertaining to its design and maintenance will be stored here somewhere. This might be the only place it exists."

In spite of their best efforts, the answers remained stubbornly out of reach. They spent the next two days trawling through the area of the *Crimson*'s memory that Monsey had gained access to. By the middle of the second day, Monsey managed to provide front-end access, which allowed them to view all the data in a logical index. This sped things up immeasurably, but only served to demonstrate that what they were looking for wasn't there.

"There's nothing here," said McGlashan at last. "At least not in this memory array."

"I might have access to another chunk soon, sir," said Monsey. She'd been so quiet that Duggan had almost forgotten she was there. The constant rattle of her keyboard had slipped into background obscurity like a droning lightbulb.

"How soon?" asked Duggan.

"Soon, sir. I'm not sure I can pin it down. I've successfully circumvented a whole load of encrypted block codes. I've got tricks the original programmers didn't know about."

Duggan opened his mouth to press her for specifics. He closed it again. He didn't want to push Monsey so hard she'd lose focus. She'd been putting in eighteen hours a day.

"Yes!" shouted Chainer, clapping his hands loudly. "Main long-range comms back online, sir! If you want to speak to someone anywhere in the Confederation I can patch you through as soon as we come out of lightspeed! Even through to Earth if you want!"

"Thank you, Lieutenant, I don't have any relatives there," said Duggan dryly. "I'd like to get through to the *Archimedes*. It's just a shame we can't do it until we come out of lightspeed."

Comms wouldn't get through at the speed they were going – it was one of the problems with lightspeed travel. You might be travelling fast, but you were also travelling blind. Still, it was positive news that the *Crimson* was now almost as good as new again and Duggan felt his mood lift slightly. It took another leap when Monsey spoke.

"Got them!" she said. "Sir, I've cracked another one of the arrays. This time I got straight in through the front door."

"Good work," said Duggan, giving her a clap on the shoulder. "That's the sort of *soon* I can appreciate."

She smiled back. "No problem, sir, I just didn't want to set your expectations and get it wrong. Glad to help. I'll grab myself a coffee and have a go at the other two arrays."

"Take a rest when you need it, soldier."

"I definitely will, sir." She looked boosted by her success.

Duggan was tired and he could see by McGlashan's face that she was running low on energy as well.

"I don't think I can stomach another coffee as long as I live," she said, calling up the new access menu. "Whoa, look at this! I can access the fission drive details here. There's something on the double-core design as well. Looks like we hit pay dirt!"

"Let's get on with it and see what we've got," he replied, feeling the tiredness ebb. He knew it would only be a temporary relief but he was glad to take advantage of it.

After half an hour, it become clear that the more he learned, the more was hidden from him. There were thousands upon thousands of new schematics relating to the *Crimson*. Duggan was no engineer, but he'd learned enough that he could understand the basics of spaceship design and he could look at a technical drawing and know what it meant and where it fitted into the whole. What they'd unearthed in the *Crimson*'s archive was a mystery.

"Look at this drawing here," he said. "It's a very high-level diagram to show the two processing cores. Over here's the model designation of the front-end core. I've checked it out and it's a design from one of the Corps labs. Not quite a standard model – they've modified it quite extensively for the *Crimson* and called it the Hynus-T. It's slow by modern standards, but dramatically quicker than most warship cores of the era. Nevertheless, it's consistent with a cost-no-object new military design."

"Yeah, I remember reading about this model series," said McGlashan. "New and improved super-cores, now too old to bother with."

"This secondary core here isn't anything I recognize at all. I call it secondary, when in reality it appears to have primacy over the known model. I can see the interfacing between the two and they expected a tremendous amount of throughput. The connections between the cores suggests that the engineers were prepared for so much data to be transferred that the front core has specially-designed buffers to prevent it from getting flooded."

"Like too much information coming at one time choking it up?"

"That's how it appears. It's hard to say more without looking at the original specifications, or speaking to some of the engineers who worked on it."

"There's no code or model number for this second core?"

"Not that I can see. Wait! There *is* something. It's been given a strange name, listed on a few of these drawings. They've called it a Dreamer core."

"A nickname? The name of a company perhaps?" asked McGlashan. "Maybe a sub-project of Hynus, designed to produce a new type of computer."

Duggan did a search on the word Dreamer, to see if it was mentioned elsewhere. It was, many times, except nowhere was there any clarification on what it referred to. "Dreamer engines," he said. "We're packing a Dreamer engine and a Dreamer core. Shame I don't have the first idea what that means."

"Doesn't look like the designers did either, sir. Must have been so classified they didn't even know what it was they were working with."

"Nothing surprises me anymore, Commander." Duggan got to his feet. "I'm going for some rest. You know where to find me."

With that, he headed to his quarters for the six hours he allowed himself. He was dog tired, but sleep didn't come at once. Possibilities swirled and spun. The face of a man he'd tried to forget came to his mind and wouldn't leave him alone.

CHAPTER TWENTY-FOUR

AFTER A LITTLE OVER five days and eight hours of travel, the *ESS Crimson*'s fission drive shut off and the spaceship entered normal space with another violent burst that shook the crew and soldiers who were onboard.

"Damn I'll never get used to that," said Chainer.

"At least you didn't knock your head again," McGlashan replied with little sympathy. "Look on the bright side – the arrival is much easier than the departure."

"Maybe they'll refit the life support systems for us," he replied. "It's clear the one we've got isn't up to the task."

"Pay attention to your stations," Duggan told them. "What's our status. Where's the *Archimedes*?"

"Sorry, Captain," said Chainer. "I'll find out for you right now."

Duggan backed off. The physical punishments inflicted by the *Crimson* weren't something he enjoyed either and it took a few moments to shrug off the effects. "No problem, Lieutenant. Let me know when you've found them."

"We've come in right on the spot," Chainer said. "I'd kind of got used to the *Detriment*'s old way of landing us here there and everywhere, half a day late or early. Checking sensors now. Yep, got the *Archimedes*, sir. Well, the *Crimson*'s mainframe doesn't know it's the *Archimedes*, but it's the only spacecraft I know that's nine kilometres long. It's coming out from the far side of the planet over there. Dion-983."

"Catchy name," said McGlashan.

"They're two hours distant, sir."

Duggan took control of the *Crimson* and pointed it towards the coordinates Chainer fed through. The repair bot had fixed the autopilot a couple of days back, but Duggan found it suited him better to guide the ship manually. "Bring up their comms man and let them know we've arrived. I'm sure they've seen us."

"Aye, sir. They've acknowledged our hail and returned the greeting. We have permission to come in close."

"What escort do they have?"

"Getting multiple pings. I'm downloading the data." The *Crimson*'s data on Corps vessels was fifty years out of date and Chainer had to send a request to the *Archimedes'* AI for each of the spacecraft in the vicinity. "Hadron *Precept* in attendance. Along with Anderlechts *Fixation*, *Extermination* and *Delectable*. Those are just the ones I can see. I'd expect there to be others still hidden behind Dion-983."

"They've got a quarter of the damned fleet here," said Duggan. "Out in the back end of nowhere."

"Maybe they know something we don't," said McGlashan.

"I hope you're right, Commander. They've got enough fire-power to waste half a dozen Cadaverons. At least we know where the *Delectable* got to. Sent here to orbit a dead planet while Ghost ships attack the *Juniper*."

Duggan chewed his lip as the *Crimson* closed the gap on the *Archimedes*. He'd expected a lot more communication than they'd received so far. The Corps flagship was practically silent and unresponsive.

"Can her hold accommodate us, sir?" asked McGlashan.

"Not a hope. It's a warship, not a cargo vessel. They might have a couple of Gunners docked. Otherwise it's the same as every other Corps combat ship: engines, weapons, armour. It's a lot more luxurious than anything else in the fleet, though. After all, it's meant to host important people."

"The sort of people who might take offence if they're not treated with the respect they feel they deserve?" asked Breeze.

"Exactly, Lieutenant. The sort of people who might decide to cut ten percent of the Corps' budget if they don't get a perfect cup of coffee from a replicator."

"Bastards," said McGlashan, almost to herself.

"Not all of them, Commander. There're plenty of good men and women on the Confederation Council. They're just too slow to react and they've been badly-informed about how the war is going. Or maybe we have too many peacetime leaders. Still, it's better to treat your superiors with respect, rather than hope for their goodwill."

Duggan heard what sounded suspiciously like stifled laughter at his last sentence. He pretended he hadn't noticed. "Let's have a look at what we've got," he said to Chainer. "Bring up the *Archimedes* on the screen."

Chainer complied and an image of the largest battleship in the Space Corps filled the bulkhead monitor. It was difficult to see the enormity of it without another vessel for comparison and to the untrained eye it looked like a functional wedge, the same way that most Corps ships did. When he looked closer, Duggan could see the thousands of pits and indentations along the flanks which hid hundreds of Lambda clusters, Bulwark cannons and defence ports. To the front and rear, there were the tell-tale bulges that showed where the particle beams were housed. The

Space Corps beam weapons were technologically inferior to the Ghasts' latest models, but from what Duggan knew, the *Archimedes* was big enough to carry power modules that were large enough to overcome many of the shortcomings.

McGlashan was the first to speak. "It's impressive," she said. "But?"

"It's too clean, Captain. Either they give it a sponge down every two weeks or it's never been fired upon."

"It's thirty years old, Commander. It came into service near the start of the war. An experiment, I believe, simply to see if we could make something that big. It's seen action and plenty of it. In the first ten years, she scored dozens of confirmed Ghast warship kills. Then the enemy ships started to get bigger and better. Someone got scared that the *Archimedes* might one day get crippled or worse. They've kept it out of harm's reach since then, refitting it endlessly with the latest technology they had no plans to use in anger. If it got destroyed, the Space Corps would look like fools. Even worse, it would have made it impossible to stop the public learning what a mess we were making of the war. I don't know where the orders came from to keep it away from the front. A faction in the council, perhaps. They couldn't have done it without some agreement within the Corps."

"Everyone knows we're losing the war now," said McGlashan.

"They do. And it took the incineration of a billion people on Charistos before the Council took proper notice. That's why I'm so pissed off to see the *Archimedes* out here...hiding from it all. Not only that, but she has a full battle escort. Orbiting endlessly around an empty planet, while the people on Angax check the skies every day to see if the Ghasts have found them. Those people are being failed, even now."

"They should have made you Admiral, sir," said Breeze. "At

least then everyone would know they had someone who would always try his best."

Duggan looked at the man and met his eyes. There was nothing other than sincerity in them.

"Sir? How can you say on the one hand that the Council are mostly good men and women, when they've spent years cutting our funding?" asked McGlashan.

Duggan sighed. Officers were expected to ask questions of their superiors, and it occasionally made things difficult. "I don't know for certain, Commander. I only have guesses."

"Can we know what those guesses are, sir?"

Duggan didn't really want to say anything else on the matter. In the end, he spoke. "It's as I've told you. The Council can only react to the information they're given. Who knows if they're always provided with a complete picture? Let's not talk any more about it. Admiral Teron told me this is the hand we've been dealt and it's the one we have to play."

"Feels like we've got a seven high at the moment," said McGlashan.

"Enough, Commander."

"Incoming message from the *Archimedes*, sir," said Chainer. "For your ears only."

"Very well. Who is it?"

"It's Fleet Admiral Slender."

Duggan didn't say anything. Anger played across his face, clear for them all to see.

"Sir?"

Duggan sat down. "Patch him through at once."

There was a humming in Duggan's earpiece, before a cold voice cut across it. "Captain Duggan."

"Admiral Slender."

"You are to bring the *ESS Crimson* to a parallel path with the *Archimedes*. A shuttle will come and pick you up. You alone."

"Sir."

The line went dead. Duggan looked over to Chainer, with an eyebrow raised questioningly.

"He's cut you off, sir."

"I think he just wanted to hear my voice," said Duggan. "To remind himself that I'm still alive."

"You don't get on with him?" asked McGlashan.

"That would be an understatement, Commander. Admiral Slender is the man responsible for everything that happened since the *Tybalt*."

Duggan's crew knew about the *Tybalt*. They knew that the Lambda modifications to the ship's aft batteries had gone untested before the vessel was ordered out of the yard. One of the launch tubes had overheated and exploded because it hadn't been properly insulated from the gravity drives. Fifteen people had died and it had been lucky the explosion didn't breach the armoured magazine where the Lambdas themselves were stored. If that had happened, the whole ship would have been torn apart. Duggan had been brought before a court martial over it, when he'd been falsely accused of powering up the launch tube in order to impress his junior officers with a display of the *Tybalt*'s fire-power. In the end, he was cleared of any wrongdoing. The truth was that the spacecraft had been ordered from its berth too early and the explosion happened without any involvement from Duggan.

"What does Admiral Slender have against you, sir?" asked McGlashan.

Duggan stared into the distance "When the launch tube exploded, one of the men it killed was a junior officer. He was twenty-two years old. An only son, loved and cherished by his mother and father. A man upon whom they pinned all their hopes and dreams. In that regard, he was little different from the other fourteen men and women who died on the *Tybalt*."

"What was special about this one man?" she asked quietly.

"His name, that's all. Frederick Lincoln Slender."

"Damn."

"Exactly, Commander. I wept for them all, but the father has not forgotten, nor has his desire to assign blame diminished during the last eleven years. Admiral Slender's son died on the *Tybalt* and his hatred for me has lasted ever since." Duggan's voice strengthened and took on a hard, dangerous edge. "I am damned if I will permit him to continue his quest for vengeance against me!"

He sat back into his seat, surprised at the fury that gripped him. If Slender had brought him out here just to drag up the past, Duggan was determined to show the man he would not take it lying down.

CHAPTER TWENTY-FIVE

A SHORT WHILE after the *Crimson* took up a parallel course to the vastly larger battleship *Archimedes*, a shuttle crossed the intervening space. After some manoeuvring, it latched onto an area of the *Crimson's* hull, close to the retracted boarding ramp.

"It's connected and sealed, sir. You're good to go," Chainer said. He paused for a moment, evidently wondering if he should say anything else. "Good luck."

Duggan left the bridge without a word and walked in his practised half-stoop to where the shuttle had clamped itself. There was a metal hatch on the floor, which he disengaged and lifted back with a grunt. Beneath, was a shaft with a ladder, leading through many metres of the *Crimson's* armour, to the shuttle's passenger bay at the bottom. Duggan slid down the ladder and sat himself on one of the eight seats in the tiny craft's bay. It was overwhelmingly metallic and utilitarian, the cream plastic of the seats the only break from the greyness. There was an odour of sweat and grease, as if the last passengers had left a bag of old clothes and food under one of the chairs. There was no one else present – his ride had been sent over completely unmanned, with nobody to greet him as politeness and procedure dictated.

Without warning, the shuttle de-coupled itself with a clanking of heavy alloy machinery. Duggan felt a momentary lurch in his stomach as it fell away from the *Crimson*. Then, its low-power gravity drive groaned into life and propelled the ship over the comparatively short return voyage. Within twenty minutes, it had docked into one of the *Archimedes'* four compact, dedicated bays. Duggan guessed the shuttles had been made bespoke for the flagship and from his recent experience with them, they'd never been updated or modified since. He climbed out through the same hatch by which he'd entered. Any visiting dignitaries wouldn't be expected to board the vessel this way. Duggan wasn't the most important man in the Corps, but he was still a high-ranking officer. This was a calculated insult.

When he reached the top of the shaft, Duggan emerged into a brightly-lit corridor which he guessed was somewhere in the maintenance area of the *Archimedes*. It was cramped and hot, with the harsh odour of barely-contained electricity. There were two soldiers waiting for him, unarmed apart from pistols. They crouched uncomfortably as if they weren't familiar with anything other than the wide, high passageways that Duggan knew were elsewhere above them in the ship's interior. The first, a woman with a hard face and her hair tied back, saluted him properly.

"Welcome aboard, sir. We've been asked to take you to the waiting area."

"Waiting area? I'm here to see Admiral Slender."

The woman shrugged to let him know that she was just doing as she was told. "If you'll follow me, sir."

The two soldiers led Duggan a short distance to a maintenance lift. They squeezed inside and he watched as the woman keyed in their destination floor number. They rose quickly and silently. Then, there was a ping and the lift door slid open. The soldiers went first, stepping onto a much wider corridor than the first. The light had the usual blue-white hue of badly-emulated daylight and the walls were smooth alloy. To Duggan it was a luxury that he could stand without bending his spine and his bones crackled as he stretched them out. The soldiers led him several hundred metres, with only one or two deviations. They passed other personnel on the way – a mixture of technicians and soldiers. Duggan wracked his brain to remember how many people the *Archimedes* usually carried. A few thousand was the best he could come up with. They could probably pack a few tens of thousands inside if they ever needed to carry troops, though there were dedicated spacecraft for that. Even with its enormous length, the bulk of the craft was still given over to the engines and weapons.

"Here you go, sir," said the man. It was the first time he'd spoken.

Duggan nodded his thanks and entered a room. At fifteen feet square and empty, it would have seemed like an incredibly wasteful use of space on anything smaller than a Hadron. Plastic chairs lined the walls and Duggan crossed the hard-tiled floor to sit on one. There was a replicator in the wall. On another day, he'd have tested it out. At the moment, he had no appetite for food or drink. He waited for twenty minutes without receiving any indication that his presence was known to anyone.

"Pointless, childish games," he growled to himself. He activated his communicator and pulled the mouthpiece loop down from the earpiece. "Commander McGlashan, please report."

Her voice came back at once, as if she'd been waiting to hear from him. "Not much to say, sir. The *Archimedes* has established a remote interface with our mainframe and it's sucking out whatever data we're carrying."

"A *remote* interface? It'll take hours to empty the memory arrays."

"What else are they going to do? We can't dock with them. At first, I thought they were only interested in bits and pieces, but they're grabbing everything."

Duggan wasn't surprised. "They can't risk missing anything, Commander. We know how important those memory arrays might be."

"Have you seen the Admiral, sir?"

"Not yet. He's left me in a waiting room."

"Like that, huh?"

"Seems as if that's the game he wants to play. Are you updating the *Crimson*'s tactical databases while we have the chance?"

"We are. We might not be here for much longer, but I'm getting us updated. It's slow, since the outbound data is taking up all the bandwidth."

Duggan unconsciously lowered his voice. "Scan the archives for any news on the war. The uncensored stuff."

"I don't think I have clearance for that, sir."

"The ship has the same clearance as its commanding officer. You have my permission to use it."

"Understood. Enjoy your wait, sir. Hopefully we'll still be here when you're done."

The earpiece went quiet, leaving Duggan to sit it out. He wasn't normally a man who'd accept this treatment. He sighed in realisation that there was nothing to be gained by taking himself off to explore the vessel's interior. His memories of the place were mostly vague, but he wasn't feeling curious enough to reinforce them. Eventually, he got up and crossed to the replicator. It vended a cup of near-perfect coffee at his command. He put it to one side and ordered the machine to produce him a sixteen-ounce medium-rare steak. It paused briefly before the vending hatch opened to reveal a metal tray with a steak upon it, which looked almost as perfect as the coffee. The aroma drifted to his nose and a growl from his stomach made him realise how bad the food on the *Crimson* was. He reached for the tray. Before his hand got there, the door to the room's only entrance slid open and a man entered. He was broad, with a pock-marked face and a lieutenant's insignia on his shoulder.

"Captain Duggan? Admiral Slender will see you."

Duggan scowled and considered telling the man that Slender could wait until he'd finished his steak. He bit his tongue on the matter and followed the lieutenant from the room. The man took him several hundred metres towards the aft of the spaceship. As they went, Duggan noticed an improvement in the décor. Here and there a picture was hung, the walls were painted and hard-wearing carpet tiles covered the floor. This was where the officers lived. The bridge was close by – above the officer's quarters and accessed by a bank of lift shafts. Duggan couldn't shake the feeling that the Space Corps' flagship was too big. When the shit hit the fan, everything was just too far from everything else.

"Here you go, sir," said the lieutenant, stopping in front of a solid-looking door. It was made of polished wood, with a sign on the front to announce the name and rank of the occupant.

The lieutenant took his leave, his receding footsteps muted by the dark blue of the floor tiles. Duggan pressed his thumb to an access panel, half expecting the door to swing open on hinges. It didn't. Instead, it slid away into a recess in the same way that every other door did. Duggan didn't wait for an invitation and stepped within.

Fleet Admiral Slender's office was large and unremarkable. Screens lined the walls and there were several consoles to provide access to whatever information a man of importance might require. There was a dark grey desk of an unknown material. It was scrupulously clean, except for a single, small pile of papers and a monitor. On one corner was a framed photo. It was turned away. Duggan didn't need to see it to know who was the subject of the image.

"Duggan, take a seat."

Duggan stared at the man he'd not seen for several years. Admiral Slender was almost the same as he remembered him – his square, clean-shaven face still looked smooth and waxy, but there was something unnatural about him. Slender must have been close to eighty, yet he looked little more than forty. His hair was close-cropped and grey. His eyes were the same colour as his hair and they locked to Duggan's. Duggan was in no mood to be spoken to improperly.

"*Captain* Duggan, sir," he said, pulling out a padded seat, continuing to meet the Admiral's stare.

"I'd like to say it's a pleasure to see you again, *Captain* Duggan." Hostility crackled about the man's voice like white-hot sparks. Duggan struggled not to rise to it.

"Have you brought me here in order to tell me you don't like me. Sir?"

"I don't know what I've brought you here for, Captain. The recovery of the *ESS Crimson* and your arrival made it seem like a convenient moment to catch up. For old times' sake." Slender gave a thin smile.

"I will not sit here and listen to you rake up the past, sir."

"You will sit here and listen until I say you are dismissed." Slender leaned back in his chair, his eyes not wavering. "If you make one misstep, I'll have you expelled from the Corps in disgrace so quickly that you'll not even have the time to thank your good luck that it didn't come sooner. However, all that is by-the-by for the moment. I am overall commander of the Space Corps warfleet and we are at war against an implacable foe. We require trained men and women to pilot our vessels against the enemy and for the time being, you are an officer of some seniority." He paused, his eyes glittering. "What do you know about the *ESS Crimson*, Captain?"

"I know there's much more to it than I've been told."

"That's not what I asked. What do you *know* about it? Don't dance around. My technicians tell me you've accessed certain parts of the vessel's data. An *unauthorized* access. Once the extraction is complete, I'm sure there'll be an audit trail."

"A warship's captain is authorized for everything on board his ship, sir. Unless *specifically* told otherwise. The *Crimson* is carrying disruptors. Engines that surpass anything we have in the fleet today. Two cores, one of which can probably outthink the *Archimedes* on many tasks. Questions without answers."

"Every question has an answer, Captain, though not everyone is privy to the details. Nor should they be. Some information is too dangerous to be widely available, as I'm sure you're aware."

"Such as why two of the fleet's most powerful warships are in the Garon sector, a place where there haven't been any reported sightings of a Ghost war vessel?"

"I'm sure you're aware that the loss of the *Archimedes* would be grist to the mill of those who would like to sue for peace."

"The Ghasts have declined every opportunity to have dialogue. Everyone knows that!"

"Have they now? There you go again, Captain. Demonstrating my point about the dangers of information."

Duggan was stunned. "We've had communication with the Ghasts?"

"On a number of occasions. Most recently we have tried forge a deal on their terms. A partial surrender, if you will. An offer to withdraw our fleet to within certain boundaries of space." The thin smile appeared again.

"And?"

"There is a lack of trust between us and it appears they

perceived our willingness to negotiate as a sign of weakness. A month after our last meeting, the Ghasts found Charistos. I'm sure you know what happened there. We assume it's a show of strength from them, in order to drive us into a total capitulation." Slender's voice climbed in anger as he spoke.

"Have they succeeded?"

"No, they have not, Captain! All they have done is demonstrated that we must do our utmost to defeat them! At the very least, we need to parlay as equals, for they seem to despise weakness. Still, there are factions amongst the Confederation Council who blame us – blame humanity - for the current state of affairs. Even in the face of what has happened, they demand that we continue our pursuit for peace - no matter what the cost. Can you imagine what might happen if we surrendered to the Ghasts and they decided to betray us?"

"Have we given up on Angax, sir?"

"Perhaps, Captain. They destroyed the Hadron *Ulterior* easily during the engagement at Charistos. Easily enough to convince not only me, but many of the Confederation Council, that further risks should be minimised. At least until our research labs have discovered new ways to combat them."

"Does this mean the *Archimedes* is now obsolete?" Duggan couldn't believe it. "Our Lambdas still work pretty well from what I've seen, sir."

"They do, Captain. Unfortunately, the Ghasts have developed a new missile and targeting system. Some of their vessels can launch from more than double our range, as the crew of the *Ulterior* found to their cost. For some reason, our Bulwarks fail to target them."

"Yes, sir. I've seen those weapons."

"Then you will know that I can't risk the *Archimedes* against the Ghasts until we have effective countermeasures."

"Will Angax be destroyed?"

"We can only hope not, Captain. The data from the *ESS Crimson* will be invaluable in helping our cause. We are re-transmitting it to several of our labs even as the *Archimedes* receives it."

"Why didn't we just keep copies of it at the time? Why don't we have those engines and disruptors aboard every ship in the fleet?"

"Those questions will have to remain unanswered, Captain Duggan."

"What now for the *Crimson*, sir? And my crew?"

"For the time being, the *Crimson* will remain in escort position until her databanks have been scoured by the *Archimedes'* AI. After that? Your fate and that of your crew is currently undecided." With that, Admiral Slender looked at the papers on his desk and began to look through them. "You're dismissed, Captain."

"Sir."

"One more thing, Captain. Don't let me catch you attempting to breach the *Crimson's* databanks again. Remember my warning."

Duggan exited the room, made his way to the same shuttle which had carried him to the *Archimedes* and returned to the *Crimson*.

CHAPTER TWENTY-SIX

WHEN DUGGAN REACHED THE BRIDGE, it was empty apart from McGlashan.

"Chainer and Breeze went for some sleep. Monsey too," she said. "Left me in charge. Is everything okay, sir?"

"It went as well as could be expected, Commander. We'll be staying here until the *Archimedes* finishes with us. After that? I don't know."

"Sometimes it'd be nice to have an idea what's going to happen more than a week ahead of us."

"I doubt anyone gets that luxury these days. We're here because they think the *Archimedes* is a sitting duck if it gets into a scrap. It seems as if those new missiles we came up against have got people worried."

"Yeah. I can see why that would happen. How was the Admiral?"

"Hostile, but he managed to keep a lid on much of it. I think he's as pissed off as we are that the Corps flagship is keeping out of the action."

"The Confederation is going to do nothing to fight back?"

"Doesn't sound like it," said Duggan glumly. "It's not about fighting back anymore. It's about surviving for long enough. We're in the middle of a race to see if we can turn out enough new warships with enough new technology to challenge the Ghasts before they master the ability to follow us through light-speed to one of the inner planets."

"They want to make us extinct, huh?"

"That's what it sounds like."

McGlashan gave her console a familiar pat. "They'll have to get past this old bird, first."

Duggan laughed. "That they will. And once we've run out of missiles, we'll strafe them from close-up with our Bulwarks."

"If that fails, we'll ram them, sir. Like we did in the good old days. Or set off all the nukes in the hold and go out in an eight-gigaton blaze of glory." Something caught her eye and she leaned forward intently over one of her screens and began to make a series of command gestures to the mainframe. "Cancel, damnit, cancel!" she said.

"What's happening?" asked Duggan, crossing over to look.

"It's the *Archimedes*, sir. It's emptied the first two memory arrays and now it's deleting them."

"Can you stop it?"

"No, sir. The flagship's AI operates at the rank of Admiral. I don't have anything like the authority to prevent it."

"Get Monsey here immediately!" Duggan said.

"I'm sending for her now."

"Admiral Slender warned me against digging through the databanks. Seems like he didn't think his warning was sufficient."

"Databanks one and two are now deleted from our memory arrays. Three and four are still intact. It hasn't finished down-loading those yet. There's not long left until it's done."

Monsey arrived, looking tired. "What's the matter, sir?"

"The *Archimedes* is deleting our data. Can you stop it?"

ANTHONY JAMES

"Yes, sir. I can hack in and block their access to the delete commands. They'll know immediately what I've done. Given time, I could write some code to hide my tracks. It'll take days to make something halfway decent. Even then it won't fool the AI for long. They'll find out what's happened eventually."

"Can we copy databanks three and four into another area of the mainframe? Or hide it in the backend core?"

"A nice idea, except it won't work. The *Archimedes* has the data locked while the transfer takes place. I could run you a copy, but again it'll set the alarms ringing."

"Very well, soldier. That will be all." Duggan knew there was a chance he might be able to talk himself out of a court martial, even with Admiral Slender gunning for his arrest. The Space Corps judiciary was proud of its impartiality. Monsey would be a much easier target.

When Monsey had gone, McGlashan spoke quietly. "Sir, do we have any right to know what's in the databanks? Shouldn't we let someone else deal with it?"

Duggan pushed his fingers through his short-cropped hair. "You might be right, Commander. Still, it doesn't sit well with me that I'm being told to risk my life and the lives of my soldiers and crew without knowing why it's happening. Information is everything. If I don't have it, I can't make the best decisions. Besides, I'm captain of this vessel until I'm told otherwise and it's incumbent upon me to learn everything I can about its capabilities. Secrecy be damned!"

"You might push it too far, sir."

"That I might." He grinned. "However, I have not once received a direct order telling me that I am not allowed to find out the secrets of the *ESS Crimson*. I have simply been ordered to stop my efforts to hack the databanks."

"Databanks which will shortly be cleaned out of anything useful."

"I need to think on the matter," he said. "At the very least, I'm relieved the *Crimson* is no longer the only receptacle for that information. They are sending the data to our war labs for analysis."

"They might think to make copies this time, and use it to make a few new engines and disruptors."

"I'm sure that's on the agenda, Commander." Duggan returned to his own console and checked through a number of status reports. "How far did you get with updating our databases from the repositories on the *Archimedes*?"

"Uh, it kind of fell off the radar, sir. We've got all we need to know about the latest Ghast ships and weaponry. The guys below wanted some TV that wasn't over fifty years old, so I've done my best to help them out. They deserve it." She shuffled uncomfortably.

"You've spent the time getting fifty years of TV?"

"It's good for morale, sir."

Duggan shook his head and paged through the updates to the *Crimson*'s databases. It looked to be in order. At least if they were given a chance to fight again, they'd have the latest information on all of the known Ghast ships. It would be invaluable assistance to know which ones were reported have the latest disruptors, beam weapons and missile systems.

"Let's have a look at the secure data on the war," he said to himself. His rank allowed him to access much that would otherwise be censored for wider release. It wasn't seen as good for morale to give exact numbers of casualties to the public. In addition to that, news about the destruction of a spacecraft would often be buried for a time.

"Does it say what happened on Charistos, sir?" asked McGlashan.

"The Ghasts detonated a series of warheads in the upper atmosphere. It caused the air to ignite all the way to ground level.

They're still analysing the exact weapons used. We've never seen them before."

"Hopefully we'll never see them again. Have the Confederation got anything similar?"

"Nope. Not unless they're keeping it secret. We've never had to develop anything suitable to wipe out an entire planet before. The nukes we're carrying would do a pretty good job of knocking out a few cities, just not an entire planet."

"I don't know what I'd think if we were told to deploy them onto the surface of a populated planet."

"Nor I, Commander. But you know what? If it was a choice between blowing the bastards up or losing the war, I'd do it in a heartbeat. I'd have to come to terms with it later."

"I wanted to be a captain once. To take charge of my own vessel and go out there to stick it to the Ghasts. Now I don't think I'd be strong enough."

"I'm an old bastard, Commander. Old and cynical. One day you'll be just like me."

Duggan's words lightened the mood and McGlashan laughed. "Twenty years until then, sir."

"Fifteen, Commander. Only fifteen."

McGlashan leaned closer, her brow furrowed. "You're still logged in to the *Archimedes* with the *Crimson's* authority instead of your own."

"It doesn't really matter. I'm permitted to do it this way if I choose."

"What do these menu options here mean? The ones with multiple asterisks?"

"I'm not sure. That would generally indicate a secured file with extra encryption."

"Like the secret stuff?"

"It could be. Or maybe stuff that's been hidden from normal view so as not to clutter up something more important."

"Captain-level stuff."

"No, Commander. I wouldn't expect to see these files."

"What's that?" She pointed at one of the options.

"Pay scales. I already know what you're paid, Commander."

"There's an option for Admiral Teron up there. The file is unlocked."

Duggan wasn't really interested in what Teron got paid. He returned to the top-level menu. "There might be a problem with the file security. I should let the *Archimedes* know."

"I don't think there's a problem with it, sir. The *Crimson* was something new at the time. Something special. It would make sense for it to have high-level access authority."

Duggan thought for a moment and then queried the command access level. "You're right. We've got clearance at a level just short of Fleet Admiral. Higher even than Admiral Teron. The *Crimson* is so old that no one seems to realise that it can act beyond the authority of a full Admiral. Otherwise they'd have revoked it immediately. Or at least as soon as they'd found someone able to do so."

"That's enough access to do a lot of things."

"Yes, Commander. A lot of things."

Duggan started a query to discover anything that the *Archimedes* might be holding on the *Crimson* or the Hynus project.

"Can you include the word Dreamers in the search as well, sir?"

"I've added it." He kept his eyes on the screen. There was no immediate response, which didn't bode well.

"They've finished off databanks three and four," said McGlashan. "The delete command will be coming soon. Here we go - they didn't hang around. You can stop it if you want, sir."

The irony that a warship which had been lost for more than fifty years technically outranked the Space Corps' flagship wasn't lost on Duggan. "I'd better not try it," he said. "It's not something that would go unnoticed."

"I think you're already treading that line, sir."

"I can cover my tracks when I'm looking for something as simple as a data file. If I countermanded the *Archimedes'* AI, that would be pretty easy to spot."

His query completed and a list flashed up on his screen, each file represented by a serial code that gave away nothing about the contents. There was a lot of information to check and the longer he took looking, the greater the chance that the *Archimedes'* AI would notice something was amiss. It was usual for even the moderately secret datafiles to be scanned regularly for locks that would indicate they were being viewed. If the *Crimson's* mainframe was found accessing something it shouldn't be, it wouldn't take long to put two and two together, at which point Fleet Admiral Slender would be on the comms, asking some pointed questions.

"For a vessel we have so little information about, there're a hell of a lot of files relating to it. Big ones."

"Can you pull them across?"

Duggan grimaced. "Not quickly. If I open up a wide data channel, someone onboard the *Archimedes* will start asking questions. If I open up a narrow channel, we'll be here all week and that'll increase the chance that a file lock will be discovered."

"It's not worth a court martial, sir."

He swore. "You're right, Commander, it's not. I don't want to give Admiral Slender the pleasure of seeing me receive a dishonourable discharge." He exited the menu and disconnected from the *Archimedes'* databanks.

"Sir? You're not going to believe this."

"What is it?"

"All four databanks have repopulated. Everything is back as it was before the *Archimedes* deleted it all."

"That can't be right," said Duggan. The lists that had reappeared on his own screen told him that McGlashan wasn't mistaken. "Are we receiving a transmission from the flagship?"

"Nothing, sir. They couldn't get the data back to us so quickly even if they wanted to."

"Some automatic undelete command to restore the data from a hidden cache?"

"Definitely not. There's no sign of an automatic command running anywhere on the system."

The answer came to Duggan. "Check the interface between the front and back cores of the *Crimson*."

"I think you've got it, sir. We've had three exabytes of data pushed through one of the links. Shame I can't see any further into the secondary core. I would love to know what's going on there."

"Any sign the *Archimedes* realises what's happened?"

"None, sir. The AI probably thinks everything's hunky-dory."

Lieutenant Chainer arrived, looking like he could happily sleep for another two days. He had a coffee with him and the smell drifted into the bridge, far more appetising than the taste. "Hello, sir. I hope everything went well."

"Thank you, Lieutenant. The Admiral and I have disengaged for the moment."

"I'm glad to hear it." Chainer accessed his console and began to run through his rote checks. He jumped up and started coughing, spraying coffee over the floor. "Sir, fission signatures! Five big ones! They're coming in with no discernible pattern around Dion-983. There's nothing on the flight plans to say they're ours."

"Get Lieutenant Breeze up here at once," Duggan barked. "Hail the *Archimedes*. I don't care if they already know. Commander McGlashan, prepare the weapons systems. What've we got Lieutenant Chainer?"

Chainer's coffee fell to the floor in his haste, spreading a pool of the thick liquid under his feet. "Negative confirmation yet, sir. I'm scanning them up now. Two Cadaverons and one Oblivion."

"What about the others? Tell me, Lieutenant!"

"Another Oblivion. A third Cadaveron breaking out of lightspeed."

Duggan looked at the feeds. The fifth vessel arrived in local space. The *Crimson*'s databanks tried to match up the dimensions against known Ghast warships and produced a list of possibilities.

"One new Oblivion, the other four unrecognized. They're either building four for every one of ours, or we're just a minor foe on the edge of an empire."

"How did they find us?" asked McGlashan.

"I wish I knew, Commander. I wish I knew."

CHAPTER TWENTY-SEVEN

ALL ACROSS THE BRIDGE, screens exploded into life. The comms burst into a frantic cacophony of signals and messages as the Space Corps fleet tried desperately to coordinate a response to the threat. Duggan knew the *Archimedes* main comms room had over thirty people inside and he pictured them struggling with the tide of information. Lieutenant Breeze arrived, already aware that something was wrong.

"Lieutenant Breeze to your post," Duggan said loudly. "Lieutenant Chainer. I need you to paint us the picture. Commander McGlashan, you will fire Lambdas when ready upon any Ghast vessel that comes close enough."

"Sir, I've got one Oblivion and one Cadaveron ahead of us and closing. They're going straight for the *Archimedes*. There's one more Cadaveron coming around Dion-983. It's fast. Four minutes until it can engage our flagship. The Anderlecht *Extermination* is almost in range of it. The third Cadaveron missed its mark and entered local space behind the planet. They're out of sensor sight. From the positioning data I've got from their fission engines, I estimate between six and eight minutes till it can engage. The second Oblivion is already firing at the *Precept*. I'm tracking six long range missiles."

"Commander, prioritise the approaching Oblivion. That's what the *Archimedes* will be aiming for as well. We don't want to divide our firepower."

"Yes, sir!"

"Keep on it, Lieutenant Chainer. I'll take over the comms to the *Archimedes*."

"Aye, sir."

Duggan pushed the *Crimson*'s sub-light engines to one hundred percent, angrily shrugging off the now-familiar dizziness. The *Archimedes* wasn't a slow vessel, but it fell quickly behind. Duggan had no idea how the Ghasts had managed to find them so far away from the usual arena of conflict between the two sides. They always seemed to be two steps ahead. They always had something in reserve, or a new weapon to keep the Corps ships on the back foot.

"Flagship *Archimedes*, this is Captain Duggan. ESS *Crimson* armed and ready to engage. Please instruct."

"I'm reading you, ESS *Crimson*. Protect the *Archimedes*. Repeat, protect the *Archimedes*."

"Understood. We're moving to intercept the approaching Oblivion."

"Anderlechts *Fixation* and *Lambast* assisting the *Precept*, sir," said Chainer. "*Delectable* out of sensor sight. The *Extermination* is under fire. Shit, nearly two hundred missiles heading their way. They've returned with ninety-six of their own. Impacts in less than thirty seconds."

Duggan's mind raced through the possibilities. The two Oblivions and three Cadaverons were outgunned by the Corps ships in the vicinity. The Ghasts didn't always act in an expected manner, but they hadn't shown themselves prone to suicide. There was only one conclusion – the enemy believed their new technology was sufficient to overcome the conventional armaments carried by the Corps vessels.

"The *Archimedes* will soon be within the estimated range of their new missiles," said Chainer. "The Oblivion's course indicates that's what they're intending. The Cadaveron's keeping close by. I'd guess they're going to ignore us and go for the big prize."

"Use the disruptor as soon as we're in range."

"That'll take our fission engines close to zero."

"We're not planning on going anywhere, Lieutenant."

"They've launched!" said Chainer. "Four missiles heading for the *Archimedes*."

"Disruptors fired."

"Fission engines at three percent and rising."

"Positron output from the Oblivion has dropped to almost zero, sir."

"Let's get close and say hello," said Duggan.

"The *ES Precept*'s taken a hit, sir. It's hard to tell the damage through the interference from her countermeasures. She's not close enough to fire Lambdas in response. The *Extermination* looks in a bad way. All six Bulwarks still firing. They've scored some hits. There's a big leak from the Cadaveron nearest to them."

The bulkhead viewscreen lit up in a flash of pure, incandescent white. The darkness of space was dispersed as countless launch ports along the *Archimedes*' flank opened up to send out a dense cloud of shock drones and pulsing plasma flares.

"Get through that, you bastards!" shouted Chainer.

Duggan wasn't convinced. These new missiles from the Ghasts had ignored their countermeasures before. It didn't seem likely they'd start crashing into the shock drones now.

"Our Cadaveron is almost within Lambda range."

"Hold onto our missiles. I want that Oblivion."

The bridge lights dimmed and a spray of interference speckled across the screen. "They've tried to shut us down with their disruptors," said Breeze. "They're out of luck."

"The Cadaveron's launching at us. Forty missiles from their front batteries," said Chainer. The Lieutenant was in danger of becoming swamped by information. There were times when you needed more than one comms man.

"Lieutenant Chainer, leave the weapons reports to Commander McGlashan."

"Sir."

"Commander, hold off the shock drones until we're close. I don't want us to overtake our own countermeasures. Then give us two fast bursts. Fire at the Oblivion as soon as you're able."

"We're in range. Seventy-two Lambdas on their way."

"There's a positron surge from their engines, sir," said Breeze. "They're coming back online. That's short of a full minute."

"Bigger ship," grunted Duggan, pulling the *Crimson* away out of range. There was no way he wanted to give the Oblivion a chance to unleash a broadside.

"Beam strike across our engines. Coming from the Oblivion" said Breeze. "We're five percent down."

"Drones away. No return missile fire from the Oblivion. Their Vule cannons are firing and they're throwing out plasma flares." McGlashan almost sounded impressed. "They're packing a lot of weaponry."

"The *Extermination*'s full of holes, sir. She's going to break up," said Chainer. "*Fixation* and *Lambast* are firing on the first Oblivion. Something's wrong with the *Precept*."

"She's drifting," said Breeze. "I can patch into her engine readouts from here. They have zero output."

"They've been hit by a disruptor," said Duggan.

"Second drone cloud launched, sir. Take us to a horizontal so the front Bulwarks can target."

Duggan adjusted the *Crimson*'s heading, in order that they could bring more of the rapid-fire cannons to bear against the incoming missiles. From the corner of his eye, he saw the four missiles from the Oblivion on his tactical readout. They were passing through the *Archimedes*' countermeasures.

"The Cadaveron's sending us another sixty. Our drone cloud has thinned out the first wave." McGlashan clapped her hands together, the sound loud and crisp. "Yes! Five successful Lambda strikes on the Oblivion! Three in their engines."

"Come on!" said Chainer to himself. Sweat dripped from his hair and he wiped it away with the back of his sleeve.

Duggan had taken the *Crimson* far above the Cadaveron. They were much faster than the Ghast vessel and he intended to keep between the *Archimedes* and the enemy craft. He'd taken them to a position from which the enemy short-range missiles could no longer target them. It wouldn't protect them from the sixty that were still inbound, but there'd be no more for the moment.

"We're out of the Oblivion's missile range. Also outside of the longest reported Ghast beam range," said Chainer. He could be jumpy sometimes, but in a real pinch he was deadly calm.

The walls of the bridge shook and there was a harsh metal-edged roar. Given their trajectory, they could only get five of the *Crimson*'s eight Bulwark cannons pointing towards the incoming Ghast missiles. Everyone held their breaths until the firing stopped.

"First wave destroyed," said McGlashan. Then the bad news. "The *Archimedes* has been hit. Four successful strikes, I think."

"I wonder what the payload is of those missiles," said Breeze. "They must be all engine to travel so far. There might be no room for a big warhead." He looked up. "Our fission engines at forty percent." The words came almost as an afterthought.

Duggan was desperate to know how quickly the Ghasts could

reload for another try. He'd seen the Ghast long-range missiles a few times, but on each occasion the engagement had been finished before they'd completed a second launch. There were several reasons why the Ghasts might not be able to fire them rapidly. Duggan kept his fingers crossed that it was a technical limitation.

"Shock drones on their way," said McGlashan. "We're running low on them, sir."

"We're running low on everything, Commander. Launch more."

"Away they go."

"The *Archimedes* is powering up her fission drive, sir. I don't think they're going to stick around."

Duggan opened a channel. "*Archimedes*, this is *Crimson*. I'm reading a fission build-up from your engines."

"We've got four big holes in our side. Four *real* big holes." The comms man's voice carried an edge of panic. No one on the *Archimedes* expected to die in combat.

"What're our orders?" Duggan spoke sharply, trying to make the man forget his fear.

"I don't know, sir."

"Find out, then!"

Duggan cut the channel. The vibration started again, an almost imperceptible thrumming that resonated through every-thing. The Bulwarks were firing at the second wave of Ghast missiles. An idea came to Duggan and he rapidly plugged in some instructions to the *Crimson*'s mainframe. He was deter-mined that this encounter would not become a disaster from which the Space Corps might never recover.

There was a rumbling sound. Deep and violent, it washed through the spacecraft. A split second later, there was another. A siren started on the bridge and a red light began to cycle from a dark hue to a lighter one and back.

"We've taken two hits aft," said McGlashan. She looked as grim-faced as Duggan felt.

"Damage report!"

"Collating the information," said Breeze.

"The Oblivion's launched another wave of long-range missiles. Four on their way." McGlashan stuttered for the briefest of moments. "We've launched two of our nukes. Sir?"

"If nothing else will target their missiles, maybe we need to try something with a bit less finesse." Duggan gave her a tight smile.

He looked back at his console. The Cadaveron had changed its course to try and intercept them. It was too late and the enemy ship was far behind them. The Lambda strikes on the Oblivion's engines had evidently done some damage and the battleship was running at less than half of its expected velocity. The Archimedes had changed course and was heading directly away from the conflict, to buy some time for her fission drives to build up.

"Sir, the Precept's back online. They're readying their fission drives," said Breeze.

"Not going to make it," muttered Chainer.

"Fission engines lighting up everywhere. The whole damn lot of them are preparing to go."

A voice broke into Duggan's ear. It was one of the comms men from the Archimedes, belatedly telling him what everyone else seemed to already know. "Sir, you're ordered to leave the scene of the conflict. Your destination is the New Earth Capital Shipyard. Good luck."

The line went dead, just in time for Duggan to hear Breeze read out the damage report from the two missile strikes. "We've got two big holes in our armour. Only one breach through to the fission engines. Negligible damage and a small antimatter leak." Breeze puffed loudly, the relief evident. "Our aft plating's going to look like a lump of cheese and we'd best hope we don't take another hit anywhere close."

"Prepare us for a lightspeed jump, Lieutenant," ordered Duggan.

"Course, sir?"

Duggan spat the words out. "New Earth Capital Shipyard."

"Dialling in the coordinates."

Even while he talked and listened, Duggan's head and hands never stopped moving as he continued to make adjustments to the *Crimson*'s trajectory. To one side, the two nukes he'd launched showed up as amber points on his tactical display. They described a smooth path along the course he'd set them, painfully slow compared to the much faster Ghast missiles.

"Too slow," he said to himself. "I took too long."

It was turning into a disaster for the Corps ships and Duggan found anger building within him, sweeping away the calmness. Without taking his eyes from the nukes, he used the *Crimson*'s override to force a channel directly to Admiral Slender. "Sir, it's Captain Duggan."

Slender showed no surprise at the intrusion. "What is it, Captain?" There was hostility, clear in the curtness of his voice.

"We're getting the crap beaten out of us here, sir. What are the unlock codes for our weapons systems?"

There was a pause, so slight that Duggan wasn't sure it had been there. "The *Archimedes* is badly damaged! Don't you think I'd have told you them if I'd known? Don't you think I'd have had someone transmit you those codes?"

"Sir, I really don't know what you'd have done."

"Damn you, man! There are no codes! We could only get the disruptors working! The final weapons systems on the *Crimson* have never worked!"

"Thirty seconds till we can go," said Breeze. "Fission drives at one hundred percent. It's going to be rough."

On Duggan's screen, the two amber dots and the four red dots of the enemy missiles coincided. The rest of the tactical map remained a crowd of missile reports and status updates, but the six dots he'd been watching vanished and didn't reappear.

"The nukes have detonated. Enemy missiles disabled or destroyed," said McGlashan almost absently. She was watching Duggan.

"We've got someone else coming to the party," said Chainer. "Whatever it is, it's a big bastard. There's nothing on the Corps transit log. It's definitely not one of ours."

Breeze had picked it up. "That's bigger than big. Sir, we need to get out of here. All of us."

Duggan heard, but didn't take his focus away from Admiral Slender. He was sure that the man was telling him the truth, which made it all the more galling that there'd been such secrecy.

"Why didn't Admiral Teron tell me there was no functioning extra weaponry in the first place, sir?"

Slender didn't answer the question. "Bring the *Crimson* to the New Earth Capital shipyard for dismantling, Captain Duggan. Those are your orders. If that vessel suffers any more damage, I'll have you dismissed from the Corps and this time you won't be able to wriggle out of it." The channel went silent – Slender had ended the conversation.

"A new Ghost warship has entered the arena, sir." Chainer sounded shocked. "It's...huge."

"Record whatever data you can, Lieutenant. We're not going to stick around to shake hands."

"The *Archimedes*, *Fixation* and *Lambast* have gone to lightspeed. They must have synchronised."

"The *Precept* tried to go and failed," said Breeze. "She's taken too much damage."

In the last second before the *ESS Crimson* tore its way violently into lightspeed, Duggan saw two images that would

229

haunt him forever. The first was the sight of the new Ghast spaceship. The unknown vessel was at least ten kilometres long, its hull an ugly mass of lumps, curves and weaponry. The second image was of the Hadron *ES Precept*, smashed into a million different pieces, each part beginning its own endless journey through space.

The force of the acceleration pushed Duggan hard into his seat. An unseen hand clenched itself around his body and squeezed. He struggled to breathe and his ribcage felt as if it would splinter, sending needle-sharp slivers of bone into his lungs. Unconsciousness came quickly, utterly denying his resistance.

CHAPTER TWENTY-EIGHT

DUGGAN WASN'T sure how long he was out. When he came to, his head was pounding and his body ached. He coughed and felt a pain across his chest, and the taste of blood was strong in his mouth. He summoned up his strength and sat upright, doing his best to ignore the dizziness. McGlashan was stirring, while Breeze snored loudly at his console.

"Commander?"

"Damn I feel like crap," she said. "Can't we do something to the engines to cut their output before we enter lightspeed? I'd rather go at seventy-five percent and accelerate afterwards, than start off at full power."

Duggan's brain wasn't ready for the challenge of the question. "I'll put your idea to Lieutenant Breeze when he wakes up," he said.

A few minutes later, Duggan was feeling much better. McGlashan was alert, but hadn't ventured out of her seat and Breeze was trying to operate his console with trembling hands. Chainer was still unconscious, though his pulse was strong and he showed no sign of injury.

Duggan checked in with Sergeant Ortiz. No one was seriously hurt, though Corporal Blunt had used his battlefield adrenaline syringe on three of the men.

"I'm sure they're faking it in order to get a jab, sir," said Ortiz with a degree of humour that Duggan wasn't feeling himself. "They try that adrenaline once when they're properly hurt and then they want it every time they break a fingernail."

"I'm pleased everything is fine," said Duggan. "Send Corporal Blunt here when he's finished up with the squad."

The words had scarcely left his mouth when Lieutenant Chainer began to groan. He coughed a couple of times and then opened his eyes.

"Whose side is this spaceship on?" he asked.

"Sergeant Ortiz?" said Duggan, catching her before she could go. "Belay that order. There's no need to send Corporal Blunt."

"Roger that, sir."

The next few minutes were filled with curses and grunts as the crew of the bridge tried to recover from the trauma their bodies had been subjected to.

"Those holes in our rear haven't slowed us down," said Breeze. "We're just about on Light-V. At this speed, we'll reach New Earth in just shy of seven days. We'll be able to fit in a week's vacation before the *Archimedes* gets there and she's not exactly slow."

"We really took a kicking back there," said Chainer. "The *Archimedes* didn't even get a shot off and now the *Precept's* gone. The Ghast disruptor managed to shut down an entire Hadron, sir."

"The Ghasts are way ahead of us, Lieutenant. We already knew that. This was just a demonstration of the fact."

"I know, sir. Sometimes you don't need your face rubbing into the dirt to know that it'll feel like crap."

Duggan understood what Chainer was trying to say. "Let's

count this as the beginning of a new war. We're facing a much more powerful foe and we're going to do everything we can to beat them. They have the upper hand, but every day that passes we'll get stronger. And if we can live long enough, one day we'll show them what happens to the Space Corps' enemies."

"They've already found out what happens to those who come up against the *Crimson!*" said Chainer.

"I wonder how long it'll take them to refit the old girl once we reach the shipyard," said McGlashan, refusing to get drawn into Chainer's sudden optimism. "I'd love to be assigned here again once they've updated it."

"I don't even know if they'll bother," said Duggan.

"You said before that they'll upgrade all the old tech," said McGlashan. It wasn't quite an accusation.

"The existing life support system should be good enough if they put in some standard engines," said Chainer. "No more blacking out for the men and women of the *Crimson*."

Duggan sighed. "I said they'd probably upgrade it. That was before I heard what Admiral Teron said about the Confederation going to total war. If there's no shipyard left to take the hull, they might pull it apart. I'm sure they could re-use some of the plating. There'll be an assessment by someone who's never seen the inside of a ship before and who's more interested in the cost. That person may decide to break the *Crimson* for scrap."

"Well, we've had some good times," said McGlashan, brightening. You couldn't keep her down for long. "We kicked some butt, that's for sure."

"That we did," agreed Duggan.

"Want me to call Monsey up here?" she asked suddenly. "We've got a week to try and get some answers from those data arrays."

Duggan smiled, though he didn't feel in the mood, He idly called up the top-level access menu for the blocked memory banks. He saw something which made him sit upright and look closely.

"What is it?" asked McGlashan, noticing his interest.

"Have a look at this," he said. She came over and leaned across.

"Four data arrays, four menu options," she said.

"Four data arrays, two of which are hidden," Duggan replied. "We shouldn't even know they're there." He punched up the option for one of the arrays. A series of sub-lists appeared immediately.

"How?" asked McGlashan.

"I don't know." He checked a few things on the file security. "You said the secondary core did some kind of data restore. Whatever it did, the file security has been removed in the process."

"Assuming the backup files even had the security in the first place," she replied.

"It doesn't matter. Let's have a look at what we've found."

"What about Admiral Slender's orders, sir?"

"I remember his words quite clearly, Commander. He told me I was not to make any further attempt to breach the databanks. These databanks are already open, so there's no need to breach anything."

"Aye, sir."

"Let's start on the third array," said Duggan.

There was a lot of information, but it was easy enough to search through when they used the right keywords. The more Duggan found, the colder he became, until the heat of the bridge wasn't enough to keep him warm. He looked at McGlashan and saw his own fears reflected in her eyes.

"This is...dynamite," she said.

"It's worrying," said Duggan.

"So, they found all this stuff – this wreckage – just floating around in space somewhere and decided to try and patch it into a spacecraft? Without having the first idea of what it was?"

"It appears that they had a good idea about what most of it was, Commander. They just weren't able to copy it."

"And they think they can now?"

"We've moved on since they found the pieces. If we can't copy it, I think we can safely assume that mankind is going to be exterminated by the Ghasts."

"What're you talking about?" asked Chainer. He looked across at Breeze. "Don't keep us waiting."

Duggan took a deep breath. "The *Crimson* isn't entirely a manmade warship," he said. "A little over a seventy years ago, one of our scout ships found some wreckage near to the Helius Blackstar."

"Helius Blackstar?"

"It's a wormhole," said Breeze. "You fly in one end and you reappear somewhere else without any time elapsing. At least that's the theory. In reality, you throw something in there and it gets crushed by the gravity. There are five or six wormholes catalogued throughout Confederation space. I think we gave up trying to figure out how to survive a trip through one decades ago."

"It looks like *something* got through the Helius Blackstar," said Duggan. "Maybe it got destroyed on the way. The point is, it actually made the transit, broke up and left pieces of itself strewn across local space in the vicinity."

"You mean something that wasn't the Ghasts?"

"The technology was completely unknown. They hauled the pieces back to the labs for study. The trouble was, what they'd found was so far advanced, the scientists had no way of reproducing it. It was made of new materials, crafted in ways we couldn't even comprehend. They assumed it had come from an unknown race of beings, living somewhere a long way distant from us."

"Aliens. I wonder if they're anything like the Ghasts."

"They gave this unknown species the name *Dreamers*. There's no indication why they chose that name."

"Couldn't they have just pulled this new technology apart for a closer look?" asked Chainer after he'd thought about it for a moment.

"Have you ever owned a watch, Lieutenant?"

Chainer looked confused. "Sure, I had one when I was a kid."

"Did you ever take it apart to look at what was inside?"

"Yeah."

"What happened when you tried to put it back together?"

"I see what you mean. I took it apart and all the pieces wouldn't fit back in the case."

"I think the scientists decided the technology was better in one piece."

"Why'd they decide to shove it into the hull of a ship? Shouldn't they have left it in a lab somewhere?"

Duggan wasn't sure. He spoke, in the hope that his words would coalesce into something that made sense. "The Space Corps found the wreckage and they kept it. Did the Hynus project come about to make use of the alien technology, or did they use the funding for Hynus as a way of trying to meld our existing technology with the new? I don't have the answers. The information in the data arrays is all over the place. Memos here, research notes there. It's hard to build the complete picture."

"I know what I believe," said McGlashan. They all looked at her and she continued. "If you ask me, the people at the top couldn't stomach the idea of leaving a load of new toys sitting in a warehouse somewhere, waiting for someone in the future to put to use and claim all the glory. I'll bet my eye teeth they decided to put it into the *Crimson* to show what high and mighty bastards they were."

Duggan could be cynical at times, but McGlashan's outburst surprised him. There again, her theory had a certain appeal, such that he found it hard to discount it entirely.

"What happened to the *Crimson*?" asked Chainer eventually. "Why'd it hide itself in that cave?"

"We're still trying to find out," said McGlashan. "There's the entirety of the fourth array to search."

"Don't let me keep you," said Chainer.

For the next eighteen hours, Duggan and McGlashan kept up the search. The longer they spent, the more they uncovered from the past. Halfway through, they had to take a break and although Duggan did his best to sleep, he found it difficult to rest. His mind continued to work feverishly and even when he finally drifted off, his sleep was disturbed by the vivid images in his head.

By the time he was done, Duggan sat back in his chair, exhausted. He didn't have all the details, but he was sure he'd found most of the relevant facts. Everything seemed to be linked – the Ghasts, the *Crimson* and this unknown alien species. He just couldn't see where the connections lay.

"How far from the Helius Blackstar are we?" he asked.

"At current speed? Just over eight days. Then another five to get to New Earth from there."

"Change our course and take us there. Admiral Slender and his threats be damned!"

CHAPTER TWENTY-NINE

WITH ITS NEW direction programmed into the navigation system, the *ESS Crimson* skimmed its way through space. Onboard, the crew sat, lost in their own thoughts. The bridge stank of coffee and sweat and Duggan's flesh prickled beneath his uniform.

Chainer was the first to speak. "You're saying the *Crimson* actually fought one of these Dreamer spaceships?"

"It's all there in the combat log." Duggan shifted in his chair. It was suddenly hard to get comfortable. "It launched over a thousand of its missiles and fired the disruptors eight times. The *Crimson*'s sensors logged a kill and recorded the Dreamer craft breaking up. Its last trajectory would place the remains on a planet near to where we found the *Crimson*."

"That Dreamer ship must have been one tough bastard to have mopped up a thousand Lambdas. What did it look like?"

"Dark green, that's the only details the sensors captured."

"Dark green? What's that all about?"

"I don't know. If I had to guess, I'd say the Dreamer vessel was protected by some kind of field that made it difficult for the sensors to pick it up."

"That's part of the reason the *Crimson* fired so many missiles," said McGlashan. "Each missile had its targeting system disabled in order to fire them out in a straight line. Without guidance."

"That'd be like trying to throw a ball into a cup from two hundred yards away," said Breeze. "The number of calculations needed to try and predict the enemy movement would be astronomical."

"We have a lot of processing power onboard, Lieutenant. Even so, it took a lot of attempts. Over a thousand missiles. We can't even guess if the disruptors worked," said Duggan.

Breeze let out a low whistle. "This is nuts."

"On top of that, the *Crimson* tried to fire its last, unknown weapon. The one that Admiral Slender said the Corps engineers couldn't figure out."

"Why didn't it work?" asked Breeze.

"The *Crimson*'s mainframe registered some type of jamming. Maybe that's not the right word. It tried to fire and it was prevented from doing so."

"Prevented? You mean by the alien ship or something?" asked Chainer.

"We're guessing," said McGlashan. "However, the combat logs show that the jamming wasn't directed against the weapon itself. Rather, it seems as if the first core tried to fire and the second core prevented it."

"Or refused to do so," said Duggan.

"The ship's own core refused to fire?"

"Not exactly. The Hynus-T battle computer tried to fire and was overruled by the Dreamer core," said McGlashan. "I've spoken to Monsey and had her run some checks. Several of the major functions on this ship are initiated by the human-built

mainframe and then passed on to the Dreamer core for processing. That's part of the reason the *Crimson* is so fast – the alien
computer is magnitudes quicker at shaping the engine output, for
example. It has a lot of grunt."

"The implication worries me," said Duggan. "It suggests the
weapon might be so devastating that the Dreamer core would
have preferred to risk its own destruction in combat, rather than
let it be fired."

"What was it doing in the cave? Why not just come home?
And why didn't the Corps send anyone out looking for it? Like
really look for it?"

"They did look for it - Admiral Teron said as much. We saw
how well it was hidden. Maybe they had to abandon the search.
It could even be they had to call off the search before someone in
the Confederation Council got wind of it. After all, they'd lost
the most significant discovery mankind has ever made."

"Great. They swept it under the rug," said Chainer. "Don't
you just love the men in charge?"

"As for why it was in the cave? The mainframe was damaged
and there was substantial other damage. I think it was acting to
preserve its own existence by hiding until it could send out its
message. *Prepare for war*. It wasn't talking about the Ghasts. It
was talking about the Dreamers. We could be facing two
enemies, each of them more advanced than we are."

The crew didn't look happy at Duggan's revelation. Eventually, it was Breeze who spoke, his voice calm and quiet. "We need
that weapon, don't we, Captain?" he said. "Something to keep us
in the game."

"We need something, Lieutenant. We're staring down the
barrel of a gun."

"Then why are we going to the Helius Blackstar?" said
Chainer. "We've got an idea of what's gone on. Shouldn't we get
on our way to New Earth and let the engineers take over? I mean,

they might be able to get it to work. Instead, we're taking the long route."

"We need answers. At the very least, I'd like to know what the enemy vessel looked like. There might be clues and wreckage we can scan. We'll be delayed by six or seven days taking this diversion. The *Archimedes* will arrive at a similar time. They can't broadcast from lightspeed to ask where we are. I guarantee that if we fly straight to the New Earth Capital Shipyard, the *Crimson* will sit untouched in a dock until Admiral Slender arrives to give instructions."

"Won't someone in the Confederation Council take charge?"

"I very much doubt they know about the recovery of the *Crimson*. They might not even be aware it was ever built. Rest assured, Lieutenant, if anyone is hauled before a court martial for this, it'll be me."

"Everything's screwed up," said Chainer.

"Everything but us, Lieutenant," said McGlashan.

As the days passed, the stress built amongst the crew. Duggan could feel it in the hot and claustrophobic atmosphere. Tempers were short and he could feel that they were one wrong comment away from being at each other's throats. He ordered them to take turns away from the bridge, doing whatever they did to let off steam when they were off duty. There was no gym on the *Crimson* and it was sorely missed. It made him realise how tough it must be for his soldiers, cooped up in their bunks for hours on end.

"No one said war would be easy," he growled to himself, wondering if the pressure was getting to him as well. He'd told Breeze they were looking for answers. In reality, he didn't know exactly what answers he was hoping to find and on more than one occasion, he was confronted by the urge to change their course to New Earth.

On the third day, he had an idea and called Monsey to the

bridge. She arrived, looking as keen as ever and carrying her box of semi-legal computer hardware.

"What did you find out about the *Crimson*'s secondary core?" he asked. "Before you got into those data arrays."

"Just what I told you, sir. It's damned fast. I'd bet everything I own it's something different to the usual nano-cores. It'd rip the AIs on the *Juniper* into shreds at most tasks. At a few bits and pieces, it's surprisingly slow."

"It's fully interfaced with the front mainframe?"

"If you asking me whether it speaks in numbers and can understand instructions given in numbers, then yes it does and yes it can. There are a few differences and there're a dozen hardware interpreters to allow the front and back to shake hands properly. It's a Ghast computer, isn't it, sir? Just goes to show, biological creatures make up their own languages, but wherever you go, computers speak the same."

Duggan smiled. He didn't want to lie. "No soldier, it's not a Ghast computer."

Monsey was wise enough that she didn't ask anything more about it. "Okay, sir. What do you want me to do with it?"

"We're carrying a weapons system that I want to access. The secondary core is hiding that weapon away. I have reason to believe that it will also prevent the weapon from firing should I ever require it."

"The rebellion of the machines, huh? My old man always warned me it would happen."

"I need you to see if you can find out how it's happened and how I can override it. After all, I am the captain of this ship."

"Right you are, sir. I'll plug in and get back to where I left off. I'll warn you – the data arrays were stored on the Hynus-T mainframe and that was quick enough to make the hacking a real test. This other core? That's something else entirely. I could grow old and die before I get around its defences. This bootbox works on brute force. It's good, but there's only so much it can do."

"Do what you can, soldier. We have no choice."

On the eighth day, the *Crimson* emerged from lightspeed into a position close to its destination. The arrivals were easier to handle than the departures, much to the relief of the crew.

"Sir, It's just clicked what this place is," said Breeze. "It's called the Hynus solar system. They might not have found names for the planets, but they sure as hell found a name for the sun."

"A short jump from the Helius Blackstar," said Duggan. "This is where it all began."

"For the *Crimson* at least," said McGlashan.

"The combat logs show that the engagement with the Dreamer vessel took place on the tenth planet. It's approximately the same size as Earth and we'll reach a high orbit in less than one hour. Hynus is a big sun and we're a long way out." He called up the image of the planet on the bulkhead screen. It was unusually large given how far away it was from the sun. It radiated an icy blue that made Duggan feel cold just by looking at it. "There we have it. The alien craft fell somewhere onto the surface."

"Scanning it now, sir," said Chainer. "It looks serene from the main screen. When you look closer, it's a tempest. Average temperature close to minus two hundred and forty degrees Celsius. Snow, ice, mountains and not much else."

"We don't have suitable kit to let us disembark, so surface work is out of the question. I wouldn't like to risk it with a normal spacesuit," said Duggan. "I'm going to take us into a mid-orbit and we're going to scan the surface. If there's anything unusual or unexpected, we're going to try our best to find out what it is."

"We have more sensors than the *Detriment* carried, sir. However, I don't know if they've been adapted for this kind of work. Things have moved on since they built the *Crimson*. Every ship in the fleet is now expected to take topographical readings whenever they're in orbit. It might not have been a priority fifty or sixty years ago. There's a lot of surface interference for us to look through."

"We'll have to make do with what we've got, Lieutenant. If there's anyone that can make sense of incomplete sensor readings, it's you."

"Aye sir!" said Chainer.

The planet loomed ahead and Duggan took the *Crimson* to an orbit ten thousand klicks above the surface. He hoped Chainer's pessimistic suggestion about the sensors would prove to be false.

"I'm owed a bit of luck," he said.

"What's that sir?" asked McGlashan.

"I said I'm keeping my fingers crossed that we don't end up circling the planet for days on end before we locate anything of interest."

McGlashan was aware of the consequences for Duggan if he was caught disobeying Admiral Slender's orders and she nodded at him. "Fingers and toes, sir."

"How fast can I go?" Duggan asked.

"I'm already getting gaps in the readings, sir," Chainer replied. "I think you should slow down. A one-hour orbit should allow us to gather what we need."

Duggan gritted his teeth at that, since the *Crimson* would comfortably do a full orbit of a planet this small in five minutes, depending on the height and hull temperature. "One hour orbit it is," he said. "How many till we've covered everything?"

"I'd say twelve if we come across any excessively mountainous areas. Ten if it's all flat rock."

With his knuckles white from their grip on the control sticks, Duggan got on with it.

CHAPTER THIRTY

AFTER TWO HOURS, Duggan relented and activated the recently-repaired autopilot. It almost felt like he was betraying himself, but he was relieved that he could take a break from sitting in the same position. Chainer was drinking what must have been his ninth cup of coffee since they'd begun the search. The man seemed to have an infinite capacity for the stuff.

"What've we got, Lieutenant?"

"We're getting a pretty good picture of what's down there. It's just slow. There're lots of mountains. It's like the entire planet is one big, damned mountain range. It's hard for the sensors to pick up details from their shadows in a single pass."

"Give me the bad news."

"We might need ten full circuits and then you might need to turn around and do another seven or eight in the opposite direction." Chainer put his half-empty cup down. "Unless you can think of a way to limit the amount of terrain we have to cover? Like when you guessed the *Crimson* might be under the surface. That gave us something to home in on."

Duggan sat back in his seat to ponder the words. An idea jumped into his head.

"Commander, can you locate the precise time and date on which the *Crimson* engaged the Dreamer vessel?"

"Checking."

"When you have that, use it to determine the exact rotational position of this planet at the time of the engagement. Lieutenant Chainer, I want you to take a break from what you're doing. I'm sending you a link to the *Crimson*'s sensor logs. There's a plot of the debris as it fell. I need you to combine that with Commander McGlashan's information. There's a chance it will show which area of the planet the wreckage fell onto."

It took some time until they came up with an answer. There wasn't quite enough data to make it a straightforward calculation and there was some guesswork involved.

"I'd say it came down here, Commander. What do you say?"

"I'd agree with your assessment, Lieutenant."

"Where do we need to go?" asked Duggan, turning off the autopilot.

"I've sent you the coordinates." Chainer grimaced. "It's an area that was on our second-last planned orbit. We may have saved ourselves ten hours of looking at mountains and snow."

"Some good news at last," said Duggan. He increased power to the gravity drive and completed a half-circuit of the planet in two minutes, leaving the hull glowing like a sullen ember.

"We are able to pin it down to a fairly narrow area," said Chainer. "A few thousand square kilometres. If you go low and slow over the area, I should be able to get what we need in a single pass."

Duggan followed Chainer's suggestion and reduced the *Crimson*'s speed to what felt like a crawl. They were less than two thousand klicks up, yet the bulkhead screen showed no more detail than it had from a much higher orbit. The surface was a bleak and featureless white. Any variation was invisible to the naked eye.

"What's it like down there, Lieutenant?" he asked.

"Rough, sir. Really rough. There's a storm right beneath us. If we were in a smaller ship and a bit lower than we are, you might have a tougher job keeping us steady. I'm going to have to tweak the sensors a bit. You get a lot more play with these old models. With the new ones, you have to do what you're told." Chainer went quiet. Duggan turned to look. The lieutenant's face had gone completely white, as if he'd seen an army of ghosts run across the bridge. Duggan realised at once he was about to hear something disastrous.

"What's wrong?" he asked, urgency in his voice.

"You need to look at this, sir. You need to look at it *now*."

Duggan sprang from his chair and stood at Chainer's shoulder. "Tell me."

"We're broadcasting, sir. We shouldn't be broadcasting, but we are."

"Tell me clearly, Lieutenant!"

"It's the sensors, sir. They send and receive external data and then pass it on to the mainframe. I was playing around with them to try and get a better picture of the surface, when I noticed one of them send out a ping. Just a single ping."

"Where did it go?"

"I don't know, sir. I don't even know if it was aimed anywhere."

"We're a vessel of war. We should be running on silent! Check the rest of the sensors in the same way. Do it now!"

"There's nothing. They're all quiet. Hang on, we sent another ping. From a different sensor."

"Does it contain any data? Anything about us?"

"No specific data, sir," said Chainer miserably. "Except if you happen to pick up that ping, you'll be able to find out exactly where it's come from."

"What's giving the instruction to send? Stop it at once!" Duggan said. He realised his voice had climbed louder than he'd intended. "Find out what it is, Lieutenant," he finished.

"We're in the shit, aren't we?" said McGlashan.

"Yes, Commander. We're deep in it," he said. "If the Ghasts can read those pings, there's a good chance we led them straight to the *Juniper* and the *Archimedes*. There we were happily doing our duty, congratulating ourselves on a job well done, when all the while we were sending out signals to every enemy vessel that was listening!"

"Sir? The instruction to send out the pings is coming from the mainframe. They're going out at semi-random intervals from random sensors."

"Block it at once," said Duggan.

"I can't, sir. I've traced the command through the Hynus-T and it's coming from the interface with the Dreamer core."

Duggan almost punched the nearest wall. "The damned alien computer's sending out an SOS! They put it into one of our spacecraft without guessing it might have an automated distress beacon, like every one of our warships! Who knows how long it's been sending?" He took a deep breath. "What do we think? Is it nothing more than an automatic response? Or is there an intention behind it?"

"I think we have to assume it's automated, sir. A call for help and nothing more."

Duggan caught sight of Monsey. "There you go, soldier. It's an alien computer, just not one that belongs to the Ghasts. We need access to it, or at least we need something that allows the front mainframe to take precedence. We have to override whatever locks or hard-coded instructions it's been programmed with."

She met his eyes, not afraid to tell him the truth. "I can't stop it, sir. I might never be able to crack it. If I had a billion times the horsepower I'd be able to give you some good news."

"We don't have a billion times the horsepower," he said. Monsey put her head down and started at her keyboard again.

Duggan paced the two or three steps there was room for. "We can't go anywhere until we can stop the pings. We might lead the Ghasts right to our position."

"At least you'll be saved from a court martial, sir," said McGlashan. "They can't prosecute you for saving humanity. Just think what might have happened if we'd gone straight to New Earth."

"They won't care about unintended, positive consequences. They'll prosecute me for gross dereliction in not finding out sooner." He swept the matter aside. "There'll be time to think about it later. For the moment, we're unable to go anywhere until I can think of a way out of this mess." He felt suddenly weary all the way into his bones.

"Want me to go back to scanning the surface, sir?" asked Chainer.

"May as well, Lieutenant. We can at least accomplish what we came here for."

For a time, the clattering of Monsey's keyboard and the humming of the ship's engines was the only sound. Then, Chainer spoke. "Sir, I'm seeing an unusual pattern on the surface."

"What do we have?" asked Duggan.

"These scars in the rock here aren't consistent with any natural formations. There have been a number of impacts and the geological data suggests they're comparatively fresh."

"Fifty years fresh?"

"Give or take. But look, where the impact scars terminate, you'd expect to see signs of whatever caused them. These three here are all clean. There's nothing there."

"Could the Dreamer craft have vaporised with the force of the impact?" asked Duggan.

"If the pieces were big enough to make these indentations, then they'd leave evidence if they broke up. There'd be something for us to see. I've run a close-in scan of the first area and there's nothing."

"Run a check on this new area over here," said Duggan, pointing to another area of the surface.

Chainer ran a number of commands. He frowned and ran another command. One of his screens zoomed in on something. He looked up at Duggan. "I'm sure you know what that is, sir."

"A Ghast dropship," said Duggan.

"It looks pretty badly beaten up and it's buried beneath forty metres of ice and snow. If I had to guess, I'd say they crash landed and couldn't get back up to their mothership."

"The Ghasts have been here? What does that mean?" asked Breeze.

"What it suggests to me, is that the Ghasts found the remains of the Dreamer spaceship, Lieutenant. They were behind our technology curve for most of the war. It's only fairly recently they've surpassed us and they've made astounding leaps. From the evidence we've got here, it's clear the Ghasts have taken away the Dreamer wreckage and have succeeded in making copies of it."

"Let me get this straight," said Chainer. "The Confederation found the remains of a Dreamer ship floating next to the Helius Blackstar. We made a spaceship out of it. That same spaceship then shot down a *second* hostile Dreamer vessel, which the Ghasts found and are now using to kick the crap out of humanity?"

"I'd say that covers the likely situation quite nicely, Lieutenant," said Duggan.

"That would also explain why there are so many Ghast ships

in this sector," said Breeze. "I wonder if they're stupid enough to go looking for another Dreamer ship to cannibalise."

"Why else would they still be here?" asked McGlashan. "I'll bet this is a regular patrol route for them now. Take a flyby every two weeks and see if there's another alien vessel to shoot at or strip down for parts."

McGlashan's words drove home to Duggan the danger they were in if they stayed here any longer than they needed to. "It doesn't seem likely that the Ghasts missed anything," he said. "Have you got enough scan data to finish up your search at a later time?"

"I've got what I need," Chainer confirmed.

"Does anyone have any preferences as to where we go?" asked Duggan. "A nice, warm planet somewhere far away from humanity, where we can put our feet up?"

"None that I can think of," said McGlashan. Her brow furrowed. "Sir, we've still got the repair bot onboard. The one we carried on the *Detriment*."

"Yes, it's inactive in the hold, waiting for something else to break."

"I can re-programme it to physically shut down the sensors if you want. It'll take me a few hours to make the changes and then it'll take the bot a few more hours to interface with each one and disable it."

"What else do we have to do with our time, eh?" asked Duggan.

"I think we're about to have plenty to do," said Breeze. "Fission signature incoming."

Duggan jumped to the controls, gripping the bars in readiness. This wasn't part of his plans. "Damnit, what do we have?" he snarled.

CHAPTER THIRTY-ONE

THE NEWS WAS as bad as Duggan expected and he cursed himself for staying too long in orbit around the ice-clad planet. He should have realised the Ghasts would pick them up sooner rather than later. His thirst for answers might have cost them dearly. *Screw those bastards.*

"Oblivion battleship, sir," said Breeze. "The same one we escaped when we found the *Crimson*. This time their helmsman has got them close by. One hundred and forty thousand klicks. Their particle beam has just hit us. Fission drive down eight percent."

Duggan pushed the control bar to maximum and the *Crimson* surged away over the surface of the Hynus system's tenth planet. He took them as low as he dared, in the hope that he'd be able to take advantage of the planet's curvature and prevent the enemy battleship getting a missile lock. The beam weapon would take a few seconds to recharge and he knew exactly what they'd launch next.

"Fire the disruptors," he said. "Before they launch a missile."

"Firing now, sir. We scored a hit."

"Too late," said Chainer. "Ghast super-missile inbound."

"Deep fission engines at sixteen percent," said Breeze. "I'm not reading any positrons from the Ghast hull. They've been shut down."

"That missile is closing at a little over two thousand klicks per second."

The *Crimson* was fast. Flat out, it wasn't vastly slower than a Lambda or one of the Ghasts' conventional missiles. These new missiles were much faster than any other ballistic weaponry on either side. Duggan kept low, hoping to fool the missile's guidance system, or force it to burn up in the thin atmosphere. It wasn't working and Duggan was forced to climb away from the planet's surface to stop the *Crimson*'s armour plates melting. The Oblivion was soon lost from sensor sight behind the planet, but the missile tracked them unerringly.

"Forty seconds to impact," announced Chainer.

"Readying the disruptors," said McGlashan. "What's our power?"

"Climbing. Twenty percent. There'll be enough juice to fire. We'll be pushing it fine."

"I wouldn't have it any other way," Duggan muttered to himself, his eyes roving across a dozen tactical displays.

"Thirty seconds."

"Engines at twenty-two percent," said Breeze. "They come back at an astonishing rate. Much quicker than they did on the *Detriment*."

"That's because the backend core is ten thousand times quicker than the *Detriment*'s mainframe," said Monsey. She didn't seem at all concerned about the incoming missile.

When he heard her words, Duggan felt as if someone had plugged him into a socket and flicked a switch. A part of his subconscious fired a thought to the front of his brain that was so intriguing, he cursed the incoming missile again for preventing him acting upon his idea.

"Twenty seconds."

"Insufficient power to target and fire."

"Ten seconds."

"Still not ready."

"Five seconds."

"Firing."

"Enemy missile free-floating. Its velocity will take it completely out of orbit in approximately fifteen seconds."

"Engines at three percent. That's as low as it'll let them go."

"Damn we're good," said Chainer, slumping back in his chair and wiping his brow.

Duggan was hardly listening. He turned his attention to Monsey and waved his hand to bring her attention away from the keyboard. "You said that if you had a billion times the horse-power, you could hack the Dreamer core?"

"A turn of phrase, sir. I meant that I'd need a lot more number crunching power to brute force it open."

"The way I understand it is that the Hynus-T mainframe does all of the bits relating to Space Corps technology. It controls the Lambdas, autopilot, life support and so on."

"You'd know as much about that as me," said Monsey.

Duggan continued. "The two cores are linked by a series of enormously wide interfaces. The Dreamer core takes over where the engines are concerned. It does the repair re-routing and deals with post-jump recovery."

"That's how it's been set up. Whoever built the *Crimson*, they were tapping into the Dreamer core processor for its speed alone. It still has its own programming, presumably from when it was embedded into a Dreamer ship. Now that I know where it's come from, things make a bit more sense. The Hynus engineers managed to block off large parts of the Dreamer core's instruction set and only let through those parts which control the weapons systems they recovered. It's a hatchet job, but I must admit I'm impressed."

"They had almost infinite resources," said Duggan. "And probably two thousand of the Corps' finest minds working on this alone. Still, it's good to see they managed to get as far as they did. What you suggest goes some way to explaining why they couldn't get the final weapon to fire. The Dreamer core must have some failsafe to prevent it working unless certain conditions are met."

"Or it obtains certain approval," said McGlashan.

"What are you getting at, sir?" asked Monsey.

"If the human-built front-end can utilise the processing power of the Dreamer core and send instructions back over the interface, can we tell the Hynus-T to brute force its way into the weapons systems?"

Monsey blinked. "You're asking if we can get the Dreamer core to hack itself?"

"That's precisely what I'm asking," said Duggan. "Can you tell it to do that?"

Monsey opened her mouth and closed it. Duggan couldn't remember seeing her at a loss for words before.

"That's a very good idea, sir," she stuttered. "But you can probably do that from your console with a few lines of code."

"That's not my field," Duggan said. "Please proceed. I want full access from my console as soon as possible."

"What are you planning, sir?" asked McGlashan.

"I'd have thought it was obvious, Commander. First, I'm going to use our access to the Dreamer core to prevent it from sending any further signals. Secondly, I'm going to evaluate the hidden weapons system. If possible, I'm going to test it out on that Ghast battleship by blowing them apart!"

"That's a plan I can go with," said McGlashan.

"I just need to find us the time," said Duggan. He changed

their heading, trying to keep it as erratic as possible. "At least we can outrun them and can knock out their super-missiles if we need to."

"They've only been launching one at a time, sir," said Chainer. "The battleships which attacked the *Archimedes* were capable of launching more."

"Maybe this Oblivion's only carrying a prototype version. Or perhaps we've been lucky so far," said McGlashan.

"Our luck's got to run out eventually. Can't we just point the nose somewhere far out and come back when we've had a chance to sort all this stuff out?"

"We're staying, Lieutenant. We're going to get something out of this. It's what we all signed up for."

"Aye sir," Chainer muttered.

The first circuit of the planet took eight minutes. It was enough for Monsey to adapt some of the code she'd already created to access the *Crimson's* Hynus-T mainframe.

"I'm setting it up for a first run, sir," she said.

"Do it as soon as you can."

"On its way. Shit, it's almost filled the interfaces with breach attempts."

"Fission drive recovery has slowed right down, sir. We're almost at full, but if we have to fire the disruptors again, you won't have them ready for a long time after. The Dreamer core must have too much on its plate."

"I wish I had access to this much grunt all the time," said Monsey. "It's probably for the best that I don't."

"Can you tell how long?" asked Duggan.

"It'll happen when it happens, sir. It takes patience to hack anything big. The same patience works well when I'm looking along the barrel of a rifle, waiting for a Ghast to walk into my sights."

"I don't have a lot of patience just at this moment, soldier."

"Sorry, sir. Nothing I can do to speed it up. This is something new to me as well."

At that moment, Duggan's luck ran dry.

"Enemy vessel coming up on the sensors, sir. High above us. Nearly three hundred thousand klicks up and over."

"Have they seen us?"

"We're hard to miss, sir. They've changed course and are coming in lower."

At that moment, Duggan realised he was about to be sucker punched. With the usual missiles employed by both sides, there was little point in sitting out of orbit and waiting for the enemy to come to you. The standard missiles couldn't target from so far out, and the opponent could easily fly out of sensor sight around the other side of the planet. This turned planetary combat into a hunt, which often relied on luck to see who got the first shot away. Not anymore, Duggan thought.

"I'm detecting super-missile launches, sir. Something tells me they were holding back before. This time it's six at once."

Duggan thumped his console with a clenched fist. "Damnit!" He took a deep breath. "I'm taking us away around the planet. Hold the disruptor fire until we're out of sight of that Oblivion. I don't want them getting a second salvo off when there's nothing we can do about it. How long till impact?"

"At least one hundred and thirty seconds, sir. It depends on how much speed you hold around the planet."

"Are we out of sensor sight yet?"

"No, sir. Nearly," said Chainer.

The next few seconds were tense and everyone on the bridge apart from Monsey kept their eyes glued on the tactical display.

"We're out of sensor sight now, sir," said Chainer after what seemed like hours instead of seconds. "Given what we know about their position, we should hopefully be able to avoid that Oblivion for at least one more orbit."

"It's the missiles I'm worried about, Lieutenant. We can't use the disruptors on all six."

With his mind racing, Duggan pushed the *Crimson* as fast as he dared, away from the incoming missiles. The hull temperature soared as it tore through the thin atmosphere.

"Sir? We'll need to activate the fission engines," said McGlashan quietly. "Else there'll be nothing left of us to take to New Earth."

Duggan looked up. He'd set his mind on the destruction of the enemy vessel, completely at odds with his ability to make it happen. He'd been about to risk everything without having a plan as to how he'd get them out of it alive. This one was lost, he'd just been too stubborn to see it.

"Thank you, Commander," he said. He opened his mouth to give the instruction for Lieutenant Breeze to load up the engines. The order didn't come.

"Hell yes!" shouted Monsey. "Got you now!"

"Give me some good news, soldier," said Duggan.

"Damn right there's some good news, sir! Cracked it open like a nut! I'm assigning command rights to your consoles now."

Duggan checked his access screen. A new tier of options had appeared for him to view. He opened up the menu for the weapons systems - there was a single additional option available to him. It had a description, but the text was a mixture of unfamiliar characters. Feeling excitement and determination build up inside him, he brought the weapon online.

CHAPTER THIRTY-TWO

"IT'S WARMING UP! It's going to be ready in less than thirty seconds," said McGlashan. She'd picked up on Duggan's excitement at once.

"Sir? The fission engines?" asked Breeze.

"Hold for one moment, Lieutenant. Until we see what we've got here."

"Still got seventy seconds until missile impact," said McGlashan. "Longer if you go higher and faster, sir."

Duggan changed course and dragged the nose of the *Crimson* into the vacuum of space.

"Sir, according to my readouts you're heading directly towards the most likely location of the Ghast battleship," said Chainer. He looked worried, like he thought Duggan was losing it.

"I know, Lieutenant."

"And at the rate you're climbing, we may well be in range of their disruptors, beam weapons and normal missiles when we reach them."

"Thank you, Lieutenant." As the ship climbed away from the

planet, the hull temperature dropped and Duggan was able to increase their speed.

"Fifty seconds to missile impact," said McGlashan. "Their rate of approach has diminished now that we've left the bounds of the atmosphere."

"Is the weapon online, Commander?"

"A few seconds left. Here we go. It's lit up and ready to fire!"

"Sir, the enemy battleship is coming into view over the edge of the planet. She's heading directly towards us at full sub-light. Two-hundred and thirty thousand klicks away."

"They're launching. Another four super-missiles. Impact in thirty-eight seconds."

"Lieutenant Breeze, fission engines please. Point us away from Confederation space."

"I thought you'd never ask. We'll be out of here in just shy of thirty seconds."

"Missiles behind, missiles in front. I should've written my will when I had the chance," said Chainer, his voice much calmer than his words.

"Commander, please target and fire our new weapon as soon as you're able."

McGlashan frowned and when Duggan glanced over, he saw her press the same area of her console several times. "The targeting must be out. Or screwed. Or both. It won't target the enemy ship."

"We've got no problems with the sensors, Commander," said Chainer. "All thirty are showing green."

"Sort it out soon, Commander, or we'll miss our chance."

"It might be broken."

"Ten seconds till we're gone."

"Target, damnit!" shouted McGlashan.

"Just fire them, Commander! Press the button!"

"There's no target!"

"Five seconds."

"Do it!"

"Firing!"

There was a shriek, coming from somewhere in the depths of the ship's hull. It rose to a crescendo almost at once, a sound which brought with it waves of punishing vibration through the entire structure of the *Crimson*. The walls and floors shook, as if something had exploded deep within. It seemed to Duggan as if the Hynus engineers had made a mistake by fitting this unknown technology into a spaceship. They couldn't have known the stresses the weapon would subject it to when fired. Before Duggan could even begin to worry that the *Crimson* was about to be ripped into pieces, something else took his full attention.

The tenth planet was still visible away to one side of the bulkhead screen. It appeared much smaller now that they'd flown so high above it. Without apparent sound, the planet shattered. Vast, gaping chasms spread across its surface in a tenth of a second. The pieces separated, each part cracking and splitting into ever smaller fragments of the whole. In the blinking of an eye, they exploded thousands of kilometres away from each other as they expanded at a speed almost beyond comprehension. None of the crew had time to say a word before the *Crimson* catapulted them into high lightspeed. Unconsciousness, when it came, was a welcome relief.

When Duggan came to, he had the usual uncertainty about how much time had elapsed. He supposed it didn't really matter. *We just destroyed an entire planet* were the first words that came into his mind. *Gone, just like that.*

McGlashan was already awake and she looked at him, her eyes dark and her expression giving nothing away about her thoughts. He stared back, sharing the bleakness of the moment with her.

"I suppose we should be happy," she croaked. "We found something that can even the odds."

"I don't think I could ever be happy knowing what we've got," he said, surprised at the strength in his voice.

Chainer woke next, driven from the sanctuary of sleep by what he'd seen. "We just blew up a whole planet," he said dumbly.

Duggan shook off his lethargy and ignored the pain of his body. "Rouse yourself Lieutenant and fix it so that our sensors stop transmitting. I want to get this spacecraft to New Earth. I don't want the responsibility for it anymore."

"Aye sir, I'll be on it when the pounding in my head calms down enough."

McGlashan came across, holding herself steady against Duggan's chair. "The Ghasts haven't shown us any quarter, sir," she said quietly. "In a terrible war, it's the side which blinks first that loses. Remember what they did to Charistos."

"I know, Commander. They're more ruthless than we are. They want to fight, while the Confederation has never been given the choice."

Something caught Duggan's eye. A message had arrived – he guessed it must have slipped in a moment before they went to lightspeed. He read the message and then deleted it.

"Sir?" asked McGlashan.

"They found Angax. Did the same to it as they did to Charistos. Almost two billion people, incinerated by those bastards." He looked at her, anger spilling across his face. "They think they've got us, Commander. They think they're going to find our planets one by one and destroy our people. We've got a new weapon now and I hope to hell I live to see the day we can fire it at their home world."

As McGlashan looked away, tears visible in her eyes, the ESS

Crimson cut a path onwards through space, carrying with it the most terrible kind of hope imaginable.

———

The Survival Wars series continues in Book 2, Bane of Worlds!

Follow Anthony James on Facebook at
facebook.com/anthonyjamesauthor

THE SURVIVAL WARS SERIES

Printed in Great Britain
by Amazon

49891911R00161